Adam Glendon Sidwell

EVERTASTER

Course of Legends

FUTURE HOUSE PUBLISHING

Cover art: Goro Fujita

Title design: Matthew Eng

Inside Illustrations: Adam Glendon Sidwell

ISBN: 0615654495
ISBN-13: 978-0615654492

ACKNOWLEDGMENTS

Alyssa Henkin, my agent at Trident Media Group, who gave Guster his first chance, and has been fighting for him ever since. She's a skilled editor who made me do twenty extra writing pushups when I thought I couldn't do one more. It's a better book for it.

Jarom Sidwell, who first helped me tell this story out loud on a long car ride one night, and lives out his own wondrous imagination every day.

My beta-readers: Furnace, Shrff, Seanny, Foodest, Mutie, Q, Rach, Chancellor, and especially the Maxes, who always gave thoughtful and valuable feedback.

Goro Fujita, a very talented artist who made the cover amazing. I'd describe it here, but the picture itself is its own praise.

Matthew Eng, an excellent artist and friend did the title design.

Nanette Harvey, who is a stern and quick editor. I appreciate her. Commas fear her.

My wife, Michelle, who married me even though she knew I wanted to be a writer, and has been several quarts of fun ever since.

This book is dedicated to Mom, who in many ways is the real Mabel Johnsonville.

Chapter 1 — The Heist

The vault was supposed to be impregnable.

And it was — for the most part. Mr. Italo Arrivederci had made sure of that. It had stopped dozens of would-be thieves over hundreds of risky years; though no one knew exactly why it was so effective.

That night, things would change.

Epiglottis pushed his mop back and forth across the marble floor of the outer hall. A guard in a dark blue uniform nodded to him as he passed, the click-clack of his footsteps echoing between the ivory columns as they did every night. For all the familiarity it brought with it, Epiglottis hated the sound. Epiglottis had waited for years, posing as a lowly janitor, casting aside his true self, enduring a Scavenger's life. Tonight it would end.

He adjusted the miniature camera housed discreetly inside the pen stuck in the left breast pocket of his coveralls. It was a direct video feed to the man with the pencil-thin tie — another source of frustration.

"Take up your position," crackled the voice through the microphone hidden in Epiglottis' ear.

"Already there," he whispered, irritated, as he ducked behind one of the two massive, polished white columns that flanked the five-hundred pound, double wooden doors. He wished the Arch-Gourmand were giving the orders. *He* would appreciate the magnitude of the task at hand.

The guard had turned the corner by now. He wouldn't be gone long. Epiglottis looked at his watch. *Now*, he thought.

There was a splintering smash, then a crack, and the doors tore from their hinges and crashed to the floor. Two huge men, each at least a foot taller and twice as wide as Epiglottis strode through the empty door frame. Their chests were bare and their bellies hung over their loose, wooly gray pants. Executioner's hoods covered their faces, except for the eyes and mouth.

The guard was back in a flash, his gun drawn. The two hulking brutes each plucked a huge door from the floor and swung them in front of the guard like a shield; he fired. There was a pop! Pop! as the bullets shattered the surface of the wood.

The first brute heaved the door on top of the guard, knocking him to the ground. And then it was quiet.

Epiglottis stepped out from behind the pillar. He was impressed. He'd heard that the giant brutes could not taste or smell — but it was their brawn that was useful.

"This way," he said, leading them down the hall. More guards would certainly come soon, so they had to work fast. They descended a steep stair that led underground. At the bottom was a locked door; this one steel. He'd never been through it; he wasn't given clearance for that. He pulled a stolen badge from his pocket and swiped it through the sensor. The lock clicked and he pushed it open.

"We're in," he said activating the microphone in his ear.

"Good," said the man with the pencil-thin tie.

The dark corridors were lit by candle. The first brute shined a flashlight on his palm. It was tattooed with a map of the inner chambers — he had probably been raised and trained just for tonight.

The brute struck out to the right. In a matter of minutes they would have what they came for. So much for impenetrable defenses!

That's when the most wonderful aroma struck Epiglottis like a mallet. It was chocolate, pure, sweet and rich as a milkshake or a slab of fudge. It filled his nose and then, like a mug filling with cocoa, his head. He bolted after it to the left.

"What are you doing? Stick to the plan!" shouted the voice in his ear. He did not care. The Scavenger was a fool, and the brutes could not smell a thing. This had to be it. He passed a hallway, then turned left, then right, closing in on the smell.

When he turned the corner he found the source of his delight: a flatbed cart stacked evenly with block after block of pure brown chocolate. It was parked in a cell, a fan gently blowing the aroma toward him.

"This is it!" cried Epiglottis. He reached through the doorway, not caring that a set of iron bars protruded from the ceiling, waiting to drop. It was within his grasp!

An enormous hand grabbed him by the back of his coveralls and yanked him back. Epiglottis winced as the second brute threw him over his shoulder like a child. He kicked. He screamed. And then the brute started to run back the way they'd come.

The precious chocolate was disappearing from sight! It had been so close. The object of their mission! Why couldn't the brutes see that? Didn't they want it? They were going the wrong way!

"Epiglottis, you fool!" said the voice in his ear. "You've fallen into their trap!"

The first brute lifted his palm at every branch in the corridors, studying the map as they ran. The scent grew weaker. Then came new breezes with similar smells — more chocolate down this corridor, or that one.

He wanted to scream, to break away and run. But the gray-hooded brute was too strong.

They followed the twisting passages until, deep inside the corridors, at the end of a long hallway, there was a room with a safe inside. A bald man in a coarse brown robe stood there.

"This is not what you seek," he said. Epiglottis sniffed the air. He had to be right. There was no smell.

Without hesitation, the first brute knocked the robed man out of the way. Then he opened a satchel slung across his shoulder and removed a block of sweet, caramel colored substance. He stuck it to the safe door, then inserted a needle with a timer on the end. He pressed a button and backed up.

The block exploded. The safe door swung open. Inside was a platter covered with a silver dome lid.

The brute removed it from the safe and lifted the lid, breaking the seal. Underneath was a stack of chocolate bars so rich and brown, Epiglottis could have sworn they were glowing. The air around them looked edible, like flavored heat from a smoldering fire. It was luxurious. It was wonderful. It was beyond compare. Every bit of chocolate he had seen up to this point was a mere distraction.

Now he understood. *This* is what they came for. He never should have been so blinded by second-rate treasures!

"Mine!" he cried. In a burst of adrenaline, he kicked the second brute. For one brief second the brute's grip loosened and Epiglottis broke free, wriggling to the ground. He leapt for the chocolate, unable to control his appetite. He knew how angry the man in the pencil-thin tie would be, but it didn't matter. He had to taste it at once.

The second brute moved quicker. His fingertips inches away from the chocolate, Epiglottis felt a hand catch him around the throat and an arm latch around his waist as he was hoisted into the air by his coveralls.

The first brute clapped the silver dome down on the platter again, hiding the sacred chocolate from Epiglottis' view. The aroma waned, then disappeared. *Bring it back*! thought Epiglottis. Couldn't they smell it?

The brute with the platter tucked it under his arm and bolted for the exit.

"It was not meant for you!" cried the brown-robed servant, lifting himself from the ground.

The remaining brute took one look at him and snorted, then ran out into the corridor, Epiglottis under his arm.

It took less than half the time to get out of the passageways as it did to get in. When the brutes reached the stairs, they charged up them as quickly as they could. The first one knocked another guard out of the way and bolted through the smashed doors to the outside.

A bucket-shaped wicker basket the size of a small car was waiting for them in the courtyard. They leapt inside. A red zeppelin floating above pulled on a set of ropes tied to the basket until they tightened, hoisting them skyward.

More guards stormed into the courtyard outside the Arrivederci vault, but it was too late. Epiglottis and the brutes were already off the ground. The guards opened fire, but their bullets only ricocheted harmlessly off the basket's bulletproof bottom.

The bottom of the zeppelin's cabin opened, reeling the basket safely inside. The hatch shut, and the second brute finally loosened his grip on Epiglottis, dropping him to the floor. Epiglottis gasped for air. His ribs hurt.

"A pity," said the man with the pencil-thin tie. He took the silver platter out of the first brute's giant hands and peered at it over his spectacles. "It seems the Arrivedercis never reckoned on invaders totally incapable of smelling their treasure." He nodded to the giant brutes who, now that they'd done their job, were stowing the basket at the rear of the cabin, completely disinterested in the prize. "We've plucked their precious gem right out from under them!" he laughed.

Miserable Scavenger, thought Epiglottis. He held such extraordinary taste in his hands — the work of the masters over the centuries. Did it mean nothing to him?

"Full speed ahead," the man with the pencil-thin tie barked to the pilot behind the controls. "I've got to get this back to my employer before the night is through."

Epiglottis boiled with anger, but he knew his duty. This was all part of the Arch-Gourmand's plan.

The man with the pencil-thin tie saw his pain, "Don't look so glum, old fellow. You elitist gourmets will get your way. After so many centuries, your time has finally come…"

Chapter 2 — The Stranger in Red

Eleven-year-old Guster Johnsonville was about to hold the fate of humanity on the end of his spoon. It never would have happened that way if he hadn't been such a picky eater, nor would he have left the farmhouse in Louisiana and set out across the world if it weren't for that wretched Ham Chowder Casserole.

No one likes to eat this stuff, thought Guster, even though his two brothers and sister didn't seem to mind. But if Mom ever made that mishmash of pig, peas, and potato again, he would be doomed.

To think! They called him picky. "You're a remarkable child," was all Mom would say to him when he told her that the potatoes in her Chowder were grown so far north, they tasted like gravel. Never mind that he was on the verge of starvation.

"Not picky! Just careful," Guster always said. How often he went hungry! How badly he needed something to eat! The way food burned or ached as it passed across his tongue — it was like eating day-old road kill. Hot dogs were like the sweaty vinyl back seat of a station wagon with its windows rolled up in the sun. Frozen burritos were like buttery squirrels infected with the flu.

And ever since the hot summer had smoldered up out of the ground that year, it had been getting worse. So bad, in fact, that he hadn't put anything in his empty beanpole stomach for three whole days. If he didn't find something — anything he could eat soon — he was going to starve.

"Guster, come down to the table," Mom cried from the kitchen on the night the Ham Chowder changed everything forever. He smelled it — that familiar smell of cheesy, potato-soaked socks — all the way up the stairs in his room.

He could make for the window and lower himself to the ground from the roof. He could bolt down the stairs, past the kitchen, and into the night, then run through the fields. But no matter what he did, no matter where he went, he could not escape it: the pain that came with eating.

"Hungry, Capital P?" Zeke jeered as Guster entered the kitchen. Zeke was fifteen, pimply and plump as a horse. He thought that calling Guster 'Capital P' was the funniest thing in the world. He said that Guster was so skinny that, from the side, his head looked like a lump on a stick.

Guster hated that name. "I served you up a real good helping," Zeke said and pushed a heaping plate full of Ham Chowder in Guster's direction.

Why does he always have to pick on me? thought Guster. He tried not to cough at the smell.

Mom — who never seemed to care what she was putting Guster through — prayed, "Lord, thanks for this Ham Chowder, and bless Henry Senior that he will come home safely from his business trip. And bless this…"

A roll bounced off Guster's head. He opened one eye. Zeke was staring at him, a grin spread across his pimply face.

"…bless this family that it will STOP FIGHTING! AMEN!" Mom finished. She scowled. Zeke had soured her mood, which was going to make it even harder for Guster to get through dinner without touching that Chowder.

"When we go camping, do you think there will be bears there?" asked Mariah, Guster's older sister. Guster loved his sister. She was much smarter than him, and she didn't tease him like Zeke did.

"Mom, why do we have to go to Camp Cucamunga again this year? Betsy's family went to Mexico!" Zeke hollered.

"You mean your *girlfriend*?" Mariah asked.

"I didn't say she was my girlfriend!" cried Zeke.

"Neither did I," Mariah said, smiling mischievously. It was enough to turn the rest of Zeke's face as red as his pimples.

"Mexico would be nice someday," said Mom without even looking up as she spoon fed Guster's toddler brother, Henry Junior. She always talked about going to far-off places, but she never actually went.

"Anyway," said Zeke, "in Mexico Betsy's brother saw these ancient stone temples with stairs leading all the way up to the top. And there were these passages that went down underground to secret chambers where they sacrificed people and ate their —"

"Zeke, that is not dinner table talk," said Mom. What it was was another one of Zeke's wild stories.

"Well, you'll notice that Betsy's brother hasn't been around ever since they got back," Zeke said.

"He's in the Army, Zeke," said Mariah. "Next you'll be telling us about the red-robed stranger again."

Zeke turned white and dropped his fork. Guster had not heard about this one. Something about the way Zeke's chubby cheeks went limp told Guster this story was different.

"Betsy's mom saw him on a trip into the city," Zeke said in a low voice, "He was lurking around down near the waterfront dressed in some kind of tall hat, red jacket and pants and apron. No one there had ever seen anyone like him before, until this week." He did not laugh or smile this time. He just stared across the room at nothing at all.

"It sounds like a chef," said Guster. There were plenty of chefs in New Orleans.

"But how many chefs come out only at night, dressed as red as the devil himself, with teeth like a gator's and a belt full of razor-sharp knives dripping with blood?" asked Zeke.

"He's probably just making some deliveries or something," said Mariah.

"Then how do you explain the disappearances?" whispered Zeke. "The way Betsy's mom tells it, people go into the city, then poof! They're gone. You could be walking down the street, sitting in a café — it doesn't matter, because the Chef in Red has got his eye on you, and everybody in the whole city, maybe even the state," he said. He was serious, and he looked more scared than Guster had ever seen him. "I know it's real. I saw it on the news. Or at least Betsy did."

Guster couldn't say if that were true or not. It's not like he watched the news.

"Who knows," Zeke said, pulling his ample cheeks down his face until you could see the red pulp around his eyes. "Maybe he's looking for something…" Zeke stood up and crept over to Mariah. "Something to eat!" he cried, and bit down gently on the top of her head.

She screamed. "Rarr!" growled Henry Junior. He banged his spoon on the table and chomped at the air, just like Zeke had.

"Enough!" said Mom. She put her round moon face in her hands and sighed. "All of you will eat your dinner now," she said, her voice quivering.

Guster froze. They were on thin ice. At times like this it was best to avoid Mom's attention so she didn't raise her voice at him. He was never sure why she got so angry. Sometimes it started with Zeke. Sometimes it started when she came into his room and he'd left his clothes all over the floor. Sometimes it started for no reason at all.

Betsy's Mom wasn't like that. Betsy's Mom let them do whatever they wanted when they went to her house. *Why is Mom always coming down on us?* he wondered. He spread the Chowder across his plate to buy him some time.

"Dinner was delicious, Mom," said Mariah, clearing her plate. In a matter of seconds Zeke was finished too, and Mom took Henry Junior out of his high-chair and into the living room, leaving Guster alone with the vomitous mass.

"Don't get up until you're finished," called Mom as she turned on the TV. She started to fold a pile of laundry. Once again she'd forgotten to remove her baby blue apron. She'd probably leave it on all night, just like every other time.

He was so hungry! If only he could get his hands on something good enough to eat! There had been a lemon meringue pie once from the bakery down the street — he could tell the sea wind had blown across the lemons as they'd ripened. There was the honeyed pork from Mac Murray's two years ago, or the mint ice cream straight from the dairy just last summer — the cows that gave the milk in the ice cream had eaten only clover. There was something special about those flavors. Something that only Guster could understand. Something that drove Guster to the fridge on those moonlit nights, when the farmhouse was asleep, to lick up the last of the crumbs. Those were the nights he was alive with taste.

Sadly, as good as those flavors were, it wasn't long before they too turned sour and lost their appeal. It didn't have to be that way! There had to be something out there that could quench his burning hunger, something that could save him. Like a dish, waiting to be discovered, that beckoned to him from far away. A dish so delicious beyond belief that once he tasted it, he would never want to eat anything else again.

The TV crackled, "And we're back with more amazing homemaking tips straight from the Queen Bee of the American Household, the Duchess of Decorating, the Czarina of Cuisine… celebrity homemaker Felicity Casa!" There was applause. Mom was watching *Roofs*, the only TV show she ever made time for. It was a silly program. The host, Felicity Casa, was always showing viewers how to make their own curtains out of grocery bags or grow the perfect gardenias in a milk bottle. Very boring stuff, even if Felicity was richer than the President and had houses all over the world. Mom practically idolized her. There was nothing she wanted more than to visit Felicity's secret, state-of-the-art kitchen hidden somewhere in France.

"Tonight I'm going to show you how to make a sumptuous, herb crusted leg of lamb," said Felicity, her middle-aged face outlined so picture-perfect with makeup, she looked like a painting. *Now why couldn't our dinner be like that?* thought Guster. The cooking demonstration was the part of *Roofs* he *did* love. Felicity described roasting the lamb from start to finish step by step, in perfect detail. If only he could taste it! "Because, after all, it is the sworn duty of the chef to provide her guests with a *taste experience*," she said when she finished.

Was that what he'd been longing for? He was certain that if he could just get his hands on it, he would eat *that*. Instead, he was stuck with Ham Chowder.

He stabbed his fork at it. And then there was Zeke's story about the stranger in red. What if it were true? What if that chef had caused the disappearances?

"Guster!" cried Mom as she came into the kitchen. "You haven't eaten a thing!"

He shook his head. "I can't —"

Mom insisted. "You are far too old for this. Now eat," she said, her hands on her tubby hips.

He shook his head again. He just couldn't. Ham Chowder was slime; it was ooze; it was a dirty, pig-filled sack of nasty eyeballs, and it tasted like poo.

"Eat," she said again, with a voice like a megaphone.

He touched the fork to his tiny lips. *Eww*. The sour cream had not soured enough. The ham was too moist. It was like eating paint.

"Swallow," she said.

He tried. He really tried. He wrapped his lips around the slime, then forced it with his tongue to the back of his throat until he couldn't stand it anymore and — *plllbbbttt*! — he spewed it all over Mom's baby blue apron.

"Guster Stephen Johnsonville!" She picked him up from his chair and pulled him over to the sink. "Look what a mess you've made! I thought you were eleven!" she screamed, and began scrubbing his shirt.

Guster spit into the sink — he had to get rid of the taste — while Mom wrestled to clean off his shirt. The stairs pounded as Zeke and Mariah came thumping down from their rooms and into the kitchen.

"What's the matter with him?" Zeke hollered.

"Ezekiel, get back up to your room," Mom shouted. He scrambled for cover.

"But Mom, all I want is a *taste experience*!" cried Guster through tears of pain. Why couldn't they eat things like Felicity made? He stuck his mouth under the running tap water.

Suddenly, Mom stopped wrestling. She let him down, dried off his shirt as best as she could, then pressed her hand to his back. It almost looked like concern on her face. "I know honey, I know," she whispered.

He just hoped she wouldn't hug him. If she did, he might run away and hide himself under the couch. He sniffed. He hadn't meant for his tears to break free.

Mom closed her eyes, as if resting herself for a minute. "Guster, go change your clothes. We're going into the city," she said.

Chapter 3 — The Master Pastry Chef

The city of New Orleans was an hour's drive away from the farm. Guster stared out the window at the cloudy night sky as the family's old rusty Suburban tumbled down the road, with Zeke behind the wheel. Maybe the city would provide something to eat — if Zeke's driving didn't kill them first.

"Eh? Eh?" Zeke turned around to make sure Guster noticed the learner's permit he'd folded and placed prominently on the dash. Zeke had shown it to Guster at least once a day since he got it. Guster smiled weakly.

"Eyes on the road Zeke," said Mom. Guster couldn't believe she was letting that maniac drive.

Sometimes Guster wondered if Zeke liked being his brother. Zeke was always throwing acorns or cow pies at him. He'd even pushed Guster out of a tree house once.

As for Mom, it was about time she got with the program. If it wasn't Ham Chowder today, it was Cantaloupe Omelets yesterday, or Toasted Lasagna Sandwiches with butter the day before. That's the way it had always been, ever since Guster could chew, his own mother shoving a scum-juice tube down his throat and cranking it on while there was nothing he could do.

Zeke steered the Suburban over the yellow dots in the middle of the road, bouncing Guster in his seat and bobbing the bun Mom wore on top of her head up and down like an apple. "Sorry," Zeke said. The country road turned into highway, and the highway turned to freeway as the bright lights of New Orleans came into view.

They rarely went into the city. The family had moved to Louisiana only three years before.

"We'll go into the French Quarter," said Mom. Guster had heard of the French Quarter — it was a neighborhood older than America itself.

"This place was built by pirates," Zeke said. "And there's voodoo magic everywhere."

Yeah, right, thought Guster. Zeke was probably making it up, just like everything else he ever said.

"Exit the freeway here," Mom told Zeke. "There are a lot of tricky streets in the French Quarter, so you will have to be very careful to follow my directions," she said in her sternest Mom-voice. She pointed to a street on their right. "Turn here."

Zeke turned down the street, then stopped at a red light. Guster rolled down the window so he could get a better look outside. There were lights everywhere. Crowds of people walked back and forth across the sidewalks or sat outside at little tables eating and drinking. It smelled of fresh gumbo in one direction, which was decent, and banana bread pudding in the other direction, which ruined everything else. *Bananas aren't ripe enough*, he thought. But there were so many choices. So many opportunities. If they were to find that perfect something, it was bound to be here — if it was anywhere at all.

The light turned green. Zeke turned the Suburban left, just as a crowd of people stepped out into the crosswalk in front of the car.

"Zeke!" Mom cried. Guster lurched forward in his seatbelt as Zeke slammed on the brakes.

"Freakazoids! What are they doing?!" Zeke cried. Guster looked up just in time to see two headlights approaching from the right. A horn blasted. Zeke threw the Suburban into reverse, turned it around and drove the opposite direction as the car zoomed past.

"This is a one-way street!" Mom cried as a green car came speeding toward them head on.

Zeke turned the Suburban a hard left down another street as Guster braced himself on the seat in front of him. Zeke was going to kill them. More car horns blared as they passed another 'One-way' arrow pointing in the opposite direction.

"Right! Turn right!" screamed Mom. The car lurched again, throwing Guster into the seat next to him as a truck zoomed past.

"Why don't we park here?" Mom said, her voice quivering. Zeke pulled the car next to the curb and screeched to a halt. Mom yanked the keys out of the ignition. Guster caught his breath.

"Did you see those guys?" Zeke asked. "Walked right out in front of me!"

Mom shook her head. "They were in the crosswalk dear," she said, and got out of the car. "You're going to have to re-read that safe driver's handbook. Let's walk."

Anything to be out of a car with Zeke behind the wheel. Guster unclicked his safety belt and hopped out.

Unlike the other streets, this one was dark and quiet. Most of the shops were closed for the night, except for a Bistro one block ahead. Mom pulled Guster toward it. It was nearly empty. The smell of cooking meat hung like a fog on the street. "How about this one?" said Mom.

Too greasy, thought Guster. There had to be something better than *this*. He shook his head.

Disappointment crossed Mom's face. For a second, Guster thought she would scold him. Instead, she tugged him onward.

They passed a bakery, a small café, and a dozen other shops. Some were closed. The rest smelled awful. He shook his head at each one. His tiny stomach was so empty, but Mom's patience was wearing thin.

"Guster," said Mom, leaning down to look him in the eyes, "You've got to find something to eat." That was easy enough to say, but it couldn't be just any old food. He looked down at the oily pavement under his feet. He wished Mariah were there, instead of at home, babysitting Henry Junior. She never got angry at him.

"Then we'll have to go home," said Mom sadly. She started toward the car.

Then a new smell hit him. One that was different from all the rest. Across the street, on a dimly lit corner, the word "Patisserie" was painted in golden letters on an old and dusty window. The most wonderful aroma of tarts and cakes spilled from it. It was so strong, he felt like he was tasting fresh berries and chocolaty crusts, all from the little pastry shop right in front of his eyes. "Wait," he said. Mom stopped. "Over there," he pointed.

Mom took Guster by the hand and led him and Zeke across the street toward the patisserie. The curtains behind the window were closed and, except for a faint sliver of yellowish light that shone between them, the shop was entirely dark. A sign that read "Closed for Business by Order of the City of New Orleans" was propped up against the glass in one corner.

"You couldn't pick a place that makes more than desserts?" asked Mom.

Guster shook his head. There was no doubt about it. This had to be it.

"Maybe the chef has a cookbook I can buy," she said, and pounded on the boarded-up door.

No one answered. *Please, someone be in there*, thought Guster.

"The place is closed Mom," said Zeke. He clutched his learner's permit in his hand. "Maybe we ought to drive back over to —"

Mom shook her head. "Walking will be just fine." She put her ear to the door. "I think I hear someone inside." She pounded again. It was silent.

"Let's check around back," Mom said. She went around to the side of the building to a dark alleyway, where there was a porch with a narrow door. She turned the knob and the door opened a crack.

"Mom, is this breaking the law?" Zeke asked. Mom held her finger to her lips. Guster grabbed hold of her baby blue apron. The dark entryway was just the kind of place where someone might break your kneecaps.

Don't be stupid, he thought. How could something that smelled so good possibly be dangerous? There was a weak coughing sound.

"Hello?" Mom said. She opened the door wide, took Guster's hand and stepped over the threshold. The place was dark and cramped. A small oil lamp burned in one corner, casting a dim light across tables cluttered with strange cooking devices. There was a tall, golden mixer with gears sticking out from every side, a set of silver measuring spoons with etched handles, an old wooden rolling pin the size of Zeke's entire pudgy arm, and a set of iron scales that balanced perfectly in the still air of the patisserie.

Zeke picked up a tiny wire whisk and held it up to the light. "What kind of place is this?" he whispered.

"Careful what you touch, Zeke," said Mom, ducking to avoid a pot dangling from the ceiling.

On the other side of the room a dim, white light shone in a glass case full of pastries: éclairs topped with cream, tarts smothered in berries, layer cakes with flaky crusts and heavy chocolate filling drizzled in vanilla. Guster let go of his mother's hand and ran to it, his mouth watering.

He pressed his nose against the glass. Finally! There were fruits; there were nuts; there was chocolate! He wanted to laugh. He had never been so near such wonderful food. If he could just touch one — He stood on his toes and reached over the top of the glass.

"Guster! Hands off!" hissed Mom.

A loud, hacking cough came from an open doorway in the back. "If pastries are not made for eating," said a voice before it started coughing uncontrollably again, "then what are they good for?" A short man with a white chef's hat that bubbled up out of his head came out of the door. Long white hairs stuck wildly out from under the hat. He wore a navy blue bath robe and slippers.

Startled, Guster snatched his hand away from the glass case. The old man was a strange sight indeed.

Mom grabbed Guster and Zeke and pulled them close. "Pardon us Sir, but of all the shops in the city, my son only wanted a taste of your pastries," she said.

"Oh?" said the old man and coughed a big, noisy cough that shook his body. His face looked pale and sweaty, like he'd eaten something that disagreed with him.

"It seemed like your shop was closed, but there was a light on. He wouldn't eat anything else, so we had to try," said Mom.

The old man steadied himself on a chair and breathed slowly. "So determined then, are we?" he said. He eyed Guster carefully as if trying to size him up. "A particular palette can be useful." He raised an eyebrow. "Or *dangerous*."

Guster squirmed. The way the old man stared at him was odd. "I wasn't going to steal anything," he said.

"No! No! Boy, you misunderstand me," said the old man and stepped toward them with his arms open wide. "I am the Maitre Patisserie! The Master Pastry Chef. I make all these creations." He put an arm around Guster's shoulder. Mom tried to pull Guster away. "I admire someone with such excellent taste as yourself! Would you like a tart?" he whispered, as if it were a secret for only Guster to hear.

Of course, thought Guster, *no matter how strange you seem*. He was very hungry, and they looked so delicious. He nodded.

"Good!" said the Master Pastry Chef. He plodded his way behind the glass counter, his slippers flopping against his heels. "Which one shall it be?"

"How much do they cost?" interrupted Mom. The family didn't have the money to buy expensive things.

"My dear," wheezed the Master Pastry Chef, "I have little use for money anymore. You may try whatever you like."

Guster looked back and forth between the chocolate layer cake and the raspberry tart. He pointed at both.

"Excellent choice," said the Master Pastry Chef with a smile. He picked them carefully out of the glass case with a tissue and handed them to Guster.

He bit into the chocolate layer cake first. At last! It was soft, dense and spongy like warm fudge wrapped in a crispy crust. There was nothing wrong with it. In fact, it tasted like the cocoa powder had been hand crushed, and like the milk chocolate had been brewed only yesterday. *Divine*, he thought, as the sugar rushed all through his body. He closed his eyes and took another bite. *I didn't know food could taste like this*!

"Guster is very particular Sir. If he likes your baking it is an extraordinary compliment," said Mom. Rain began to drum softly on the window outside.

There she went, calling him particular again. If this were any other moment, he might have opened his mouth to protest, but right now, it was full of the most delicious raspberry tart, and he could not miss a moment of taste.

"Do you, by chance, also cook other things? Like healthy, stick-to-your-ribs kind of meals?" Mom asked.

The Master Pastry Chef laughed a laugh that quickly turned to a cough. "Food should never stick to your ribs Madam, so much as it should linger on the tip of your tongue — like a butterfly kissing a flower."

"I need some new recipes, you see. It is very difficult for me to find something that my boy likes. He tells me that he tastes things — things that are impossible — like the size of a sugar grain, or which part of the country oranges were grown in."

"Indeed?" said the Master Pastry Chef. "So he does have such clever and discerning buds?" He leaned on the counter as if to get a better look at Guster. "Would you like one of my specialties?" he asked.

"Please," whispered Guster.

The Master Pastry Chef turned his back to them and rummaged through a cupboard. He turned around and placed a small tray on the counter in front of Guster with two identical, crescent-shaped cookies dusted in powdered sugar.

"Go ahead. Choose one," he said. Guster took the one on the left and placed it in his mouth. It was dense, but sweet.

"You like it?" said the old chef.

Guster nodded, then swallowed. Of course he did.

"Good. Then have another," said the old chef, pushing the tray toward Guster.

Guster took the second cookie and bit into it. It would easily be as good as the first. But then — there was a foul, sour taste at the back of his throat — he spat. "What's in this?"

"Aha!" cried the Master Pastry Chef, throwing his arms into the air. "So it is true! I knew it! This is wonderful! So wonderful!"

He hopped around the counter and took Guster by the shoulders. "Just one extra drop of lemon, my boy, and nothing more. But that's too much for you, now isn't it?"

Guster was annoyed. He'd done it on purpose.

The chef peered down at Guster. "Some have the eyes of an eagle. There are others who can hear a pin drop in a crowded shopping mall. But there are few indeed who can taste the stories of the world with their tongues. You have a gift," whispered the Master Pastry Chef.

Zeke could crack jokes, and Mariah was really smart. But him? A gift?

"And that is why I need a new recipe," said Mom. "Somehow I have to make a meal that he'll eat."

"A recipe!" hacked the Master Pastry Chef. He hobbled over to a cluttered book shelf, shuffling his slippers as he went. "Very well! Let me see!" he said and pulled a yellowed piece of parchment from the shelves. He peered at it in the low light, muttering to himself, then tossed it aside.

"No, that won't do," he said. He opened a drawer, yanked out a scroll and untied the ribbon around it. The scroll unrolled across the floor. He turned it over then tossed it aside too. Next he limped to the book shelves, and while standing on his tip-toes, ran his finger across the titles written on their spines. *The Creams That Crippled the Crown*, read one. *Tastes and Treachery*, read another, *The Forbidden City of Flavor and Pain*, read a third. He stopped at a large, red, leather bound volume as thick as his head. His finger lingered on the title, *The Final Season*. He turned to face Mom, taking his shaking hands away from the book. "I don't know if I have what you are looking for."

But he had to! As strange as the Master Pastry Chef was, this was one of the few times Guster had tasted something that did not hurt him. It was his one hope. If anyone could give them a worthwhile recipe, it would be this chef, and now he was saying he couldn't help them?

"Those tarts, you like them, don't you?" he asked Guster.

Guster nodded. He liked them very much indeed.

"It took me years to find the perfect combination of ingredients. Thousands of trials before I finally made them into the mouthwatering treat they are. You may eat one hundred in a row, savoring every particle." He shook his head, "But alas, you would even tire of them. Their taste too, would fade. And so it is for all cuisine."

There was sadness in the old pastry chef's voice. Those tarts were the best taste Guster had ever had. He wanted to help the chef somehow, tell him that it wasn't true, that his tarts would never grow old.

"Except, there is —" the old man shook his head, "No, I shouldn't. I cannot tell you. The burden would be too great," he said, then bent over in a fit of coughing. He coughed for over a minute, sucking in a great lung full of air. Sweat poured from his face and his cheeks turned deep red until he finally collapsed in an easy chair in the corner.

The Master Pastry Chef seemed like he'd grown older, as if decades had passed since they'd come to the Patisserie. He breathed slowly, muttering, arguing with himself. "But they're here, and I don't see any other way. No, no other way." He paused, turning back to them with a piercing glare. "Are you sure you want a dish so exquisite, so luscious, that, once you taste it, you will never care to eat anything else again?"

Guster looked to Mom. He couldn't cook. She had to be the one to agree. She wiped the last of the tart from his cheeks, sadness in her eyes. "Yes," she said.

"Very well," sighed the Pastry Chef. "I am about to tell you a secret you must take to your grave. Do I have your word?"

Mom hesitated. "Yes," she said.

"Any gourmet historian will tell you how merchants risked their lives to sail their ships around the horn of Africa just so they could trade spice. They will tell you that tea was the final straw that started the American Revolution. They know that Kings define their countries by the dishes they eat! They know the power of flavor! They know that history hangs in the balance, and taste will tip the scales! Since the day Paris was founded, gourmets everywhere have been seeking — baking, cooking and experimenting endlessly.

"See these books?" he nearly shouted, pointing to the hundreds of cookbooks stuffed into his shelves. "Across the world there's a trillion more! Why write them?" he shook his head and threw up his hands. He wasn't making eye contact anymore, like he was talking to himself. "Why make yet another recipe? What is it that they want to find?

"*It* of course! The One Recipe."

The rain pounded on the roof like bullets as the Pastry Chef's eyes grew wide. "I will tell you this night that the legends are true! The One Recipe exists! The One that is delicious beyond compare. It is shrouded in legend, but as real as you and I. The One Recipe that none have tasted, but men have killed for in hopes that they might be the first to savor just a teaspoon of it." He coughed, then leaned dangerously close, "And those killers are among us!"

Mom clutched Guster's hand. She was trembling. "Zeke, will you please go get the car?" she said, handing him the keys. He was stuffing tarts into his mouth with both hands. Mom must have been as scared as Guster if she was letting Zeke drive again. Zeke tip-toed carefully out the back door, taking a look back before he closed it.

"That One Recipe, as they tell it, is the Gastronomy of Peace," said the Master Pastry Chef.

He motioned to a large red cake high up on the shelf behind the counter. It was several layers thick, like a tower, covered in a smooth frosting, with intricate designs across the borders. "Boy, would you be so kind as to get that cake down from the shelf?" he said.

Was that it? thought Guster, *the Gastronomy of Peace?*

"Go ahead honey," Mom said without taking her eyes off the Master Pastry Chef. Guster squeezed his mother's hand before letting go, slid a stool up to the shelf, and started to climb — keeping an eye on the chef all the while.

Shiny pearls of sugar shined across the cake's edges in the dim light. On the top was an intricate drawing in frosting of a dove on a spoon with an olive branch. The smell was so heavenly that the strange chef, the dark alleyways outside and his talk of killing for food didn't seem to matter so much anymore. The frosting would be perfect; there was no doubt about that. Guster lifted it down from the shelf and stepped to the floor carefully. It was much heavier than it looked.

"Bring it here," said the Master Pastry Chef. Guster took it to the old man. "Now drop it," he said.

"No!" Guster cried. He couldn't destroy a dessert as beautiful as this one — not without tasting it.

The Master Pastry Chef looked pleadingly into Guster's eyes, the veins on his forehead throbbing like they were about to burst. "Please," he said.

The old man was so pitiful, so frail and weak he seemed like he could die at any moment. Guster could not refuse. He dropped the cake.

It fell to the floor and broke all over, smearing bits of frosting and sponge everywhere. Something hard clanged against the ground. In the middle of the mess lay an old, oversized metal eggbeater with a long wooden handle. A faint hint of pickled ginger seeped into the room.

"Take it!" The Master Pastry Chef stood up, grabbing Guster by the shoulders, his aged eyes popping from his skull. Guster reached for the eggbeater.

His fingers almost touched it when lightning flashed and the electric lights in the glass case went out. There was a crash of shattering glass and a grunt, then more smell of pickled ginger. Guster turned. The lightning flashed again, and standing next to Mom was a man dressed as red as the devil himself.

He wore a tall, red, cylindrical chef's hat pulled over his face with two eye holes cut in it like a mask. His red apron was as long as a snake, streaming out the window through which he'd come. His chef's jacket was red as blood. He pulled a giant shining metal meat cleaver from his belt and raised it into the air.

Guster was too scared to scream. He was too scared to move. He felt Mom grab his hand and drag him to the back door where they had come in. The lightning flashed again. In that split second Guster saw more than he wanted to. The old Master Pastry Chef coughed one more time, "Get it to Felicity!" he said, then fell back into his chair, clutching his chest. His eyes rolled back into his head as the red-aproned chef sprang toward him.

"The eggbeater!" cried Guster as he realized what was happening. He lunged for the eggbeater, scooping it up as Mom pulled on his shirt and dragged him from the room. The doorframe of the back door bumped his shoulder hard as she yanked him into the alleyway.

The old Suburban screeched to a halt in front of them, knocking over a trashcan.

Zeke honked the horn. "Let's get out of here, Mom!" he yelled. Guster had never been so glad to see Zeke in his life. He jumped into the back seat, slammed the door shut behind him, then smashed his hand down on the lock as the Suburban accelerated. The red-aproned chef burst into the alley, his cleaver wound up and ready to throw.

Guster ducked as the red chef hurled the giant knife. It flew, spinning straight toward the back door of the Suburban. The engine roared then metal clanged where the knife struck the car as they zoomed off into the night.

Chapter 4 — The Eggbeater

"We're safe now. We're safe now," Mom breathed over and over as they drove home from the city. Guster could tell that she was crying, and it scared him. She reached behind her seat, put her hand on Guster's knee, then moved it to Zeke's shoulder, then back to Guster's knee again, as if making sure her boys were really there.

"What happened?" Zeke yelled.

"Zeke," said Mom — Guster could tell she was trying to keep calm — her voice cracked anyway, "The Chef in Red is real."

The words sent a wave of cold fear through Guster. It had all happened so fast.

"What?" Zeke screamed. The car swerved violently, then straightened again. Zeke seemed so terrified, he hadn't noticed he'd cranked the wheel. "What did he want?"

Guster cradled the eggbeater in his lap. Perhaps this was the answer.

"I don't know!" cried Mom. Her eyes darted around the car. "I've got to call Dad," she said. She flipped open her phone and started punching keys.

"Oh no oh no oh no oh no oh no oh no no no no," Zeke muttered. His eyebrows wrinkled, like he'd done something to feel guilty about.

"Henry, Henry! We need you!" Mom hung up. "It went straight to voicemail," she said.

"Mom!" Zeke yelled at the top of his lungs.

She put up her hand to silence him. "Not now. I have to call the police," she said. The car swerved again.

"I left my learner's permit in the pastry shop!" he cried.

Mom closed her phone. She turned to Zeke and looked him carefully in the eye, as if studying him. "You what?" she said calmly.

"I didn't mean to. I just set it down when I was putting cookies in my pocket!" he said.

Fear crept from Guster's chest up into his neck. Zeke had shoved that permit in his face every day since he'd gotten it. The address to the farmhouse was printed on it, for anyone who picked up the permit to read. This changed things. Two seconds ago, they'd merely been in the wrong place at the wrong time. Going home was supposed to fix all that. Now nothing was certain.

"We can't go home," breathed Zeke. "We can't."

"Henry Junior," Mom muttered to herself. Her round face bent with worry. "Zeke, drive as fast as you can."

"But I don't have my permit! I'll get a ticket."

"I'll make a ticket look like a piece of candy if you don't step on it right now!"

Zeke smashed down the gas. The Suburban's tires burned into the asphalt as they sped along the highway. Mom was quiet the rest of the drive home.

Guster watched the shadows beside the road pass, the memory of the shining cleaver gleaming in his mind. How long did they have until the Chef in Red came for them? An hour? Two?

It seemed like days before Zeke finally pulled the Suburban into the garage. "Mariah!" Mom called as she rushed inside. Guster followed, clutching the eggbeater in hand.

Mariah came down the stairs into the family room. Mom grabbed her into a tight hug. "You okay?"

"Fine," said Mariah, her chin-length black hair still wet from a shower. She looked confused.

"Where's Henry Junior?" asked Mom.

"Upstairs. Sleeping," said Mariah.

Mom bent down to her level. "You know that story Zeke told you about the Chef in Red?" Mariah nodded. Mom looked straight into her face. "We saw him."

Mariah's eyes widened in horror. "Where? How?"

Mom explained everything as quickly as she could. "Get upstairs. Pack your backpacks. We'll go to Aunt Priscilla's in Key West. We can drive all night. We'll try calling the police from there. It'll be safer than staying at home."

Suddenly, the farmhouse wasn't the same anymore. It was as if the walls weren't as thick, like anyone could see right through them; like someone had broken in.

"Go," said Mom. Her voice was shaky.

It only took a minute for Guster to climb the stairs to his room, grab a jacket and throw a change of clothes into his backpack. Zeke was right behind him. Guster had never seen him so eager to obey. "You okay Capital P?" Zeke asked while they packed. Guster didn't know what to do; Zeke had never talked to him like a human before.

"Yeah," Guster said and tromped downstairs, but he wasn't so sure if he was. Zeke zipped up his pack and followed.

When Guster got downstairs, Mom was in the kitchen throwing a loaf of bread, pickles, tins of sardines — whatever food she could find — into a basket with one hand while Henry Junior slept on her shoulder. The little toddler, with Guster's same wispy brown hair and blue eyes, was practically a miniature version of Guster — brave and a little bit reckless. Guster felt a sudden urge to protect him.

"Guster, I want you to go out back and throw that eggbeater down the well," said Mom to Guster when he entered the kitchen. It was lying on the kitchen table where Guster had left it.

He opened his mouth to protest. Mom cut him off before he could. "Honey, I don't know where that pastry chef got all those wild ideas about secret recipes, but I think it would be best if we got as far away from the whole thing as possible."

"But —" Guster said.

"Go," she said, cutting him off again, then put her clenched knuckles on her hips. It was her Mom stance, and that always meant the argument was over.

Guster slipped his backpack over his shoulders, took the eggbeater in hand, and trudged out the back door. The screen door banged shut behind him. He stopped at the edge of the porch, clutching the eggbeater to his chest with both hands and absorbing the night. The old stone well lay in a patch of weeds on the far side of the wide backyard.

The Master Pastry Chef had promised so much — the perfect dish — a taste that could fill Guster's aching, empty stomach. A reason to hope. The One Recipe he'd called it. He could have at least told them where to find it.

Instead, all he'd given Guster was an eggbeater. But it was the last thing the Pastry Chef had done before he died. It had to be important for something!

Guster stepped off the porch and turned toward a rusty spigot at the back of the house. Whatever Mom said, he couldn't throw it away. Not yet. It was the only link to the Pastry Chef and the One Recipe they had.

He pumped the spigot's lever and rinsed off the cake. The eggbeater's crank and metal beaters gleamed under the porch light. It was a strange contraption — the giant cylindrical handle was carved with irregular, tiny grooves. It was layered too, like an extra tall stack of wooden silver dollars fastened together in a column. There were five symbols skillfully imprinted around the edge of the crank that turned the beaters: a lemon, an olive, a pile of salt, a honeycomb, and a steak. Guster turned the crank. It clicked like a dial, spinning two dozen intricate gears fitted like clockwork between the crank and the beaters. They whirred.

What if the One Recipe really was so delicious that if you ate it, you would never want to eat anything else again? He couldn't even imagine what dish it would make. Was it a certain kind of filet mignon? Or A sorbet?

He felt a sudden pain of loss, a longing to know. The Pastry Chef had promised so much, but it seemed so far away. Guster was empty inside, and now his poor, beanpole stomach was drying out. He needed that recipe more than anything.

He shoved the eggbeater down into his backpack and zipped it closed.

Mom couldn't know that he had it; she'd be mad at him for keeping it, and worry too much like she always did. The long shadows cast by the barn at the side of the yard suddenly seemed to darken.

"Guster! Are you finished packing?" cried Mom from inside. There was an urgency in her voice he'd never heard before.

"Not yet!" he called, and banged through the screen door. She was still in the kitchen desperately packing food for the car. He did not look up at her as he clomped up the stairs. He had to talk to Mariah.

He found her in Henry Junior's room, furiously packing the toddler's things into a duffel bag. Her backpack was already strapped to her back.

"I think I know what the Chef in Red was looking for," said Guster. He opened his backpack and pushed it toward her, showing her the eggbeater inside. She looked at it for a second, then back up at Guster; she looked surprised.

"An eggbeater?" she said. She reached inside and pulled it out, then turned it over in her hands. "It looks like it could be in a museum." She traced her finger across the markings on the crank. "How fascinating. These look like the five flavors: bitter, sweet, sour, salty and savory."

Guster knew he could count on his sister to be interested. Mariah was always so curious about everything. "But why would some Chef in Red want this?"

Guster told her as quickly as he could about the pastry chef, what he'd said about the mysterious dish called the One Recipe, and how it had been kept a secret for a very long time. She listened intently, her dark eyes lighting up with a mixture of excitement and terror. "And so he was willing to kill for it," she said when Guster was finished. Guster nodded.

"Exactly how old is it?"

"I dunno. He said something about the Renaissance."

Mariah glanced down toward the living room where the old family computer was plugged in. Guster could tell what she was thinking. This was enough of a curiosity to send her off scouring the web for hours.

The car horn honked in the garage. "Guster!" called Mom from downstairs, panic in her voice.

Mariah stomped her foot. "If only Mom had let me get a smart phone, I could look things up while we drive!" she cried. She pinched her chin. "We'll take the encyclopedias!" she said. "We'll find out what we can on the way, then use Aunt Priscilla's high speed connection when we get there."

She stuffed two flashlights in the duffel bag and headed toward the stairs. "Mariah," Guster said. He had to let her know how much this meant to him. She turned. "Mom doesn't know," he said, glancing down at the eggbeater in his backpack.

"Guster —" said Mariah. He could tell what she was thinking. She wasn't likely to hide things from Mom.

"Please," he said. "I need this." He had to find out what the One Recipe made.

She reached out and touched the handle of the eggbeater lightly with one finger. If anything, her curiosity wouldn't let her pass up such a mystery. "Alright," she sighed. "But we'll tell Mom as soon as we find out what this is."

Guster nodded. The two of them went down the stairs where Guster helped her jam the big, dusty, red A through K encyclopedia volumes into the duffel bag, then grabbed the M, P and Z ones. They would have to make another trip if they wanted the rest, but there was no time for that. It took all their strength just to drag the heavy duffel bag across the floor into the garage.

“Hurry up, slow-bots!” said Zeke. He still looked more scared than anyone. So scared that he didn’t seem to notice the duffel bag was full of more than a dozen heavy books when he helped Mariah load it into the back of the Suburban.

Guster jumped into the fold-up seat in the very back. “Wait,” said Mariah, and ran back into the house. She came back a second later with one more big red volume under her arm. “Had to get the R,” she whispered as she climbed in next to Guster and buckled her seat belt.

“For Renaissance?” he whispered.

“For Recipe,” she said, her teeth gleaming in the dark.

“Seat belts!” Mom said, then punched the gas and peeled out of the driveway. In seconds, the farmhouse was out of sight.

Mom drove through the center of town on the way to the highway. The old shops where Guster had gone in search of treats seemed different somehow, as if — like the patisserie — they had something to hide. It was as if the town Guster once knew had lost its innocence; as if it was changing forever. Guster, Mom, Mariah, Zeke, and Henry Junior might never come back; and it had all started with a chef in a blood-red apron.

Chapter 5 — Late Night News

Guster woke to his head thumping against the window. His neck was sore. It was still dark out. Mom was up front driving, Zeke sprawled across the seat in the middle, his leg draped over Henry Junior's car seat, his foot swaying so close to the little toddler's face that whenever they hit a bump in the road, Henry Junior tried to bite Zeke's toe.

Guster did not recognize the shadowy trees or the open marsh. He'd never been to Aunt Priscilla's summer home, and as far as he could tell, the family had never been so far east either. 'Welcome to Florida' read a sign on the side of the road.

Mariah was asleep in the seat next to him, flashlight in one hand, her chin resting on her chest, the 'E' encyclopedia open in her lap. Guster glanced at the article. "Eggbeater" it read. From the looks of it, it was a short and useless entry.

He unzipped his backpack quietly, so Mom couldn't hear, and removed the eggbeater. Now that they weren't evacuating the house he could examine it more closely. It was larger and far more intricate than the ones pictured in the article.

He turned the crank until the salty symbol on the crank's edge lined up with a tiny needle protruding from the wooden handle. He was hungry, and the symbols on the crank only reminded him of what he'd tasted in the patisserie — how delicious food could be. He turned the crank to the honeycomb symbol for sweetness, then back three-quarters turns to the olive branch for bitter. Then, almost as if in a daydream, he turned it one and a half times back to salty again. Something in the handle clicked.

Startled, Guster shined Mariah's flashlight on the eggbeater to make sure he hadn't broken the old thing. Instead, the tiny grooves in the handle had rotated; they were lining up. From the looks of it, they were forming the picture of a man's face.

He shook Mariah. He had to show her. "Wake up," he whispered, "You have to see this."

Mariah opened her eyes and stretched. "Are we there?" she yawned.

"Not yet," Mom called from the front. "Just a few more hours."

Guster put his finger to his lips to quiet his sister. Mariah blinked her eyes, then looked down at the eggbeater. Her face brightened with understanding.

She grabbed it and turned it over in her hands, peering closely at it from every angle. "Guster, do you know what this is?" she whispered. Guster shook his head. The face in the carving was strange — with a huge nose and pointy chin — it wasn't anyone he recognized, if that's what she meant.

"It's a combination lock! Dad used to have one on his briefcase. There are five numbers in a row, and you have to line them all up so that the locks will come undone. Only this one's got hundreds of these little rows, and it works the other way around." She pointed to the discs that had lined up. "See?" she said, pointing to where the grooves formed the outline of a man's forehead and nose. "But everything below that is still messy."

She peered at symbols on the crank, then turned it a few times back and forth. The grooves shifted and the face was gone. “I lost it!” she said. “How did you get it to work?”

“Let me see,” said Guster. He took the beater and turned the crank back to the olive branch. *What would I eat?* he thought. *Something bitter. Something sour*. He turned the crank to the lemon. *Something sweet*. Then back to the honeycomb, just like he’d done before. The grooves in the wooden handle began to line up again, one by one, until the carving of the face reappeared.

“You're doing it!” whispered Mariah, amazed. “Keep going.”

Guster tried. He carefully turned the crank back and forth, sometimes to the olive, sometimes to the pile of salt. Sometimes he’d turn it twice in one direction before coming to the next symbol; other times he’d turn it the opposite way one-fifth of a turn, depending on how much of the taste he craved. Whichever way he went, he followed his instincts, like an invisible hand was guiding the crank handle. Slowly, the grooves lined up down the length of the handle until they were no longer just grooves, but a complete row of intricately carved symbols. The last disk clicked into place.

“How did you do that?” Mariah cried.

“I dunno, I just turned the flavors to whatever I wanted,” said Guster.

Mariah eyed her brother. “You truly are remarkable,” she said.

Guster blushed. Whenever anyone called him remarkable, they were usually talking about how difficult he was to feed.

Mariah picked the eggbeater out of Guster’s hand. “It’s like a totem pole,” she said. The handle was divided into rows of carvings, each one wrapping around the circumference. Mariah pointed to the set of symbols on the top row.

"See, here's the entire face," she said, pointing to the man's nose. "And that looks like a tree with some kind of large oval fruit," she said, pointing to the second symbol on the row. "And these, I don't know what these are," she said pointing to the smaller ones.

Guster peered closely at the symbols under the flashlight. So this was why the Master Pastry Chef had given the eggbeater to Guster. It wasn't for mixing the recipe, nor was it some kind of key. It was far more important than that. "Mariah, this *is* the One Recipe," Guster said, "or a map to it."

"Encoded on the eggbeater so no one can find it," she said. "It's brilliant." She opened up the encyclopedia again. "We've got to find that face. I'm almost positive I've seen it before."

The car hit another bump and Zeke's foot swung straight into Henry Juniors open, waiting jaws. The little boy bit down.

"Ow Carumba!" cried Zeke. He bolted straight up in his seat. "That little muskrat chomped my toe off!" he screamed. "Check him for rabies! Check him for rabies!" Henry Junior started to cry.

"Don't make me pull over!" Mom snapped, turning in the driver's seat.

"It's not my fault!" said Zeke. He got quiet; Henry Junior's wailing filled the car, then lessened. Guster stowed the eggbeater back in his backpack. He didn't want to have to explain it to Zeke.

"I have to go," said Zeke quietly.

"How bad?" asked Mom.

"Niagara falls bad."

"You'll have to wait five minutes at least," said Mom.

They pulled off the highway onto an exit and turned into a gas station with bright fluorescent lights. There was a car at the pump and a row of cars parked in the shadows behind the station. Some of them looked abandoned.

Zeke bolted from the Suburban before Mom had even switched off the engine. Guster shoved his backpack under his seat and climbed over the seat in front of him and out the door, with Mariah right behind him. He might as well see what snacks Florida's gas stations had to offer, though it probably wasn't much. He was glad to stretch his legs at least.

He pushed open the grimy double glass doors Zeke had gone through. There was a woman with a stained gas station uniform behind the counter chewing loudly, her eyes glued to the TV set mounted on the wall. Guster made for the snack aisle. Orange Styrofoam puffballs and shoelaces made out of beef. *Might as well have them with a warm cup of used motor oil*, thought Guster.

The late night news blared a headline from the TV, "The smoke from the Foodco Instant Dinners Factory explosion can be seen from several miles away," said the anchorwoman. "The fire department suspects arson, but police have yet to make any arrests."

Guster dropped the bag of orange puffies. The TV screen showed a wall of flames and firemen. An explosion at an instant dinner plant? He'd never liked instant dinners, but who would want to blow up a factory like that?

"Roastin'!" said Zeke, returning from the restroom and looking up at the television. Mom came through the doors, Henry Junior on her hip.

"In other news," continued the anchorwoman, "famed celebrity homemaker Felicity Casa was arrested today for robbery of the world famous Arrivederci Chocolate Vault."

Mom gasped. *Felicity Casa? Under arrest?* Guster thought. He glued his eyes to the screen.

The anchorwoman continued, "The vault contains a treasured collection of the Italian chocolate-brewing family's most valuable chocolates. Felicity's spokesman Benjamin Arnold had this to say at today's press conference —"

The TV showed a tall, slender man with slick black hair and a pencil-thin tie. He spoke into a microphone. "We are disappointed that such serious accusations would be leveled at our dear Ms. Casa. Our legal team is working around the clock, and we are absolutely confident that Ms. Casa will be proven innocent in a court of law."

"We know how much the public admired her, and are certain they will show their support," he said.

"Italo Arrivederci, descendant of the famous chocolatier of the same name and heir to the family chocolate fortune, made the following comment —" said the anchorwoman. The scene switched to a man in a trim navy suit.

"So Felicity Casa wanted some chocolate. 'We have aplenty to sell you,' I says. But that wasn't good enough. She wanted the prize jewel from the vault — the family fortune! Ha! Like we'd ever sell that! Not for a million dollars a pound!"

The anchorwoman continued, with a slight sniffle, "The Arrivederci Family has been making the most exquisite chocolate in the world since the Renaissance. The Arrivederci chocolate vault, therefore, has often been a target for many failed robbery attempts — until now. The chocolate has yet to be found.

"Currently, Felicity is imprisoned in the Lovelock, Nevada Maximum Security Prison where she awaits trial."

The camera showed an angry mob protesting outside a high rise building labeled "Casa Brand Industries."

"Fans everywhere are throwing out their 'Casa Brand' curtains and cookware. I for one, will be keeping mine," said the anchorwoman. She stared straight into the camera.

Guster couldn't believe it — Mom's hero, behind bars. "It can't be!" said Mom.

"Why not? The woman'll do anything to get ingredients!" sneered the lady behind the counter. "She's a billionaire! You'se gots to break a few eggs to make an omelet!"

Mom steadied herself on the candy shelf. "She seemed like such a good woman. She made homes into such splendid places."

"She was a celebrity! Only an actor," said the lady behind the counter. "You can put 'em all in jail to rot if ya ask me!"

Mom stood up again. Guster thought about the shelf of video cassettes she had back at home that she'd used to record every episode. She looked like she was trying not to cry. "No matter. Guster, Zeke, no dawdling, we've got to get back on the road." She hurried back outside.

Guster lingered at the TV. To think, Felicity was nothing but a common criminal. It made all her past episodes seem different somehow. But hadn't the Master Pastry Chef said, just before he'd died, "Get it to Felicity?" There were millions of Felicity's in the world. Had he meant *the* Felicity Casa? That made sense, if the symbols on the eggbeater were indeed the One Recipe.

"Let's go, Fanboy," said Zeke bumping Guster with his shoulder on his way out.

"It's all so strange," said Mariah.

"I dunno," said Guster, "Maybe she did it." The worst part was that Felicity wasn't going to have any more cooking shows. Those demos had been his only hope that Mom would learn to make a decent meal. Guster cast a final glance at the snacks. It was useless.

"That's not what I mean. The fire at the Foodco plant," Mariah said as they made their way to the car. "Why would anyone want to burn down a food factory?"

Guster knew she was right. It was strange, but there were bigger things to worry about right then. They climbed into the back of the Suburban and shut the door.

"No way! Check out the cream colored caddy with those stainless steel rims," said Zeke, opening the driver's side door. Mom stepped between him and the car and pointed her thumb at the passenger seat. Zeke reluctantly obeyed and went around to the other side.

"That's the same killer ride I saw behind us in Mississippi," he continued, pointing to a Cadillac parked behind the gas station. Its lights were off. "It's like it's following us or something."

Guster felt a knot form in his stomach. "What did you say?" asked Mom, her voice serious.

Zeke's cheeks quivered. "Maybe it's a different one?"

"Maybe," Mom said, and turned on the ignition. "Buckle up kids. I don't want to find out."

She pulled out of the gas station and took a right onto the freeway onramp. The cream-colored Cadillac's headlights switched on. It followed slowly after them.

"I didn't know!" cried Zeke. Guster twisted in his seat and looked out the back window. The Cadillac was only a few hundred feet behind, motoring along, maintaining a healthy distance. Mom kept feeding the Suburban more gas. The engine shuddered; the orange speedometer needle crept up on 100 miles per hour.

"They're going to kill us!" cried Zeke.

Then suddenly, Mom switched lanes, slowed down, and pulled off onto the shoulder. "What are you doing?" cried Zeke. "They'll catch us!"

"You'll understand when your older, son," said Mom with a curt smile. She turned off the road and plowed over a dirt mound into a dark orchard. The suburban hit the bump so hard, it nearly knocked Guster's head against the ceiling. Mom shut off the lights, leaving the orchard darker still.

The Cadillac slowed where Mom turned off the road, then sped on. "No 'killer ride' can follow this 4x4," said Mom, imitating Zeke. She steered through the trees onto a narrow, crumbly road and switched the lights back on.

Guster felt his heart beating. Why did it seem like everyone in the world was after them?

Mom took back roads for a few miles, then finally made her way back to the freeway. The sun was rising. Guster leaned against the window again. The daylight made everything feel just a little bit safer. He was so tired.

He woke a few hours later. Mariah was flipping through the encyclopedias, comparing every portrait she could find with the face on the eggbeater.

"You find anything?" Guster asked.

"Not yet," she said. "It's not like I can just open up an article, and see the matching picture, since we don't even have a name. So I have to scan by article. I've looked at almost every portrait of famous chefs, kings, or generals I can think of, but nothing matches up. I even looked at actors. I'm almost positive I've seen this face before." She held up the eggbeater. "He looks like his eyes are closed, and he's smiling, almost like he's got a secret."

"What about the tree?" asked Guster.

"Can't find anything about that yet either. I've never seen a tree with such big fruit."

Guster shrugged. It was like trying to read Egyptian hieroglyphics. "Doesn't look like anything I've ever seen either."

The swamps gave way to high-rises and the high-rises gave way to open beach until the Suburban was driving along a bridge that stretched out over the ocean for miles and miles. "Aunt Priscilla's is just at the end of this bridge," said Mom. She sounded tired. "I didn't tell her we're coming so everyone will need to be on their best behavior."

There was nothing but blue water on either side for as far as Guster could see. He felt like a toy car on a track, with nowhere to go but forward.

He turned around in his seat to see how far they'd come, when his heart gave a start. There behind them, not more than a few hundred yards back was the cream Cadillac. "Mom! They're back!" he cried. There was no doubt about it. They were being followed.

"How did they find us?" yelled Zeke. He slammed his hand down on the locks. "What are we going to do? We can't turn off now!"

"We're going to gun it!" said Mom and pounded the accelerator. The engine roared. The big orange needle dipped past 110 mph. Guster could feel the car floating over the bumps in the bridge, they were going so fast.

The Cadillac was closing the gap anyway. The long bridge was ending; "Hurry Mom! Hurry!" screamed Zeke.

It took five agonizing seconds to reach the island. Mom cranked the wheel hard at the first side street, slamming Guster into the side of the Suburban, Mariah pressing up against him like they were all lumps of Jell-O.

The tires squealed as Mom made two more quick turns then slammed on the brakes at a little call box next to a huge wrought iron gate. She reached out and smashed a button next to the speaker.

It buzzed. "Hello?" said a bored, nasally voice.

"Priscilla! It's your sister! Let us in!" screamed Mom.

"Mabel? What are you doing here? Do you have an appointment?"

"Priscilla, we're being followed. We're in danger!"

"Oh, very well, come in and we'll have a late lunch," said Aunt Priscilla. And then in the background, "Open the gate, they've got themselves all worked up about dying or something."

The wrought iron gate rolled open. The Cadillac rounded the corner and zoomed down the street. Mom squeezed the Suburban through as soon as the gate was open wide enough.

The Cadillac hit the driveway as the gate slid closed again, blocking the car. The driver slammed on his brakes, inches away from the gate. Guster could see him — a man with a thick neck and aviator sunglasses staring him down from the other side of the iron beams, his black leather gloves gripping the wheel.

Chapter 6 — Aunt Priscilla

Mom sped up the driveway toward Aunt Priscilla's house. It was about four times as big as anything else they'd passed on the island, with a carved, weathered wooden façade that made it look like an old ship. The best part was the stone walls surrounding the grounds. They were twice as high as Zeke was tall and thicker than a giant stack of Mom's blueberry pancakes — plenty dry and sturdy enough to keep the man in the Cadillac out.

Mom stopped the Suburban and they all piled out. The long trip was finally over, and none too soon. Guster glanced back at the gate — the Cadillac was turning around.

A skinny old man in a dark jacket, gloves and cap came out of a set of wide stained-glass doors. "Let me help you with those," he said, taking Mariah and Zeke's backpacks. When he reached for Guster's, Guster held it back.

"I'll carry it," Guster said. The eggbeater was inside, and he didn't want to let anyone besides himself or Mariah get near it.

"I understand an unwelcome fella has followed you home," said the old man in the cap to Mom. "I wouldn't worry too much about that now. We keep a tight watch on the grounds. You'll be safe inside these walls."

"We're grateful," said Mom.

"Woah! This place must cost a billion dollars!" said Zeke as they entered the house. The entryway was decorated with silver candlesticks, and the spiral stair at the far end had a shiny gold railing. Mom shot Zeke a stern look.

"I should warn you though," the old man in the cap said, setting the backpacks down inside the entryway, "Ms. Priscilla has had some special 'circumstances' develop lately." He pointed to his nose and winked. "She got one of them upgrades, if you know what I mean. Best not to mention it."

"No way! She got a nose job?" Zeke said. He smiled mischievously.

"Mabel, darling sister? Is that you?" came a bored voice from a spacious living room next to the entry. A tall, slender woman with shiny black hair who looked like a skinnier, more elegant version of Mom was draped across a red leather couch, her left hand resting on a ship's wooden steering wheel. She sounded like she was holding her nose when she talked. "Mabel dear, I'm in here," she said without getting up. "I'm resting. Doctors say I'm to relax for a few days — well, for certain reasons." She touched the cast on her nose when her face suddenly grew grim. "But never mind that!"

Guster followed Mom across the hardwood floor into the living room where Aunt Priscilla sat up and put her arms gingerly around Mom in a weak hug. "How are you?"

"Wonderful, Priscilla," said Mom, hugging her sister back.

"Glad to hear it. My don't you look —" Aunt Priscilla forced a grin, "lovely?" she said, smoothing out Mom's baby blue apron. "Braxton? What are you still doing here? Get those bags stored in the upstairs rooms. This is family time."

Braxton tipped his black cap and hauled the backpacks up the spiral staircase.

Aunt Priscilla leaned over to give Zeke a hug. He reached his arms out to wrap around her back when he bumped her cast with his shoulder. It did not seem like an accident.

"Aaaa!" howled Aunt Priscilla in a nasally voice. She held her hands up to her face and tried to straighten the cast. "It hasn't set yet! You'll ruin it!"

"Ruin what?" asked Zeke innocently.

Aunt Priscilla stood up straight. "Hmmph! Nothing. Never mind," she said, waving her hand toward the rooms upstairs. "Why don't you go have a rest?"

"Nose problem!" said Zeke, following Braxton up the staircase and laughing to himself the whole way.

Instead of hugging Mariah, Aunt Priscilla carefully patted her head from a distance then shook Guster's hand.

Mariah went up the stairs after Zeke. Guster followed. At the top, thick red carpet covered a hall that led to dozens of rooms. "Here're your quarters, little lady," called out Braxton from down the hall. "It's got a nice fluffy bed and your own bathroom." Guster and Mariah went inside.

"A computer too!" said Mariah. "Is it connected to the web?" she asked.

Braxton nodded. Mariah smiled at Guster. He knew what she was thinking. She'd be able to look up whatever image she wanted now.

Braxton showed Guster to the room across the hall. It had a window that overlooked the backyard, where a sleek, silvery jet was parked on a runway that pointed out to the sea. "This room's yours," he said. "Your brother will be down the hall."

"My own room! Finally, I'll be stink-free!" said Zeke. He made a face at Guster, then ducked out of sight. Guster ignored him. The further away Zeke was, the easier it would be for him and Mariah to do research.

He waited until Braxton was gone then tiptoed into Mariah's room. She'd already booted up the computer.

"Here," he said, laying the eggbeater down on the table next to her. "I'm going to go check on Henry Junior."

He went down the staircase. Checking on Henry Junior was only half the reason to go downstairs. He wanted to see if the cream colored Cadillac had really gone, so he opened the giant front doors just a crack and slipped outside. Down at the far end of the driveway the iron gate was still shut fast. The street beyond was empty. Whoever it was with the thick neck and aviator glasses had given up — at least for now.

Guster slipped back through the door. He heard dishes clanging, so he passed through a dining room by a long varnished table with clawed feet, and peeked inside a set of swinging double saloon doors. Aunt Priscilla had pried herself off the couch, and she and Mom were in the kitchen. Henry Junior was sleeping in his car seat on the counter. Mom was doing dishes.

"Honestly Mabel," said Aunt Priscilla, "The help will take care of this. I just hired a new chef today — a top chef. He'll be here to cook us our late lunch. We can have him or Braxton do this. There's no reason for you to be your usual obsessive self over this sort of thing."

"It's habit," said Mom.

"Hmmph," Aunt Priscilla said under her breath, and leaned lazily against the kitchen counter. "I've got to tell you Mabel, the press has been absolutely hounding me ever since *Billions* magazine named me top businesswoman of the year. I had to come out here to Key West to get away from it all; though sometimes I think this ship-décor is just awful rubbish. I assure you though, it was designed by someone very expensive," Aunt Priscilla yawned and scanned Mom's baby blue apron, then glanced at Henry Junior. "You know, it's quite a shame that you never did anything with that history degree of yours," she said.

Mom blinked at her. "I met Henry," she said. "And marriage — and then the children — well, it sort of took over." She rinsed another dish and put it in the dishwasher.

"Ah. Of course. Don't know if you can do much with a history degree anyway," said Aunt Priscilla. She laughed. It sounded more like a bark. "Too bad though. There would have been so many ways for you to use that sharp mind of yours."

Mom turned off the sink. "What do you mean?" she asked, her eyes narrowed.

"Oh, don't get me wrong, Mabel!" said Aunt Priscilla sitting up and putting out her perfectly manicured hands. "You had the children!"

Mom didn't flinch.

"And such precious little ones they are!" cried Aunt Priscilla. "It's just that I wonder what could have been, had you moved to the coast when I did, years ago. Would it be different? Would you have achieved great things?"

"But I live on the farm. With *them*," said Mom motioning toward the upstairs.

"Yes, of course! Of course! But do you want to stay there forever? Have you ever even left the United States of America?" asked Aunt Priscilla.

Mom shrugged her shoulders and started wiping the counter. She pressed the countertop so furiously, it looked more like she was sanding than washing it.

"It might be good for you to go abroad, Mabel. To have an adventure. Someday I ought to take you off to Paris in my private jet. It's parked out back on my own personal airstrip," she boasted, "You could see the world. Then you could *do* something with your life."

Mom threw the rag in the sink. "I may just take you up on that," she said. There was a shortness to her voice, something wholly different than she used when scolding Guster.

The kitchen doors swung open and Mom charged through them, past Guster, and up the stairs, stomping all the way.

Guster waited a moment, then followed her. He veered off at Mariah's room. "Mom seems mad," said Mariah, her eyes glued to the computer.

"How can you tell?" Guster asked.

Mariah turned to look at Guster. "It's just something we women know about."

Guster figured he could worry about that later. For now he had bigger things on his mind. "Is the net helping?"

"It is, but it's still difficult. It's not like I can just scan the image and get a result. I have to search by trial and error. Believe me, I've already tried the words 'the One Recipe.'"

Guster sat on the bed and watched. He wished he could be more help, but he couldn't think of anything to search that Mariah hadn't already tried. It wasn't long before his eyelids grew heavy again.

His dozing stopped when Zeke jumped on the bed. "Aunt Priscilla says lunch is ready. Even you'll love this one, Guster. She says she's got some new fancy chef." Guster rubbed his eyes.

Mariah was still on the computer, clicking furiously. The backpack was zipped up next to her, and the eggbeater was nowhere in sight. She must've hidden it before Zeke came in the room.

"Go ahead," she said. "I'll be there in a minute."

Guster trudged downstairs, working the blood back into his legs and arms, trying to wake himself up. He entered the dining room and was jolted alert by the most delicious smells.

The table was covered with summer salads, simmering meats, rice with fish in a succulent-smelling sauce, and pork chops smothered in applesauce. Mom was already seated with Henry Junior next to her at the table. Guster's poor starving beanpole stomach nearly shoved him down into the chair across from the kitchen doors all by itself. He could hardly wait. He reached for a pork chop.

"Not until your brother and sister get here," said Mom. Her words were like a jail door slamming shut between him and the food. He wanted to scream.

Zeke pulled up a chair across the table from Guster. Mariah wasn't there yet. What could be taking so long? Guster needed this meal. It looked so delicious, and it felt like he hadn't eaten in years.

A minute later she came rushing down the stairs, Guster's backpack in her hand. "I found something," she whispered to Guster.

"You did?" Guster exclaimed. Mom glanced over at them.

"Not now," mouthed Mariah silently. Guster nodded. They'd talk about it when Mom wasn't around.

"It looks lovely Priscilla," said Mom.

"Just wait until you see the main dish," Aunt Priscilla said.

The double doors to the kitchen swung open and Guster nearly choked. Standing there, with a silver platter in hand, was a chef dressed as red as the devil himself.

Everyone froze — except Aunt Priscilla, who didn't seem to notice anything strange about her new employee. Guster dropped his fork. It clattered on the china.

"Oh, wonderful. Meet Sophagus. I know the name's a bit odd, but he's foreign. That's why he's such a good cook." He was clothed exactly the same as the chef from the Patisserie, just shorter, and with more muscle.

"You! It's one of them," stammered Zeke under his breath. The chef snapped his head around and stared at Zeke. A sudden fire of comprehension blazed in his eyes.

He set the silver platter on the table — it held a juicy goose — and whisked back into the kitchen.

"Let's remain calm, kids. We don't have anything he wants. Just don't eat anything," said Mom as she set down her fork. Guster thought of the eggbeater hidden in his backpack next to Mariah. Only the sound of Zeke's breathing broke the silence, then Henry Junior started to whimper.

"What do you mean, don't eat? These are fine dishes of the highest quality prepared by a top-rate chef!" exclaimed Aunt Priscilla.

"Priscilla, your chef — he's the reason we had to leave New Orleans. It's not safe."

"Nonsense!" she said. "Look at all this deliciousness! I can't eat it all myself."

Guster knew it was dangerous, but oh how badly he wanted to try just a bite!

The chef came back a moment later, placed a steaming pie on the table, and whispered something in Aunt Priscilla's ear. She laughed. "Wonderful!" she said. "Sophagus has prepared something extra special, just for you! It's a pie, a raisin-rhubarb Bubalatti!" she exclaimed.

"A what?" Guster asked. It smelled amazing, like the raisins were sweetened with fire.

"My boy! You've never heard of a Bubalatti?!" Aunt Priscilla cried. "It's not the swill you're used to eating." She glanced at Mom. "Bubalatti's is the finest pie maker in all of New York City! There's only one of these little shops, down in lower Manhattan. You have to be on the waiting list for a year to get one. Sophagus here got a hold of the recipe. Maybe you'll finally get some real delicacy in you for a change!"

Sophagus cut the pie into pieces and served Guster a slice, then disappeared into the kitchen. How delicious and spicy-sweet it smelled!

Guster picked up his fork. *This*, now *this* had to be worth the risk.

"Guster, don't," hissed Mom.

Aunt Priscilla's lined eyebrows bent like daggers. "Don't deny my hospitality, Mabel! Eat the pie, boy!"

Guster couldn't help it. Mom was going to kill him, but he had to. He opened his mouth and put a forkful to his lips — when he tasted something strange. A raging cinnamon fire burned across his mouth before he even had a chance to close it. He dropped the fork and spat. "Something tastes funny."

"Don't be ridiculous!" cried Aunt Priscilla. "It's a Bubalatti! You cannot be so presumptuous!"

"Priscilla, I'm telling you, this meal is not to be trusted!" shouted Mom, rising from her seat and picking up Henry Junior.

"First you just barge into my home unannounced with these little monsters," she glared at Zeke, "Then, you have the audacity to insult one of New York's finest pies!" She dug out a heaping forkful. "I'll show you how to enjoy fine dining!" She shoved it into her mouth. Then she downed another forkful, and another, until finally she stopped to chew. Almost immediately, her lips began to swell, her cheeks flushed red-hot, and her eyes poured tears like faucets. "Ga!" she mumbled as her cheeks and forehead swelled up like red balloons. She stumbled, then held herself up on the table.

She clutched a crystal pitcher of water in both hands and guzzled it down. "Ack!" she said, when the swelling popped her nose cast right off. It shot across the room. Underneath, she looked like a bloated frog with a plump tomato stuck to her face. A moment later, she fainted.

The chef came smashing back through the double doors, a torch in one hand, and a bowl of bananas in the other. He lit it. It burst into a curtain of flame. "Who are you?" he demanded, holding the dish overhead like he was about to throw it. "Tell me what you know!"

"Nanas!" cried Henry Junior. Guster could feel the heat on his cheeks.

The chef threw the burning bowl onto the table. The table cloth caught on fire.

"Let's get out of here!" cried Zeke, crawling under the table to Guster's side. Mom picked up the pork applesauce and threw the entire dish at the bananas flambé, dousing half the flames.

"Run!" she said. She grabbed Henry Junior, Guster grabbed the backpack, and they all dashed out into the entryway.

Mom looked back over her shoulder where Aunt Priscilla lay prostrate on the dining room floor. "Zeke, get my sister!" Mom cried. Zeke turned back, when the chef stepped into the entry, blocking Aunt Priscilla from view.

Guster shoved open the front door and bounded onto the porch. The Suburban was parked in the driveway where they had left it. At the far end, on the other side of the wrought iron gate, was the cream colored Cadillac. Guster skidded to a stop. *Cadillac outside, maniacal chef inside*, he thought. *No way out*.

"The plane!" shouted Mom. She grabbed Zeke by the hand and sprinted round the side of the house, Mariah hot on her heels. Guster followed, cinching the backpack tight to his back.

Braxton was in the side yard, pruning the hedges. "We're taking Priscilla up on her offer to see the world!" shouted Mom.

"Where's Ms. Priscilla?" Braxton asked.

"Indisposed!" said Mom.

"And we're going without her?" asked Braxton.

"Wish we didn't have to!" said Mom without slowing. Braxton dropped his pruning shears, held onto his cap and ran after them. Mom reached the silvery jet first, took the steps up to the door two at a time, and disappeared inside with Zeke and Mariah. Guster pounded after them. Braxton arrived last and yanked the steps upward and latched them shut like the door to an oven.

The plane was lined with velvet seats down the mid-section and a small cabin with two beds and a bathroom in the back. There was even a refrigerator. It reminded Guster of a motor home he'd been in once, but much fancier. Braxton ducked through a short door at the front of the plane and started flipping switches and twisting dials. Guster sat down on one of the seats.

The engines hummed to life. Guster stared out the window. The chef was coming toward them, a cleaver drawn, his crimson apron blowing in the jet stream. "Hurry Braxton!" shouted Guster.

"I've got pre-flight checks to run through. You can't just get a bird off the ground without notice."

There was a clank-clank against the fuselage. The chef was hacking into the plane with his cleaver. "Braxton!" cried Mom; there was a thrust and the jet lunged forward, pressing Guster into his seat.

In seconds, they were airborne.

Mom buckled in Henry Junior then flopped down in her chair, panting. "Please, everyone make sure you have on your safety belts." Zeke undid Mariah's while she stared out the window back at the ground below.

"So where to?" asked Braxton as he leveled out the plane.

"Somewhere far away," Mom sighed. They could breathe, for the moment.

"Peru!" shouted Mariah, nearly jumping out of her seat.

Mom gave her a funny look. Mariah pulled a folded up printout from her pocket. "I've been researching it. It's so far off the beaten path, no one will come looking for us there. I can help us find our way around."

"Okay," Mom said. She closed her eyes. "We can slow down a little bit. Strategize. Hide out for awhile until this blows over — but only until we can figure this all out," said Mom. Guster could tell that the idea of knowing a little something about where they were running to was going to help Mom feel better about the whole thing. She talked about going to unfamiliar places, but when it came down to it, she seemed nervous about actually doing it.

"There's a place there called Machu Picchu," said Mariah. "It's supposed to be absolutely spectacular." She dropped the paper into Guster's lap. He picked it up. On it was the picture of a mountain range, that, when turned on its side, looked exactly like the carved nose, chin and forehead of a very familiar face.

Chapter 7 — The Cuisine Capital of the World

Guster awoke hours later with a crick in his neck. He was exhausted. He rubbed his eyes and moved next to Mariah, who had an atlas open on her lap and the eggbeater on the seat next to her. Mom was in the cabin in the back, sleeping. "Peru is right here," she said, pointing to a country on the western edge of South America. "Braxton says we're going to land in a town called Cusco, and I've convinced Mom that we might as well take a train or a bus from there up the mountain to the ruins."

"She actually agreed?"

Mariah looked perplexed. "Surprising, right? I wonder if her conversation with Aunt Priscilla had anything to do with it."

Guster looked at the map. He was never any good at geography, and now he was going to a whole new country. They'd lived in Montana before moving to Louisiana and now they were in Florida, but Peru? He wasn't sure what to expect. "What do you know about it?" he asked.

"There are lots of jungles there, and everybody speaks Spanish," said Mariah. It was a good thing she was there to figure all this stuff out.

He sat down next to her and picked up the eggbeater to see if he could read any of the symbols. “It just doesn’t make any sense.” he said.

Mariah nodded. “I know! It seems that whoever made this eggbeater wanted the One Recipe to be kept a secret. Even after you unlocked it, it’s still quite the puzzle.” She looked frustrated. “As near as I can tell, each of these symbols points to the location of an ingredient, with a bunch of extra instructions at the end. Look. Besides just the face and the big round fruit, there are these —”

“I can’t figure out what the chickens are for. Something about it doesn’t seem quite right, like they were carved there by mistake,” she said.

Guster frowned. He couldn’t tell what kind of fruit it was from the carving. As a clue, it was a dismal one.

“And these symbols tell us where to find the second ingredient.” She pointed to the second row of carvings:

"This looks like an island, a bear, and a barrel with a wooden handle sticking out of it. The odd thing is these baking instructions inscribed under the bear. They're the only part written in English."

seventy-four degrees, thirty-one minutes
nineteen degrees, one minute

That clue wasn't very clear either. Guster was no cook, but baking something for thirty-one minutes at seventy-four degrees, then baking it for one minute at nineteen degrees seemed pointless to him. Nineteen degrees was actually really cold.

"On the third row it looks like a gorilla," said Mariah.

"The rest I can't read. It's in French. I think it must say what the actual ingredients are, and maybe the baking instructions." Couldn't the Master Pastry Chef have just written it out for them? It was going to be harder to figure out how to make the One Recipe than Guster thought. Especially since they had to hide their search from Mom.

In a few hours the plane began descending and Braxton's voice came over the intercom, "Zero ten niner! Flight Squadron breaking formation and preparing to hit the tarmac!"

"Huh?" said Zeke, waking from his nap.

Braxton turned around and hollered through the open cockpit door, "Never mind, just some old Air Force talk. I used to fly the Vice President, you know." He winked, a twinkle in his old watery eyes.

Mariah stashed the eggbeater and map away in Guster's backpack just as Mom emerged from the cabin in the back. They flew lower and closer to the jungle-covered earth, then landed smoothly, Braxton jabbering over the radio to the flight tower. He brought the plane to a stop.

"I'll wait here with the plane and get some shut-eye. You go on out there and stretch your legs," he said.

Mom looked worried.

"Oh, Ma'am, there's no sense in going straight home with all those nasty fellas running around back there in the USA. Besides, Ms. Priscilla can take care of herself indeed."

Mom looked stern. "We shouldn't have left her."

"You think she would've come?" asked Braxton. "If anything, I'd be worried more that she's going to give the what-for to those gents back home!"

Mom straightened herself up. “I suppose you’re right,” she said. “There’s nothing we can do for her now.”

“Here, take this,” said Braxton, removing a backpack from an overhead compartment and handing it to her. “You can put the little guy in there.”

Mom slid Henry Junior inside and zipped it halfway up so that his big round head stuck out the top. He looked pleased as pie.

Guster shouldered his backpack and Mariah led them out the hatch, down the steps and into the noisy, bustling airport. There were tourists from every country with big cameras around their necks, and shops selling brightly colored blankets. Guster couldn’t understand a word of what people were saying.

“Oh dear,” Mom said looking around. She cinched up Henry Junior in his backpack. “Stick close to each other.” Mariah grabbed onto Guster’s backpack.

“This is total Español-land, Mom! How the heck are we going to find this place?” said Zeke.

Before Mom could answer, a short man with weathered brown skin and a bright woolen cap approached. “Would you like ride to Aguas Calientes?” he asked. He smelled strongly of salt.

“You speak English?” said Mom.

“Yes,” smiled the man. He was missing three of his front teeth, and he wore a small cob of red corn on a string around his neck. “I can show you to ruins.”

“Oh.” said Mom. She glanced around at the busy airport and hesitated for a moment. “Well… that’s what we came to see. Sure,” she said. She grabbed Zeke’s hand, probably for reassurance.

The man smiled at Guster. “You like to know about history?” he asked.

Guster nodded. He wanted to know anything that was going to get him closer to the recipe.

"I can take you there in my truck," he said. He pointed to an old, faded orange truck parked outside on the curb, then held his palm out flat.

"Okay," said Mom. They waited for the man to move, but he didn't. He just stood there, his hand open.

"Oh," said Mom, and fished a few dollar bills out of her apron pocket. She pushed it into his hand. He still didn't move. Mom pressed another handful of bills into his hand and he sprang back to life. "Ah, the beauty of Peru!" he said with a smile, spreading his arms out to the mountains. He led them to the truck. Wooden planks nailed together formed three walls around the bed. They all jumped in the back, except Zeke, who sat up front.

The man opened the back window. "My name is Estomago," he said. "Please be careful for the chickens." At the front of the truck bed were five chickens, each clucking and scratching in their own individual, padded cages. "They are my children," Estomago said. He started the truck and drove down a rough road, dodging bicyclists and busses as he went. Guster held on tight. The houses and buildings looked so different from back home. Some of them were painted bright orange or yellow, with open fronts where shopkeepers could sell their wares. In many places, there were no sidewalks. Even the road signs were strange and unfamiliar.

"This place you go to — Machu Picchu — it was built five hundred years ago by the Incan Empire," said Estomago as he drove. "It was a place for kings and nobles to live. They had running water, magnificent stone work, and temples for worshipping the sun and moon." Estomago tapped the side of his forehead. "The Incans were very smart. They built that city like a fortress, way high up in the mountains, surrounded by jungle, where it was very difficult for their enemies to find. In fact, it was so difficult to find, that when the Spanish came and conquered this country, no one even knew the city was there. They didn't even find it until, mmmm, about one hundred years ago. Some people think that they were hiding treasure up there," Estomago shook his head. "Me? I think they just wanted to be alone, so they could grow their crops close to the sun, away from everything else, where they could remain pure."

That made sense to Guster. A fortress high in the mountains was the perfect place to hide a precious fruit.

They drove out of the city along a winding highway that went higher and higher into the mountains.

"I can only imagine what an Incan feast would taste like. By the way, you hungry?" said Estomago.

Everyone nodded, except Guster. He hadn't eaten anything besides a handful of crackers on the plane, but he doubted Estomago could offer him anything he wouldn't hate.

Estomago stopped the truck in a small town nestled between a ring of steep, tree covered mountains. "My friend has a shop here," he said. He called out in Spanish toward a small roadside booth. "Lengua! Amigo! Queremos empanadas!" A short man with dark black hair and dark brown skin came to the counter. He also wore a red corn cob around his neck. He nodded and set to work. In minutes he presented the family with a steaming plate full of small meat pies.

To Guster's surprise, they smelled quite good. It was worth chancing it, so he took a pie and nibbled on the corner. The firm crust was decent, but there was something inside between the tender [illegible] and cheese that was just perfectly divine — a chopped hard-[illegible] egg. It was cleaner than any food he'd ever tasted, with a strong, almost almond-flavored yolk. "These eggs are delicious." he said.

Estomago raised his eyebrow at Guster. "You can taste my eggs in the middle of Lengua's delicious meat?" he laughed. "You certainly know quality! Some people have come from across the sea, just to taste one egg from my chickens.

"My friend Lengua and I are descendents of the Incan priests. And just like them, we know good flavors when we find them."

Lengua chattered something quickly to Estomago in Spanish.

"Yes, and as my friend reminds me, Peru is the Cuisine Capital of the Americas. The best vegetables in the world grow here, so we must be careful to protect our crops and meats from cross-breeding with foreign influences," Estomago frowned. "We have to preserve the flawlessness of the Peruvian tastes."

Guster carefully picked out the eggs from his empanada and discarded the rest. Then he had another. They were so good, the eggs could've been sold in the Patisserie.

He reached for a third, when Zeke snatched it right out from under him and stuffed it in his chubby mouth. "Way better than anything those stupid chefs in red made, eh?" said Zeke.

Guster could have kicked him. First, because that was the last empanada, and the few morsels Guster had weren't enough to feed a mouse; second because Zeke had blabbed. He'd already blown their cover once back at Aunt Priscilla's.

Estomago squinted like he was about to ask something, then decided against it.

Mariah bought a book on Machu Picchu from the shop next door. Mom paid Lengua, and they got back in the truck. Estomago drove them up a steep, winding road through the jungle. They drove in silence for a long time. Finally, Estomago stopped the truck where the road ended at a parking lot. "Tell me something," he said to Mom, then glanced at Guster. "Is your interest in the great Lost City of Machu Picchu purely for sightseeing?"

Guster squirmed. Something in the way Estomago said it made him feel uncomfortable.

"This was an excellent chance for a family vacation," said Mom. She picked up Henry Junior and got out.

"Then I will wait here until you are finished," Estomago said, "To take you back down the mountain." His eyes fixed on Guster.

With that, they started across the parking lot toward the Lost City of Machu Picchu.

Chapter 8 — The Lost City

The lost city of Machu Picchu hadn't been lost ever since it was found about a hundred years before Guster got there.

Now the parking lot outside the city was bustling with tourists just like the airport had been. There were several busses parked there, and a small store selling soda pop.

They followed after a crowd that went down a short, winding path, then hiked back and forth along more than a dozen switchbacks. At the end, the jungle opened up and Guster found himself standing at the top of a broad, uneven stone staircase that descended into the ruins. The city sprawled up and down over a narrow hilltop.

"Well," said Mom, as she looked around, "it's nice to see that this place is well-kept enough to host so many visitors."

"Let's check over there first," whispered Mariah to Guster. She pointed to a lone tree growing on a grassy area in the middle of the city. Guster scanned the maze of crumbly stone walls and patches of green grass below. Plant life was sparse — only the grass and a few bushes growing amid the stone buildings. That tree was the likeliest place of all to find the fruit. Guster started down a broad staircase toward it.

"Stop right there Guster," ordered Mom. Guster froze. "You have to stay within eyesight! No climbing things, and you must take Zeke with you."

As if we need extra rules right now, thought Guster grumpily. Making it all the way to Machu Picchu was a step in the right direction, but they couldn't let Mom's overprotective nature get in the way of finding the One Recipe. Hiding it from her was hard enough.

"I don't want to go down to some stupid lawn when there are ruins to explore," Zeke complained.

"I need you to go to protect your sister," said Mom. "Besides, you may explore the ruins the whole way there. Henry Junior and I will catch up with you in a bit." Mom smiled and looked at the city. "We really are out seeing the world, aren't we?" she said taking in a deep breath.

Guster, Zeke and Mariah descended the broad staircase until they came to a stone wall with a rectangular archway that marked the entrance to the city. From what Guster could tell, the city was a series of smooth-cut stone buildings and corridors built in levels right into the mountainside. It looked like a web of interconnected staircases.

Mariah bore to the right and took another staircase down further toward the center of the plateau. Guster followed, staying as far to the left as he could. The right side dropped off into what looked like a moat, and beyond that, at the edge of the city, the mountain fell straight down to the jungle far below. The cliffs surrounding the plateau were so steep, and the plateau itself so narrow, it was like they were balanced on the head of a pin.

They scrambled down a few flat, wide, grass-covered terraces 't like giant steps down the side of the slope.

“These terraces were probably used for growing things,” said Mariah, as she lowered herself down the stone wall that separated the levels. “The air is so thin, and the city so much closer to the sun, fruits and vegetables grew differently here than in cities down below.”

Zeke gasped for breath and leaned on his hiking stick. “The people probably grew differently too — grew tired of it. Why do you think they all left?”

Guster followed Mariah down to the next level, carefully jamming the toes of his cowboy boots in the gaps between rocks for footholds. He could care less if Zeke was going to be his usual, complaining self. There was nowhere Guster would rather be.

They passed a row of stone buildings, none of them with roofs, dodged a group of tourists snapping photos, and found the lonely tree Mariah had pointed out earlier.

It was very skinny with a bushy top, like an extra-tall piece of broccoli. Guster got as close as he could to the trunk and stared up into the branches for signs of anything round. Even a blossom or a bud would do, but all he could see were tiny leaves. He shook the trunk. Nothing fell. He could try climbing it, but it was no use — there was nothing up there.

“What are you looking for?” asked Zeke.

“You wouldn’t get it,” said Guster. He didn’t have to explain himself to Zeke. He wondered though*, what did this fruit taste like*? Maybe like a strawberry or a peach.

Mariah opened her guidebook and flipped through the pages, reading silently to herself. “We could check the bushes,” she said.

“What exactly are you guys up to?” said Zeke. He looked suspicious.

"Nothing interesting," said Mariah, "Just looking for some local fruits." Good. She was playing it down, keeping Zeke in the dark.

"Why don't you just go buy a watermelon or something? You'll never find anything up here!" said Zeke and plunked himself down on a rock. Though Guster hated to admit it, Zeke had a point. The bushes didn't sound any more promising than the tree.

Mom and Henry Junior caught up to them just as a tour group passed by.

"I hope you are learning all sorts of things about the way of life up here," said Mom. Guster made a show of peering out over the city. He could pretend it was an educational experience if that's what would make Mom happy. As long as they got to keep looking.

"We certainly are, Mom," said Mariah. "According to this book, there's even more to learn up there, on that peak." She pointed to a steep rocky peak that overlooked the city. It was the big nose in the face on the eggbeater. "That's where something called the Temple of the Moon is. Can we go?"

"Okay, but we'll go together," said Mom. "I need to be able to keep you in sight."

They crossed a wide, green plaza surrounded by stone walls in the center of the city, climbed a few levels, passed a tour guide with a wide brimmed straw hat, and came to a massive piece of granite that shot up from the ground like a miniature mountain. A man with a llama stopped them at the rock. "If you want to go to the peak, you must be back in a few hours, before we close the city," he said. "It is a very steep climb, but the sights are worth it."

"Let's be quick about it then, kids," said Mom. They started down the steep trail that led toward the big nose.

They climbed up and down on the high, narrow trail for over an hour. They were so high, that if there had been any clouds that day,

Guster could have reached down and scooped up a handful of white fluff.

The trail dead-ended at a steep stone slab that rose upward for more than fifty feet. A thick orange rope dangled from the top. Guster took hold of it and pulled. It held fast. The only way up was to climb. Guster planted a foot on the stone.

Mom's eyebrows scrunched together with concern, "Hmm," she muttered. It was like Mom was trying on her adventure shoe, but just wasn't sure she could make it fit.

"It's not like it's straight up or anything," said Mariah. "Besides, look up there, there's a whole tour group of people that made it." Sure enough, there were a dozen folks above them, hiking down the trail toward the rope.

"I guess if they climbed it…" said Mom. Before Mom could object, Guster took hold of the rope and pulled himself upward. Mariah followed right behind.

It was steep, but if he kept his weight on the rock instead of the rope, he found that it wasn't too bad. Still, it was a long way down if he let go. He tried to keep his eyes on his cowboy boots instead of the sheer drop. At one point, he nearly lost his balance; he had to scramble that last few feet to keep from falling. Mariah got to the top a second later.

Mom tugged nervously on the rope down below.

"We'll wait for you ahead," said Guster.

"Stay in my sight!" shouted Mom.

Pretending like he hadn't heard her, Guster ran down the path. He and Mariah passed the tour group they had seen from below, hiked around a bend, and came to a wide but shallow cave in the side of the mountain. A tour guide in a straw hat spoke with a few tourists in the opening. "The Temple of the Moon is the remains of a ceremonial temple," he said, pointing to the crumbling stone work. Most of the white granite wall at the back was covered by the shade. There were a few bedroom-sized niches carved into the sides. In the center, there was a throne made of rock. To the side of the throne were five stone steps that lead further into the shadows. It didn't look like much, but it was obvious from the crumbling stonework that it was very, very old.

"The caverns in the Temple of the Moon were used to bury mummies and perhaps to record a history of the people," continued the tour guide while he pointed out some of the tiny carvings. There were hundreds of them, all lined up in rows and columns like letters on the page of a carved stone book: there were jaguars, men with spears, steep pyramids, and the shining sun. Guster felt a surge of excitement — down near the floor, barely visible on the white granite, was a tiny carving no bigger than Guster's hand. It was a tree with a large oval fruit.

"Mariah," Guster whispered, tugging on his sister's sleeve. He pointed. "It's just like on the eggbeater."

"Indeed," she said, squinting at it. "And there's another one," she said, pointing near the steps to a carving of a chicken hatching.

Guster's head whirled with the possibilities. Before this moment, the eggbeater had been nothing more than a hope for something far away that may or may not exist. But this was different. These carvings were real.

The tour group snapped a few photos, then the guide ushered them away from the cave back toward the main ruins. "It's closing time soon," he said to Mariah as he was leaving. "You will want to be back at the main city before long."

"We'll only be a few minutes," she said. They would have to work fast, especially if they didn't want Mom finding out what they were up to.

As soon as the tourists were out of sight, Mariah felt around the edges of another stone carving. It was a chicken eating a bone. "I think it's a button!" she said, pressing it with both palms and leaning up against it. "Help me."

Guster leaned into the stone, adding his weight to Mariah's. The button made a grinding sound and slowly gave way, sinking back into the wall. The cave was quiet.

"We have to try the other ones," said Guster, starting for the carving of the fruit.

"Wait, let's do them in order," Mariah said. "We'll need the eggbeater."

Guster unzipped his backpack and pulled it out. Mariah took a flashlight from her pocket and shined it on the handle. Chicken eats the bone, chicken lays the seed, a tiny sapling, a tree with a big round fruit, a chicken hatching. It was a good thing they had the eggbeater. The carvings were so strange, almost like they were trying to tell a story, but they just didn't quite make sense.

Guster found the chicken-laying-the-seed-symbol near his feet. "Here," he said, pressing it. It barely moved, then gave way under his hand and sunk deeper into the rock.

There was a rumble and a grinding behind the back of the throne. Mariah focused her flashlight beam. Barely noticeable in the darkness at the back of the cavern was a giant, hideous carving of a twisted face. It was at least twice as tall as Guster, with bulging eyes and slightly open lips.

"He looks mad," said Mariah.

"Like he's never been able to find anything to eat," said Guster. He swallowed. Guster knew how it felt. All that hiking had only made the pit in his stomach worse.

"Let's hurry," said Mariah, studying the eggbeater handle again. "The sapling is next." She scanned the carvings until she found the sapling near the cave's entrance and pressed it. It gave way, and the stone face's mouth opened another foot.

Guster took the other flashlight out of his backpack, reached inside the face's mouth, and pointed the beam down its throat. He could barely make out a long staircase leading down a dark tunnel hewn out of the mountain. "It's a passage!" Guster said. His voice echoed into the hole. So the carvings were like another combination lock — press them in the right order and the door opens.

Mariah handed Guster the eggbeater and heaved herself against the carving of the large oval fruit on the stair that led up to the throne. It clicked, and the huge mouth ground open even wider, bits of stone crumbling away from the lips until they finally parted so wide, Guster could've walked through without ducking.

"Of course. What better place to hide a large oval fruit than the Temple of the Moon?" said Mariah.

"More like Temple of the Dumb!" said Zeke. He was standing behind them.

Guster spun around. Zeke looked down at the eggbeater in his hand. A wave of guilt flushed over Guster. He was caught red-handed. "Wow. Mom's gonna kill you," Zeke said, obvious relish in his voice.

Zeke was right. A second later Mom's stern voice sounded from the crest of the hill. "Guster Stephen Johnsonville!" she cried, "I told you to stay close! Don't make me count to ten!"

Guster tensed. If Mom saw the eggbeater, she'd make him do every single chore she could think of for the rest of his life. But without the eggbeater, they'd never have come this far. They couldn't turn back now. He had to see what was down that tunnel. Mom couldn't deny him that.

"What is that in your hand?" she cried. Even from far off, Guster could see the steam building up in her eyes. "I told you to get rid of that thing!" she exploded, charging down the hill. He slipped the eggbeater in his backpack. *Better in there than out here with her*, thought Guster. He slammed his hand down onto the final carving and dashed through the stone mouth and down the first few steps before he could talk himself out of it.

It was dark and the way was steep. He paused to glance up at Mariah. She hesitated, then ducked through the stone mouth and into the passage after him.

Zeke poked his head through the lips. "Fine! Go down there and finish your fancy grocery shopping!" he called. He looked torn, like he was trying to decide whether or not to tell on them, or join them. Zeke rarely missed a chance to be mischievous.

"Just because you're scared of the mummies doesn't mean you have to ruin it for everyone!" shouted Mariah.

Her taunting worked. "I am not!" Zeke said, then charged down the tunnel after them.

Guster picked his way carefully down the stairs, the heels of his cowboy boots clicking on the stone in the darkness, two meager flashlight beams lighting their way. He was glad to have Mariah and Zeke's company. He doubted Mom would have the gumption to follow. Either way, she was not going to be happy with him.

It was strangely quiet except for the sound of their own footsteps and water drip-dripping onto the ground. They must have gone down more than three stories before Zeke spoke. "What if there are traps or something?" he whispered, clutching the back of Mariah's shirt.

"Shh," Mariah shushed him, though there was little confidence in her voice.

Guster hated to admit it, but Zeke could be right. They would have to tread as carefully as possible.

The stairs went deeper and deeper, when something like twigs breaking crunched under Guster's boot. He shined his light down and stifled a scream. The floor was covered in hundreds and hundreds of white bones. He turned his light away before Zeke could see.

Zeke's screech told Guster it was too late. "What do you think ate all these?" stammered Zeke.

"They're probably just rat bones. I'm sure they got old and died," said Mariah, nervously. Her face was worried.

Guster had to be brave, or at least pretend to be. He stepped out onto the bones. Step, crunch, step. The passage leveled out ahead, and a dim glow shone at the far end of the tunnel. Guster tried to concentrate on the light, since it meant there was something — maybe an end to the tunnel — on the other side. Crunch, crack, crunch. He crunched across the bones for what seemed like a full, agonizing minute.

"Guster!" hissed a stern voice in the darkness. It was Mom. She sounded like she must have come down the steps.

"Ba baa ba ba!" babbled Henry Junior, breaking the cave's silence.

"That's far enough!" Mom said, her voice a mixture of anger and worry.

Guster couldn't let her stop them now. He was so close to the light, and now it was obvious: it was a way out. He broke into a run.

Whump! A massive stone pillar shot down from the ceiling and smashed into the ground only inches behind him. "Guster!" cried Mom.

He jumped to the wall and flattened himself against it, his heart racing. He'd nearly been squished, like a juicy grape underfoot. "I'm okay," he said, panting.

"Guster! How many times have I told you not to go into dark secret passages in the middle of ancient cities? See? This is exactly what happens when you disobey your mother!" Mom shouted. She was hysterical, her voice echoing off the walls and ringing in Guster's ears.

Guster looked back up the tunnel. The stone pillar blocked most of the passageway, except for a narrow space on either side just wide enough to peer through.

"I'm coming through," said Mariah as she pushed herself through the gap.

"No you are not!" said Mom, her voice getting closer all the time.

"I've got to go with Guster!" she said. Zeke took one look back up the passage, then squeezed himself through the gap like a fat worm.

"So help me, Guster! You are going to get yourselves killed!" shouted Mom. She was usually exaggerating when she said that. This time, she might be right. It was better that the gap was too narrow for her to follow. She and Henry Junior would be safer if they didn't.

Guster switched off his flashlight and climbed out of the tunnel into the sunlight. It was so bright, he had to blink several times before his eyes finally adjusted. There was a mound of boulders surrounding the tunnel's end, and beyond that a ledge as wide as a small soccer field with row after row of trees growing out of its fertile ground. Beyond that was a sheer drop that looked over a narrow valley far, far below.

Guster scrambled over the boulders, Mariah and Zeke right behind him, when they saw the most amazing sight. There, on the ledge, right in front of him, hanging from the trees' branches, like a flock of golf balls, were hundreds of smooth, white oval fruits.

The big round fruit. Exactly what they'd been looking for, just like the eggbeater said. It was real, and they'd found it.

"It's an orchard!" said Mariah.

Guster smiled triumphantly and Mariah, then, without hesitation, ran to the nearest tree, reached up, and picked the lowest fruit. It was gleaming white, hard, smooth and a little bit sticky on top where it had grown out of the branch — not at all like what he expected. He shook it. What felt like a thick liquid swirled around inside the hard shell.

Why hadn't he seen it? It was right in front of his face this whole time. This was no fruit. "It's an egg," he whispered.

"An egg?" said Mariah and picked one for herself.

"That's impossible!" cried Zeke.

But it wasn't. Guster was holding one with his own hand. "No, it's all too possible," he said. He cracked it on the tree's trunk. Sure enough, a crystal clear egg white and golden yolk poured out of the shell. Guster caught as much as he could in the broken halves. It smelled so full and sweet to him, even raw, unlike any other egg Guster had ever smelled. He dipped his finger into the yolk and tasted it.

It was so good, his tongue laughed; his head whirled. Every particle of yolk unfolded across his taste buds, as if five hundred years of sunshine were poured inside a single shell. It was better than empanadas, better than the Master Pastry Chef's raspberry tart. It was by far the most delicious thing he had ever tasted, and it was only an egg. He drank the rest down like a vanilla milkshake.

"Egg-static!" Zeke said, his eyes wide. He plucked an egg from the nearest tree, then cracked it and ate it too. Guster wanted to say 'I told you so,' but if he hadn't tasted the egg himself, he wouldn't have believed it either. "Shouldn't these come from chickens?" asked Zeke, the yolk dribbling down his chin.

"Normally, but it's kind of reasonable, though, if you look at the carvings," said Mariah. "The eggs ripen on the trees. The trees are grown from a seed. The seed is laid from…" Mariah shook her head. "No, it's too extraordinary."

Yet there they are, thought Guster, hundreds of eggs growing from tree branches all around them. He cracked and ate another, then another without stopping to wipe his mouth in between. The yolk coated his stomach; it soothed his burning hunger. For the first time he could remember, he started to feel full.

Zeke collected a whole armful and shoved them in his backpack. He zipped it up and slid it back on his shoulders. After that, he shook the trunk of the next tree. A few dozen eggs fell, where they shattered and spilled golden yolk all over the ground.

That's when Guster spotted it — the mother of pearl — a large white egg the size of a watermelon, gleaming and glistening like polished marble in the sun.

Mariah noticed it too. "It's gigantic!" she said.

It hung from the center branch of a massive tree on the far end of the orchard. The tree was enormous — its trunk was as wide as five of the other trees, its branches spanned outward, low to the ground, like a giant bush.

"That thing's bigger than my head!" said Zeke.

"Just barely," said Mariah, running toward it.

Guster slurped down the last of the egg he was holding. "It must be the one we're looking for." He started toward the massive tree. The smaller eggs were good, but to make the One Recipe, they needed the best.

Something still puzzled him, though, as he picked his way through the trees. The eggs ripened on the trees, which were grown from seeds, which were laid by the chickens. But where were the chickens? And what did those chickens eat?

That's when he saw them: bleached-white bones piled twice as high as they were in the tunnel, scattered at the roots of the massive tree. There were broken femurs, ribs pointing skyward, and skulls with deep, hollow eyes.

Suddenly, the symbol of the chicken eating the bone made sense. The life cycle of the trees began with one thing: meat. Panic burst inside him. He dashed after Mariah. "Don't!" he cried.

Just then, two giant chickens the size of tigers scrambled from either side of the massive tree, straight toward Mariah, thrashing their wings, chomping with their beaks, and striking at her with razor-sharp talons.

"No!" Guster cried. He lunged, yanking Mariah back by her backpack as far as he could. The chickens' beaks slashed inches from her body. Cringing, he threw his arms up to block their attack.

It never came. The two chicken-monsters hissed at them, struggling wildly in place, more like feather-covered dragons than birds. Their ankles were latched to a heavy iron chain anchored to a pair of stone columns rooted into the ground on either side of the huge tree. Somebody had put them there to guard the egg.

Guster pulled Mariah behind a tree and tried to calm his pounding heart. That egg had to be the one they were looking for. She let out a tiny sob.

"Who comes to disturb the Sacred Orchard?" wheezed an angry voice from somewhere in the trees. The chickens went quiet, the wind stopped stirring and the leaves stopped rustling, casting an eerie silence over the orchard. Zeke froze in his tracks.

"Who comes to disturb the Sacred Orchard?" the voice wheezed again, angrier still.

Again, silence. Maybe if they answered, they could bargain with him, "Guster Stephen Johnsonville," Guster said aloud.

Someone came out from behind the base of the leftmost stone column. It was a skinny, weathered, brown-skinned man. He wore a large feather headdress and long, colorful robes. His neck and hands were covered with golden jewelry. His skin was very, very old, like brittle autumn leaves that could crumble and fall at any moment. In his right hand he held a long wooden staff. He wheezed, "You have come to taste the fruit."

Guster stepped cautiously out from behind the trunk. The man knew they were there; Guster might as well take a chance. "Yes sir," he said.

"Many have come to seek the treasure, though it has been so very, very long since then," said the ancient man.

Zeke came up behind Guster. "Are you a mummy?" he asked. Mariah jabbed him in the ribs with her elbow.

"Be polite," she said. *Please don't mess this up, Zeke*, thought Guster. He didn't want to end up as shredded chicken feed.

The ancient man struck the stone with his staff, his eyes blazing. "I am the Priest of the Tree of the Fowl," he said. "And this is the Sacred Orchard protected by the Lost City in the clouds which was built by my Fathers! I have guarded this place for one hundred years, and when I'm gone, another shall protect it for a hundred more. We have bred these trees from the seeds laid by the chickens which have hatched from the fruit!

"You have eaten the fruits. For that I can forgive you this once, but now, you must go your way!"

"We only want one more," said Mariah. Guster tensed. She was brave to ask, but he knew it was impossible.

The priest glanced at the great gleaming white egg. "That I can only grant to the Great White Chef who came long ago! It was he who gave our people the tastes which built our empire! It was he who prophesied the destiny of this pearl. It was he who said that it would be part of the greatest taste ever known. It is only to him that I can give this fruit."

But that wasn't possible. Any chef who came to the orchard that long ago would have been dead for hundreds of years.

The priest's eyes narrowed on Guster. "Are you the Great White Chef?" he asked. The chickens snarled.

"Sure he is," Zeke interrupted. Guster cringed. Like anyone was going to believe that.

"Ha!" laughed the priest cruelly. The chickens clucked, as if laughing with him. He pointed his staff at Guster, "If you are the Great White Chef, then tell me boy, what is your name?"

Thanks a lot Zeke, thought Guster. He shot an angry glance at his brother. Whatever he said would be a shot in the dark.

"Felicity Casa?" said Zeke, pointing to Guster, a sheepish grin on his face.

"Lies!" cried the priest.

"We have the One Recipe!" said Mariah. She pulled the eggbeater from her backpack and held it up. Surely the priest would recognize that.

"Buc-cah!" clucked the priest, striking his staff on the nearby column. "Your weapon will not harm me!" he said. Gears groaned and the iron links clanked together as the chain slackened. The chickens charged forward, talons slashing. "The Guardian-Birds will have their flesh today!"

Wrong answer! thought Guster, jumping out of the way. He felt the chicken's beak swish past his leg. It was too close. For whatever reason, the priest did not recognize the eggbeater.

Mariah lunged toward Zeke, pushing him behind a tree. They were on their own. Both chickens took a sharp turn toward them, and Guster saw his chance. He dropped his backpack and dashed round the far side of another nearby trunk.

He ran hard to the massive tree, one of the birds striking dangerously close to his ear as he reached the trunk. He planted one boot on the bark and leapt up, grabbing hold of the lowest limb. He hoisted himself up, just as a beak clamped down on his pant leg. He kicked out with his cowboy boot and struck something soft. *Hope I got its eye*, thought Guster as his jeans tore in the chicken's beak. It fell backward, wings flapping.

He didn't stop to see it hit the ground; he was already climbing outward on the limb toward the giant egg.

"Do you not see the bones from the flesh they have eaten?" shouted the priest. "You will die the same as the thieves before you did!"

Guster hoped the priest was wrong. The chicken below leapt upward again, trying to take flight, but the heavy iron chain kept her from getting more than two feet off the ground.

Guster ignored it. The limb was sagging under his weight; he had to get that egg. He scooted further out, his arms and legs wrapped around the branch. Just a few more feet.

Out of the corner of his eye, he saw Mariah lead the second chicken around a tree then dive out of the way, tangling its chain. She was alive — for the moment. Zeke was nowhere in sight.

The chicken below him leapt again, narrowly missing his foot. One more push and Guster stretched out with both hands, closing them around the egg. It was hard and smooth like porcelain. And it was heavy. He snapped it from the branch.

There was a crack as the limb broke beneath him. Guster fell, twisting himself between the egg and the ground. *Can't let it break!* he thought as he slammed into the ground. The pain nearly knocked him out.

The branch struck the chicken as it fell, knocking her over. Guster struggled to get up, to breathe, but he couldn't — it felt like an elephant had stomped on his chest.

It didn't take long for the chicken to recover. In a flurry of feathers she was on him, beating him with her wings. Her beak struck down like an axe.

He rolled, clutching the egg with one arm to keep it safe. He barely escaped the attack. The chicken reared its head again. He had to get away; he had to breathe.

In a flash, the second chicken struck from the other side, slashing at his legs. Guster covered his face as the chicken's talons tore into his leg, slicing it with pain. Warm, wet blood oozed over Guster's skin. This was it; they were going to tear him apart.

"Run for it, Capital P!" shouted Zeke. Zeke charged out of nowhere like a football player, smashed his shoulder into the closest chicken and knocked it to the ground. Guster pushed himself up with his free arm and ran, his leg burning with each step.

Something sharp scratched his back then yanked his shirt backward. The first chicken clamped down on his shirt like a pit bull. Guster tried to shake himself free. "Zeke!" he cried.

Zeke smashed his walking stick down on the chicken like a mallet, beating it to the ground, feathers exploding into the air. Its grip slackened, and Guster broke free. He ran for it, the blood pounding in his head.

Mariah picked herself up off the ground as he ran past her. She was right behind him. "Let's get out of here!" Guster cried, glad she was able to move. More than half an orchard length stood between them and the tunnel.

"You shall not escape!" cried the Priest. Guster heard the grinding of metal again, then a loud clanking. He chanced a look over his shoulder. The two chickens flapped after them, chains dangling loosely from their feet.

Guster dashed as fast as he could, but Mariah was quicker. "Inside!" she shouted, scrambling over the boulders and down toward the narrow tunnel. She slipped through the gap between the stone column and the wall.

Mom was waiting for them on the other side. "You have never been in so much trouble!" she cried.

Mariah took the egg from Guster as he pried himself past the column, Zeke right on their heels and the chickens gaining.

"Zeke!" Mom cried as she realized what was happening. The two birds caught up and struck at Zeke's face with their beaks. He turned and blocked with his stick, knocking one's head aside while the other chomped the stick in two. “That’s my son you foul fowl!” Mom said, kicking one of the chickens through the gap and knocking it backward. “I’ll bread you and eat you for dinner!” Zeke dove into the gap and Guster pulled him through to the other side. The chickens flapped hard against the stone, trying to squeeze through. Mom grabbed Guster by the hand and led them all up the tunnel at a run.

“The tourist office will certainly be getting a strongly worded letter from me on this!” Mom exclaimed as Henry Junior began to scream.

“Mom, I don’t think this has anything to do with —” said Mariah.

Mom threw up her hands. “I know, but somebody needs a talking to!” she shouted. Guster was shaking. They had nearly been killed. All that for an egg.

He whirled around, frantic. Mariah was cradling it gently in her arms. It was safe.

When they emerged from the tunnel, he took it from her. There was no visible yolk or cracks. Mariah had been quick enough to pick up his backpack from behind the tree. She gave it to him, and he gently stuffed the egg inside.

“No one should be allowed down there; they’ll just get hurt,” said Mom, pointing to the angry stone face.

“We’ll make sure no one is,” said Mariah and pushed the carvings in the opposite order from before. The mouth ground shut.

They came out of the shallow cavern into the light. “My boys!” Mom exclaimed at the sight of their dirty, bloody legs and arms. She looked like she didn’t know whether to scream at them or hug them. She pulled a handkerchief from her apron, dipped it in a water bottle from her backpack, then wiped the gashes on Zeke's arms and legs, all the while shouting at him.

Guster cringed when it was his turn; his back felt bruised from landing so hard on the ground, and his leg was hot with pain. "And you! You kept that eggbeater when I clearly told you to get rid of it!" Mom yelled as she cleaned his wounds. "You've put the whole family in danger because of your own selfishness!" Guster winced. She was mad, and he knew he'd only seen the start of it.

"Let's go," Mom said when she was done. She led them to the rope. Guster was just as eager to leave as she was. They climbed down the steep rock and hiked back to the parking lot as fast as they could go. It was much easier than going up, though Guster stepped more gingerly this time.

Mom didn't stop lecturing the whole way back to the city, while Mariah tried to explain everything that happened. They passed the last remaining tourists who eyed their ragged, bloody clothes. Some even took pictures, but Guster didn't care. When they got to the road, Estomago was waiting for them.

"You saw beautiful sights, yes?" asked Estomago, a quizzical look on his face.

Guster hoped that no one would say anything about the orchard. Something told him that they ought to keep the egg a secret.

"Yes. Yes we did," said Mom hesitantly. "The… ruins were breathtaking."

Estomago smiled, but his eyes narrowed.

They got back in the faded orange truck and rode down the mountain as clouds filled the sky. It started to rain. After an hour of driving, Estomago stopped the truck on a muddy patch of ground just outside the airport. Guster could feel his heart start beating a little softer. It would be good to get back on the dry, safe plane again.

Guster got out of the back of the truck. Estomago opened his door and stood with his arm holding something inside the cab. "I just wonder. Is there something that you found in the ruins? Something you want to share?" he said, his face growing grim.

"You know about —" Zeke said, before Mariah clapped a hand over his mouth.

"About what?" asked Estomago. Zeke shook his head.

"What is it that you are hiding boy?" Estomago took whatever it was he held in the cab and put it behind his back. He inched forward, pointing to Guster's backpack. "You have something there, don't you? Show it to me!" he said, swishing a rusty old machete from behind his back and brandishing it in the air over his head.

Mariah screamed and swung the eggbeater like a baseball bat at Estomago, who knocked it easily out of her hand. It rolled through the mud.

"Boy, you have something I want. Am I going to have to take it from you?" Estomago said. Guster backed away slowly. Estomago was serious — and dangerous. But Guster couldn't give up the egg. Not after they'd come so far.

Mom spoke, "Guster, maybe you ought to —"

Suddenly, Braxton sprang out from behind the truck and, before Estomago even knew he was there, landed a swift karate chop to the back of Estomago's neck. Estomago's eyes closed and his knees buckled as he fell to the ground with a thud. "I can't have anyone disturbing my passengers on their vacation!" Braxton said. He bent down and pulled on Estomago's closed eyelid. "He'll wake up in a few hours, but what do you say we skedaddle before then?" He motioned toward the plane.

Guster let out a long breath of relief. He would never have guessed that old Braxton could move so fast. “How did you do that?” he asked.

“Old trick I learned in Vietnam,” said Braxton. He winked at Guster.

They boarded the plane quickly, and before night fell, were flying through the skies, far away from Peru.

Chapter 9 — Lovelock, Nevada

Guster placed the giant egg inside the jet's fridge as its engines hummed.

"I'm sorry. I didn't know that it would turn out like this," Mom sobbed out loud. She held Henry Junior tight in her arms, while he clucked at her like a chicken. "I didn't know what we were getting into — no, I was being selfish. I wanted to see the world. But we should have stayed home, on the farm. Housewives shouldn't be off wandering the planet." She frowned at Guster. "I'm disappointed in you."

That's all it took to make him feel hot all over. He hated it when Mom cried. It meant she was blaming this all on him. It wasn't his fault that Estomago had attacked them, or giant man-eating chickens had almost bitten Zeke's legs off, or that they had taken Henry Junior into a cave full of traps, or even that the Chef in Red had burst through the window that night in the Patisserie. He wasn't picky! Just careful. *Besides*, he thought, *We wouldn't be out here if Mom knew how to cook a decent meal*.

Mariah sat down next to Guster. She was probably mad at him too; he did not want to talk to anyone right then, so he stared out the window.

"Who do you think that 'Great White Chef' the priest told us about was?" asked Mariah. It would be hard to make her go away, determined as she always was.

"I don't know," Guster said. "But, whoever he was, he knew that the egg was supposed to be used in the One Recipe."

"I suppose it makes sense that the priest didn't recognize the eggbeater," Mariah said. She'd carefully cleaned all of the mud away, so that it gleamed like it had after the first time he'd washed it. "This beater is old, but it's not that old. And it sounds like no one has been back to Peru to claim the egg since The Great White Chef saw it there, five centuries ago."

"Until now," said Guster.

"Until now," Mariah echoed, a grin spreading across her lips. Guster had the funny feeling that she saw this as a kind of game. They had almost died. At least she wasn't mad at him.

"If we could just figure this out," Mariah said, pointing to the carving of the bear. *Seventy-four degrees, thirty-one minutes, nineteen degrees, one minute,* read the inscription underneath the symbol. It just didn't make any sense. Though it probably didn't matter anymore anyway — Mom would probably never let them go adventuring again.

Braxton turned around from his captain's chair in the cockpit. "If I may be so bold, Mrs. Johnsonville — I'm not usually in the habit of asking questions, especially to Ms. McStock — but some villain with a machete tried to attack you back there. And I don't take too kindly to that, especially with these youngsters around. If you're in trouble, I'd like to be of assistance."

Guster was grateful for the old man. Braxton had saved them, and the least they could do was tell him what was going on.

Mom wiped her tears and sat up straight. "Very well, Braxton. You have been extremely helpful, and proven yourself as a friend. It is only right that you know exactly why we are on this journey," she said. Mom explained everything that had happened to them since they met the Master Pastry Chef in the Patisserie. Mariah piped in, adding details here and there, while Guster remained silent, hoping that no one would mention that it was his particular tastes that had sent them to the Patisserie in the first place, or how he'd kept the eggbeater when Mom told him to throw it down the well.

Mariah showed Braxton the eggbeater and the symbols carved on the handle. "And this next one is a bear," she said.

When they got to the part about the priest and the orchard, Zeke told the rest. "And then this old mummy came out and was moaning, and there were like fifty chickens that attacked us, and Guster grabbed the egg while I fought them off using all my karate black belt skills."

Zeke had only ever made it to orange belt, but that didn't matter now. Zeke had saved Guster, and that made Guster wonder if maybe ol' Zeke liked being his brother after all.

Braxton took a long look at the eggbeater. "Hmm," he said, and stared out the front of the cockpit for a long time, flying the plane in silence. "Now Madam, I am not one to offer advice, but I would be doing you a disservice if I did not mention that going back to the farm at this point would be dangerous. Or going anywhere, so it seems. I'm afraid that the only way out of this bubbling stew may be to somehow get to the bottom of it."

Guster felt his tongue tingle. He knew that after what had just happened to them, Mom was unlikely to allow any more adventuring. But at this point, she didn't have many options.

"Is there anyone who might know something about that eggbeater of yours?" asked Braxton.

Mom stared for a long time at nothing, her lips tight, her face hard. "Yes, there is one person," she said. "Felicity Casa."

***

It was noon when Braxton brought the plane to a halt on the airstrip in Lovelock, Nevada. The airport was almost as empty as the one near the farmhouse in Louisiana, except for a lone tumbleweed blowing across the runway. There was nothing for miles but small shrubbery, gritty sand, and a tiny gas station that looked like it was closed. It was deathly hot. *At least we're back in America again*, thought Guster, though that is where they'd last seen the Chef in Red. He could be anywhere. They would have to be on guard.

"Lovelock, where they love to lock you up!" said Zeke as they stepped off the plane.

"You should definitely save that joke for Felicity," said Mariah.

"You'll have to write her a fan letter, Zeke," said Mom. "You and everybody else are going to stay behind with Braxton."

"But Mom! I've never been to prison before!" shouted Zeke.

Mom smiled. "Let's keep it that way," she said.

"Do you think that Felicity Casa is really the Felicity that the Master Pastry Chef was talking about?" asked Mariah.

"I don't know, honey, but we're going to find out."

Braxton called a cab, and a few minutes later, it pulled up next to the hangar. Mom opened the door. "Guster, you're coming with me," she said.

Guster looked up from the tar melting in the cracks in the sidewalk. He felt his face flush. She'd taken the eggbeater from

Mariah, and now she'd probably give him a lecture about it on the car ride over. They got in the cab.

"Lovelock Maximum Security Prison, please," said Mom. The cab driver sped off. They drove on Interstate 80 for a few miles until they turned off the freeway and headed down a crumbly road between two mountains. Guster wondered why people would ever live out there, in the dry, lifeless desert, when he remembered that they weren't doing it by choice.

Mom was staring out the window, silent. There was no doubt she was still upset with Guster. Any second now she would probably tell him how if he would just obey, the whole family wouldn't be in so much trouble right now, or that he was eleven years old now, and he should know better than to lead his little brother into danger. The usual Mom stuff. Instead they rode without speaking. *I didn't want to hear a lecture now anyway,* thought Guster. Somehow though, silence was worse.

The cab rounded another hill, and there, on the other side, was a giant cement wall, twenty feet high, topped with barbwire and a dozen guard towers. The words "Lovelock Maximum Security Prison" were spelled out in gigantic red and blue neon letters that flickered on a sign posted out front. The driver stopped the cab next to a white guard booth in front of a huge iron gate.

A guard in a drab gray uniform stepped out from the booth. He pulled his gun belt up around his portly middle as he did so.

Mom rolled down the window. "We're here to visit a prisoner," she said.

"Visiting hours don't start for twenty minutes," said the guard gruffly.

"That's fine, we'll wait," said Mom.

The guard pushed a button and spoke into an intercom. In a moment, the huge iron gates swung slowly open. The cab drove through the open gate into the outer courtyard of the prison.

After filling out forms and showing identification and insisting that Guster's health depended on seeing Felicity, Mom and Guster were ushered out of the lobby by a burly guard with a shiny badge into a secure hallway. "You're lucky ma'am," said the guard from under his huge handlebar mustache. "We don't usually let unknown visitors see celebrity prisoners like this, but no one has been to see Ms. Casa at all. My guess is her fans just gave up on her. I don't blame 'em if you ask me."

The frowning guard took out his night stick and tapped a metal detector with it. "Through here, please," said the guard. Guster recognized the freestanding doorframe and blinking lights — he'd seen one before on TV.

"Go ahead, Honey," Mom said. Guster didn't like being called 'honey' in front of strangers, especially big, sweaty prison guards. Still, it was better than the silent treatment. He passed through the metal detector without a single beep.

"Your turn, ma'am," grunted the guard.

Mom stepped through. The metal detector flashed red and beeped wildly as soon as she was under it.

"No metal objects!" roared the guard. "Let me see what's in your pockets!"

Mom smiled innocently. "Oh, you mean this?" she asked, and pulled the eggbeater out of her apron. Guster was glad she was the one carrying it.

The guard took out his nightstick, and rapped it in his hand, eyeing her suspiciously. "Ma'am, why would you try to sneak an eggbeater into a prison?"

Mom turned on the guard. “Because I’m a mother, young man, and these are the tools of the trade. No matter how tough you may think you are, you had a mother once too, and you would be smart not to forget it,” she said, shaking her finger at him and shoving her face at his. The guard took one bewildered step backward.

Guster had never seen Mom reprimand an adult like that before. “Um, okay. Right this way then, Ma’am,” said the guard sheepishly.

They came into a small room with a glass wall that was divided by partitions into private booths, kind of like Guster had seen at a bank once in New Orleans. Mom sat down next to the glass divider and he took a chair beside her.

“I’ll get Ms. Casa right away, Ma’am,” said the guard.

In a few minutes, a lady about ten years older than Mom, with blond hair cut like a picture frame around a flawless, aged face, teeth that shined like porcelain toilet bowls, and paint-by-numbers makeup came out of a door on the other side of the glass wall. She wore a bright orange jumpsuit with numbers stitched over her right breast and an orange floral pattern embroidered across the collar. A small black ball and chain earring dangled from each ear. Except for the grim expression on her face, she looked exactly like Felicity Casa, the Czarina of Chocolate on TV. She was perfect as a painting. Guster wanted to laugh. Weren’t prisoners supposed to be hard-as-nails scary? Then again, Guster didn’t worship her homemaking. He worshipped her cooking.

Felicity sat down on the other side of the glass divider and stared at Mom. “Ms. Casa, I’m delighted to meet you in person,” said Mom, smiling. She had clearly been looking forward to this.

“I'm sorry, I don’t know you,” Felicity said in a voice polished enough for radio. She turned to go.

“But Ms. Casa…” said Mom.

Felicity waved her hand. “I’m not interested in talking with anyone I don’t know right now,” she said.

The smile left Mom’s lips. She set the eggbeater down on the counter in front of her with a thud, like it was a pair of aces. “I don't think that matters one way or another,” she said.

Felicity gasped. Her eyes narrowed suspiciously. “Who are you?”

“A fan. But more importantly, a friend,” said Mom.

Felicity stared at Mom, dark circles hanging from under her eyes. “I don't trust fans,” said Felicity. “I trust friends even less. Trusting friends is what got me here.”

“Then you don’t want to know where I got this?” asked Mom.

Felicity sat back down. “You got it from Renoir, a Master Pastry Chef operating out of a small patisserie in the French Quarter of New Orleans.” Felicity scowled. “My network of informants is spread far and wide, even if you people put me in here.”

“What happened to him?” asked Mom.

Felicity studied Mom for a full minute. The wrinkles in her forehead disappeared for a moment, then snapped back. “Poisoned, by the Cult of Gastronimatii,” she finally said. *So that’s why he’d kicked the bucket right in front of their eyes,* thought Guster.

“Who?” asked Mom.

“The Cult of Gastronimatii,” said Felicity. “A 500 year-old order of chefs dedicated to preserving the purity of cuisine. Perhaps you’ve seen them? Aprons trailing in the wind like dragons, toques pulled low over their eyes, the smell of spice pungent in the air?”

“Yes! They attacked us on two separate occasions!” said Mom.

“And you escaped?” said Felicity. She did not seem convinced.

“Yes,” said Mom.

"Really…" said Felicity, seeming to question how likely that really was.

"What do they want?" asked Mom.

"You are in over your head, aren't you?" Felicity laughed, exposing her toilet-white teeth. "They want what any Evertaster wants. Flavor that is pure, unpolluted by foul history, tantamount to perfection! A perfect combination of ingredients, blended in ecstasy! They don't want to eat, they want to taste!

"Since the Renaissance, they've met in secret, drawing up their plans, gathering strength, initiating those few they deemed worthy into their ranks."

"Are they chefs?" asked Mom.

"So much more!" said Felicity. "They are guardians. Protectors of flavor. They despise the simple or distasteful things that the common people eat. To them, we are scavengers. To them, if it is not perfect gourmet, it is filth! And they will not tolerate their world being filled with filth, lest it mix with the pure flavors! They seek the few dishes that will please them, then they protect them like they were endangered species — preserving them from extinction."

"So they love food," Mom said.

"No! They will kill for food!" hissed Felicity.

"Like assassins."

"Close enough."

"Then we'll go to the police," said Mom.

Felicity laughed. "Do you realize how easily the police can be swayed by a couple dozen fresh gourmet Austrian donuts? The Gastronimatii can give people exactly what they need. They know the power of taste and they wield that weapon with more skill than anyone."

"Then what do they want?"

"To find it. They are searching, and they can never be satisfied — not until they get it — the one they have been seeking since it was first invented, five hundred years ago."

"What?" asked Mom.

Felicity leaned forward, her nose almost touching the glass, "The Gastronomy of Peace!" she said. "The One Recipe! Don't you see? Why is it that every chef for centuries has been cooking, experimenting, inventing, breaking new ground? They are all seeking the same thing! The greatest dish on Earth! And now you hold the instructions to make it in your hand!"

"Why would Renoir give it to my boy?" asked Mom.

"Why indeed?" Felicity asked, staring at Guster.

Guster squirmed in his chair. If he hadn't been so insistent on getting something new and delicious to eat that night, Renoir would never have given him the eggbeater.

"It's just a recipe," said Mom.

Felicity shook her head. "The Gastronomy of Peace is much more than that. It is *the* recipe. Haven't you seen my program?"

"Recorded every episode," said Mom.

A faint smile seemed to cross Felicity's face, but then it was gone. She had called it by the same name as the Master Pastry Chef — the Gastronomy of Peace.

"Then you know what great lengths people will go to in order to eat the perfect meal. You know that you cannot underestimate the power of food."

"I suppose, but —" said Mom.

"Then imagine a dish so delicious, so complete and perfect, that anyone who tasted it would have all their sorrows washed away, all their regrets and burdens forgotten. All their hate would be replaced by ecstasy, their sadness with joy."

"But it's just food," said Mom.

"No! It's cuisine!" said Felicity.

"I just can't imagine it," Mom said.

But Guster could imagine. He had believed in the One Recipe ever since the Master Pastry Chef had first told him that it existed. It only made sense that it would be as powerful as Felicity described.

"Have you ever tasted it?" asked Mom. Guster was wondering the same thing.

Felicity cackled darkly. "Of course not! No one ever has! There are only a few who even know what the One Recipe will make! And most of them died hundreds of years ago. Not even the Gastronimatii know."

"Then how can you know that what you say is true?"

"Because I believe in perfection," said Felicity. "And because I believe in the legend of Archedentus."

"Who?" asked Mom. The name sounded regal, like it was someone very, very important.

"Only the most gifted chef that ever lived and the creator of the Gastronomy of Peace."

The Great White Chef, thought Guster. The one the priest was talking about. "He made the eggbeater," said Guster.

"Not quite," said Felicity. "He lived over five hundred years ago, and that eggbeater was made at the beginning of the last century, but it contains his recipe." *Which is why the priest didn't recognize it*, thought Guster.

"So why do the Gastronimatii want it so badly?" said Mom.

"To taste it for themselves!" said Felicity.

"Then why don't we just give it to them?" Mom asked.

"So no one else can have it?!" cried Felicity.

"We'll make them a copy!"

"And how will you copy the ingredients?" asked Felicity.

Guster knew she was right. That egg had been hard enough to get. Getting whatever else was on the list could be next to impossible.

Felicity shook her head. "I'm afraid that you don't understand the power of this recipe. It was said that Archedentus could create a rabbit stew with a red wine sauce so delicious, it made cowards fight for their nation. He made soups so divine that one taste of it, and men and women would fall in love. The Gastronomy of Peace, his most powerful recipe ever, has the power to wipe away mankind's sorrows and present him with that which he has always sought: peace."

Pictures of Archedentus' creations swirled through Guster's head. If only he could taste just one of them! He sighed. And to have his greatest creation of all — Felicity stared at him. Was he that obvious?

"It sounds so wonderful, but —" said Mom.

"Imagine! Presidents, kings, and tyrants dining on the most exultant cuisine possible, then forever dismantling their war machines," said Felicity, glancing at Guster. "Madam, the Gastronomy of Peace is not a selfish quest to satisfy the cravings of a boy. It is the quest to end all war upon the Earth."

"All that from one little recipe?" said Mom.

"Yes, from one little recipe."

"Then what can I do?" asked Mom.

"Make the Gastronomy of Peace!" Felicity said. "If you don't do it, who will?"

Mom was silent. She pushed the eggbeater toward Felicity.

"If only I could," said Felicity. She pressed her hand to the glass, as if trying to grasp the eggbeater.

Mom stood up to go.

"Your boy, he knows what I'm talking about, doesn't he?" said Felicity desperately.

Mom nodded. Guster blushed. How was it that everyone knew about his tastes? He was only doing what was normal — tasting the good and avoiding the bad. He didn't see how that was any different from everybody else.

"Your boy is an Evertaster! Otherwise, Renoir wouldn't have given the eggbeater to him! That is not a gift to be treated lightly! If not taken care of, it can turn into a curse!" said Felicity.

"You must be mistaken, Ms. Casa," said Mom. "Guster is no Ever — whatever you call it. He's just a bit particular."

"No, I can tell. He is an Evertaster — you've seen it in him. Someone who tastes every flavor that ever touched every ingredient in his food. They taste time. They taste history. You know how it is. Nothing satisfies him. Maybe a morsel of the finest cuisine here, or a bite there, but it never lasts. He has more taste buds in one square inch of his tongue than in all of Iowa! He is hungry, always hungry."

Everyone gets hungry, thought Guster. She was only guessing. It was strange though because, for the first time ever, someone understood a part of him that no one else had.

"We've managed so far," said Mom. She grabbed Guster's hand and dragged him toward the exit, leaving the eggbeater on the counter in front of Felicity. He turned, reaching back to grab it; Mom pulled against him. They couldn't leave the eggbeater behind. He had to think of something fast.

"It gets worse with age!" cried Felicity.

Mom stopped. She was silent. She looked down at Guster with the same sympathetic look she made when he'd fallen off his bike or skinned his palms. He looked away. She squeezed his hand.

Felicity spoke, "There is a cure," she said, both hands pressed up against the glass. "You know what it is!"

Mom bowed her head and sighed. She stood there for a long time, her eyes closed. *I don't need a cure*, thought Guster, *I just need something to eat*. He searched Mom's face for a sign that she would not abandon their search. He needed that recipe. He needed her to do her duty as his mom.

Finally she reached over, picked up the eggbeater, and tucked it in her apron pocket. "Goodbye, Felicity," Mom said. Guster followed her as she made her way out the prison doors.

Chapter 10 — On the Road Again

Mom cradled the eggbeater in her lap as she stared out the window of the cab on the way back to the airport.

Finally, thought Guster. She was on board. He wouldn't have to hide things from her anymore. She could tell Braxton to fly them where they needed to go and he would listen because she was an adult. It was times like this that he loved her most.

He felt lighter too, knowing that their search for the Gastronomy of Peace was not just for him, it was for all mankind. *We're doing this to stop wars*, he thought, though he'd never seen a real war for himself. They were doing it for everybody. For all the people in America, and in China, and Africa. For people everywhere. For peace. He could only imagine what it would have been like to live in Paris long ago, to taste Archedentus' work.

"Guster, I need you to start taking responsibility for this recipe," said Mom as they drove back to the airport in the cab. She looked very, very tired; that meant he had to be careful not to set her off. She slid the eggbeater across the seat toward him.

I'm the one who kept the eggbeater in the first place, thought Guster. She was the one who told him to get rid of it. He was eleven. She was the adult. What did she want him to do, fly the plane himself? *Responsibility* was one of those words she liked to use all too frequently. As usual, it was easier to nod his head than to disagree out loud.

"Good," said Mom. "Because you're the Evertaster, and you're the reason we're doing all this."

He was the reason? He felt himself flush with anger. That was like a punch in the stomach. *Evertaster*. For as long as he could remember, Mom had called him picky, and now a celebrity chef thought she was right. *Evertaster*. He wasn't as bad as *that*. He couldn't let Mom blame all this on him.

He turned away from her. He was not in the mood for her scolding right now.

When they got back to the airport, Guster told Mariah everything Felicity had said about the Gastronimatii, Archedentus, and the cuisine that would bring peace to all mankind. He left out the part about her calling him an Evertaster.

"If the Gastronomy of Peace will stop wars, then why did Archedentus want to keep his recipe a secret?" Mariah asked.

"I don't know," said Guster. He hadn't thought about that. It did seem strange to him that Archedentus wouldn't share it with the whole world. It also seemed strange that Felicity wouldn't either.

"In those days, an ocean voyage from Peru to France could take months. If Archedentus needed the egg-fruit of Machu Picchu in order to make his recipe, he would never be able to get it back to France before it spoiled," said Mariah.

"Good point," Guster said. He wished he would've thought of that, too. Mariah was always one step ahead.

"Hey, guys, look over here!" cried Zeke from a newspaper vending machine outside the hangar. Guster and Mariah trotted over to him. "Check out this headline!" he said.

The front page of the paper read in bold letters: "Canned Soup Factory Tainted with Raw Sewage."

"Isn't that weird?" said Zeke. "It's so totally slobulous, it makes me want to vomit!"

Mariah slid some quarters into the slot, pulled out the paper, and started reading the article. "'Cambini's Soup Factory in Pennsylvania was shut down yesterday when a pipe containing raw sewage was found spliced into their main line. Thousands of gallons of soup were filled with human waste from the city sewers, making the soup completely inedible.'"

"Duh!" said Zeke.

"There's more," said Mariah, ignoring him. "'A note written in spicy hot mustard was scrawled across the floor of the factory in huge letters, "Because your soup is already poop, here's a little more of it." The saboteurs still remain unknown and at large.'"

"Woah, that's totally cool!" said Zeke.

Mariah finished reading the article before she gave Zeke a glare. "Zeke, the factory is going to be shut down for months. According to this, Cambini's produces over half the soup consumed in the United States. No one will be able to buy Cambini's soup!"

"So what? It's just one factory!" said Zeke.

Guster felt his stomach turn. It wasn't just one factory. There were more. They'd seen that factory on the news go up in smoke right before they'd left home. "The Foodco Factory!" he cried. Two food plants destroyed in only one week, as well as the Patisserie back in Louisiana. It couldn't be a coincidence. Someone had to be behind this. Someone to whom food meant everything.

He opened his mouth, just as Mariah said it. "The Gastronimatii!" she gasped. Guster nodded. It had to be. The Gastronimatii were advancing. There was no way to tell how many factories or restaurants or supermarkets they'd destroyed. The same innocence they'd burnt and mangled near Guster's little town was dying all around them. It was spreading. And then where would they go? Where could Mom take them? They needed peace more now than ever.

Mariah started for the plane.

"Gastro-who?" Zeke asked.

"We have to tell Mom!" Mariah called back.

Guster hesitated. He didn't want to talk to Mom right now, especially after her lecture in the taxi. Zeke shoved past Guster from behind. "Can't you stop talking crazy for just once!" Zeke shouted after her.

"Mom!" Mariah called as she pounded up the plane's steps. Guster couldn't miss anything either, so he followed, reluctant. They found Mom lying on the bed in the back, resting.

"Gastronimatii!" Mariah gasped holding up the article for Mom to see as she jabbered an explanation.

Mom listened without saying a word. She read through the entire article quietly. When she was finished, she folded the paper and set it down. "Mariah, please get me the eggbeater. We need to find out where that second ingredient is."

Guster followed Mariah to the main cabin where the eggbeater rested on a seat cushion. At least Mom was going to try and help them a little.

"Haven't you looked at that second ingredient a million times?" Zeke said.

"Yes Zeke, I have. It says, 'seventy-four degrees, thirty-one minutes' and 'nineteen degrees, one minute'. Those are the baking instructions; now we just have to discover the location," said Mariah, pinching her chin in thought.

"Why don't you discover your own brain?" Zeke asked. As much as Guster didn't like his tone, Zeke was right. Temperature and baking time were useless without knowing where to find the ingredients to bake. "Don't know if even Christopher Columbus could find that," Zeke whispered to Guster.

Mariah's eyes suddenly lit up. "You mean like a sailor?" She nearly dove for the eggbeater, plucked it up and scanned it with her eyes.

"Yeah, a sailor without a map."

A smile spread across Mariah's cheeks. She didn't seem to be listening. "You may not be as useless as you try to be, brother."

Guster stifled a laugh. Mariah must've been on to something.

"Braxton?" said Mariah, switching directions. She knocked on the cockpit door and he opened. "Do you have a world map with geographic coordinates?" she asked.

"Sure thing, little lady," he said. He rustled through a pouch of charts and maps on the wall until he found one and handed it to Mariah.

"See, 'seventy-four degrees, thirty-one minutes' and 'nineteen degrees, one minute' aren't baking instructions at all," she said, spreading the map out on a table. "They're coordinates!"

"Well of course," said Braxton, looking at the map over her shoulder. "That's latitude and longitude."

"Which is always written in degrees and minutes," said Mariah. "Each degree is broken up into 60 minutes. Seventy-four degrees is the latitude, plus 31 minutes," said Mariah. "And 19 degrees, one minute is the longitude."

Braxton looked over her shoulder. "I wish you would have said something 'bout that earlier," said Braxton.

"Which means that the next ingredient is right there," said Mariah. She pointed to a tiny little island way up in the Arctic Sea north of Norway. Mom stood at the back of the main cabin, smiling. She had heard the whole thing.

"Look," Braxton said, reading the name of the island in fine print below it. "It's called Bjørnøya."

"Braxton, how soon can you have this jet off the ground?" Mom asked.

"Two shakes of a lamb's tail," said Braxton.

"How about one?" Mom said.

Braxton smiled. "Now you're talkin'," he said.

***

Hours later, they were flying over the Atlantic Ocean, far away from home. Leaving the country again was scary, but there was no way around it if they wanted to make the One Recipe.

Then there was the matter of the chickens. Five-foot chickens and egg-trees that grew from chicken seeds. It sounded like one of Zeke's crazy stories, but it had been real, and they'd almost been killed. The bloody wounds on Zeke's leg proved it.

And now they were going to some tiny Norwegian island in the middle of the sea.

Mariah stirred on the bench across the cabin. She rubbed her eyes and went up to the cockpit to sit next to Braxton. "Oh, good. You're awake," he said, "There's something I wanted to show you." Guster craned his neck to see. Braxton pulled out a laptop computer. "We've got a satellite linkup here, so you can get the internet." They muttered back and forth to each other, Braxton showing Mariah how to log on and use it. Eventually, Guster grew tired of trying to listen and drifted off to sleep.

When he awoke, the sun had risen. Mariah sat across the aisle from him, the computer on her lap, the eggbeater on one side, a pencil on the other. She was typing on the keyboard furiously. Occasionally she wrote something down on a piece of paper.

They stopped off in London to refuel. As soon as they were back in air, Mariah switched the computer back on and started working again.

"What is she doing?" Zeke asked when he woke up.

"I don't know," said Guster.

"Looks like homework to me," grumbled Zeke and went back to sleep.

"I've got it!" said Mariah. She smiled at Guster. Her eyes were bright.

"What?" asked Guster.

"I know what the next ingredient is!" she shouted. Mom came from the back room. "I found a website that translates whatever you type in from French to English. It took me awhile to get a translation I was sure of, but I got it working. Here's what I've translated so far." She held the eggbeater up and pointed to the lettering with one hand while she read her notes off the paper.

"The Fruit of the Fowl, sixteen shekels sunshine, sixty-three cloud," she said.

"The eggs!" said Guster. "But what is the sunshine and cloud?"

"Egg yolks and egg whites, of course," said Mariah. It made sense.

"And a shekel?"

"It's some kind of measurement they used in the old days." She pointed to the text below the symbol of the bear and the barrel with the stick. “This means twenty-one shekels of the Buttersmith’s gold.”

“Buttersmith’s gold?” asked Zeke. “What the hecknacious is that?”

Mariah smiled. She seemed proud of herself. “It’s butter, Zeke. It’s so obvious now, it was right under our noses. See the barrel? It’s a butter churn. That’s how they used to make milk into butter way back when.”

“So we’re flying all the way to some island out in the middle of nowhere for butter?” asked Zeke. He made a face.

“Think of the egg, Zeke,” Guster said. “There must be something special about it.” Something about it that would make it more scrumptious than any butter on the whole planet. If only he had a loaf of oven-fresh white bread he could use as a sponge to soak it up…

“If it’s anything like the egg, then the butter probably comes from some crazy place, like a cow,” said Zeke.

Mariah looked at him, as if she was waiting for Zeke to comprehend what he just said. “Are you sure that you live down the road from a dairy? Butter does come from cows, Zeke. It’s made out of their milk.”

Zeke’s cheeks flushed red, hiding his pimples. “Are you sure you don’t live down the road from a mental institution?” he said.

Mariah smirked. She knew she’d won. “Here’s another thing. I looked up Bjørnøya in Norwegian. It means bear island.”

“We’re going to Bear Island!” said Zeke, the smile coming back to his cheeks. “This is totally awesome! I’m gonna wrestle one, and make a rug out of its fur, and —” Zeke acted out the entire scenario right there, growling at Henry Junior as his victim.

“Rar!” laughed Henry Junior back at him.

"So you think we have to find a bear and it will lead us to the butter?" asked Guster.

"I don't know," said Mariah. She looked worried. She got so scared of bears every time they went camping.

Mom smoothed Mariah's dark brown hair. "You are a very clever girl," said Mom. "And I am quite proud of you."

"There's more," said Mariah. "See the next set of symbols?"

She pointed to a carving on the handle of a river with pyramids at one end, and a lake at the other. There was a gorilla with a group of gleaming diamonds next to the lake. "Fifteen and a half shekels of the Mighty Ape's Diamonds," read Mariah from her notes. She pointed to the symbols below that, "Twenty-six shekels Dark Milk Bricks from Arrivederci's Bean," she read. Then finally, "Seven Drops of Sweet, Black Tears. It looks like the rest is instructions for baking and mixing. I'll see if I can get those done before we land," said Mariah.

"Hmm," Mom said. She paced back and forth down the aisle. "Eggs and butter — that makes sense, but diamonds? Dark Milk Bricks? Sweet, Black Tears? In all my years of cooking, I've never heard of anything like it. What could an ape make that was like a diamond?" Mom continued to pace the floor.

There was something strangely familiar about the phrase 'Dark Milk Bricks from Arrivederci's Bean.' Guster was certain he'd heard that before, though he couldn't remember where.

In a few hours, Braxton called back from the cockpit, "I talked with the control tower back in Heathrow. They said that the island is used by meteorologists to study the weather from time to time. Other than that, hardly anybody ever sets foot there. There is supposed to be a landing strip on the southwest corner."

Hours later, the plane was circling over an island partially covered in snow and surrounded by dark gray seas. "There's the airstrip," said Braxton. "Hold on."

Guster felt his stomach leap into his throat as the plane dropped. A minute later, Braxton pulled up on the stick and it hit the runway, bumping furiously. Guster braced himself against the arm rests. The plane slowed, then skidded to a halt.

"Gather your things, and you will all need to put your jackets on," said Mom. Guster zipped his up.

"I'll stay behind with the plane and make sure everything's in good working order," said Braxton. He opened the plane's door and Guster stood on the stairs. The runway was old and cracked, like no one had been there in a long time. Beyond that was a desolate, brown and gray landscape with snow covered mountains looming in the distance. There was no sign of any settlement, no hint of any place that butter could hide.

"Guster, you are the Evertaster. Show us the way," Mom said.

He cringed. There she was, calling him that word again. How was he supposed to know where to go? It wasn't like he had a built-in ingredient detector. And if he somehow did, wouldn't that just prove he was an Evertaster? Wouldn't that just prove to Mom how picky he was — that he was everything she'd always accused him of being? He couldn't let her get away with that.

"Whatever," he said, shrugging his shoulders to pretend like he didn't care.

"Very well," said Mom, standing up slowly. "Then we will go north." She strode past Guster down the stairs with Henry Junior on her back. Guster saw a flash of disappointment in her eyes as she passed.

I'm in trouble again, he thought as they hiked over the gravelly plain. She had been angry with him for keeping the eggbeater, and now she wanted him to make more decisions she could get mad at? For as long as he could remember, she wanted to tell him what to do. Then suddenly, on a deserted Arctic Island, she was going to change all that?

But a lot of things were changing. Mom, who a couple of days ago thought that building sandcastles on the shores of Lake Cucamonga was an adventure, was now hiking decisively toward the inner landscape of the island. The same Mom that didn't let Guster ride his bike into town alone wanted him to take charge — it just didn't make sense.

The plain was so broad, the great sea so wide, and the white mountain so far in the distance it made him feel like a tiny ant in a giant parking lot.

At the end of the gravel plain they came to the beginning of a snow pack, where a pile of boulders reached up toward the sky. Mom stopped and stooped down in the snow. "Tracks," she said. "Something was here."

Just then, a loud roar split the cold air and echoed between the rocks. "What was that?" cried Mariah.

A huge white polar bear came lumbering out from behind a boulder on all fours, straight at them. Its shoulders were taller than Guster's head, and its eyes were like deep, black holes. It snuffed warm steam out of its nostrils.

Mariah screamed. Henry Junior wailed. Desperate, Guster looked for a place to run. There was nothing but boulders and a desolate landscape — not a single place to hide.

"Get behind me kids," said Mom. She spread her arms wide and pushed Guster, Mariah and Zeke behind her. "You will leave my children alone!" she said; she picked up a rock and threw it at the bear's head. It found its mark between the eyes. The bear roared in pain, spit flying from its bared fangs.

"I don't know if you should've done that, Mom," blubbered Zeke between sobs. He was no match for a beast that size. None of them were. It was hopeless.

The bear charged. It raised its massive claws; Guster braced himself. If it ripped his stomach out, at least Guster wouldn't feel hungry anymore. At least death would bring that.

Suddenly, a huge man wearing furs and a horned helmet leapt down from a stack of boulders on Guster's right. He held a huge battle-axe, which he dropped onto the snow, then heaved himself between Mom and the beast. He stared the bear straight in the eye — he could because he was so tall.

"Rar!" he roared, his mouth opened like a lion's.

"Rr?" growled the bear weakly, almost like it was asking a question. It glanced over its shoulder as if it were looking for help.

"RARRR!" The giant man roared so loud in answer, his chest shook.

For a second, it was hard to tell which one would eat the other. Then the bear dropped to all fours and ran off as fast as it could, whimpering the whole way.

Mom plopped down in the snow, her head between her knees. The giant man turned around. Guster hadn't realized he'd been holding his breath. *Now who is going to save us from him?* he thought.

"Unnskyld, men jeg mener at han gjerne ville spise deg!" said the giant man. Though they made absolutely no sense, his words slid up and down like notes on a trombone.

"Torbjorn! They do not speak the mother tongue!" grunted a second huge man as he came lumbering out from behind the rocks. He was even larger than the first. His shaggy silver hair was tied in long braids, under a helmet with horns as thick as elephant tusks. He too, wore thick brown furs and his words bounced high and low like a song.

"Sorry, Storfjell," said the giant named Torbjorn. "It is not so often that we get strangers here," he said, looking at Mom. Even when he spoke English, his voice was melodic. "It is a pleasure to welcome you to our island."

Guster tried to stop his knees from shaking. So they weren't hostile. That bear had only been inches away from tearing them apart, and these men had saved them from certain death.

Guster had to act quickly. He couldn't let the bear get away — not if it would lead them to the prize. "Stop that bear!" he cried. "We need its butter!"

The giant named Torbjorn looked at the giant named Storfjell, and the giant named Storfjell looked back at the giant named Torbjorn. They both began to laugh so big that their chests echoed like hollow garbage trucks. "Oh, my!" said the giant named Storfjell, trying to control himself, his eyes twinkling. "Bears don't know where to find butter! But, don't worry! You outlanders have certainly come to the right place!"

Chapter 11 — The Buttersmiths' Gold

Torbjorn was at least ten feet tall, as broad as an ox, and had the thickest forearms Guster had ever seen. Storfjell was at least a foot taller. At least they *seemed* friendly.

"We're the ones who make the butter around here! Oh it is so excellent — very fresh. If you would like to try some then it would be our distinct pleasure to take you back to our longhouse for some refreshment," Torbjorn said in his sing-songy voice as he picked up his battle-axe and hooked it to a loop on his belt.

"Oh ya!" said Storfjell, "We have some most fresh and delicious blueberry muffins baking in the oven! In fact, we must hurry back so we can get them out before they burn!"

Mom hesitated. She was trying to calm Henry Junior, who was still wailing at the top of his lungs and pounding on her with his fists. "Well, we uh —"

"Oh, you don't like blueberry muffins?" asked Storfjell, a frown forming under his heavy, silvery moustache. "Maybe the boy would like his butter plain?" He looked at Guster.

Guster smiled. Men this hospitable could hardly be dangerous — no matter how big they were. They had already saved their lives. Besides, they had butter, which was bound to be the butter they were looking for. It was worth the risk. "No, butter with muffins sounds delicious," he said.

"Very well, we will accept your hospitality," said Mom.

"Oh, ya! This is very good!" said Torbjorn, his mouth open wide, his teeth sticking out like a row of polished rocks. "Let me get my sled!" He pulled an enormous wooden sled the size of a minivan from behind the boulders. It was just like the ones sled dogs pull, with two very long runners and a place to store gear in the middle.

"Would you be so kind as to have a seat here?" Torbjorn said.

"In that?" asked Mom. Torbjorn nodded. Mom took a seat in the middle, carefully cradling the crying Henry Junior as Zeke and Mariah huddled close. Mariah's face was still streaked with tears. Guster sat on edge of the sled, as far away from Mom as possible.

Torbjorn kicked off the ground with one foot, and the sled lurched forward. Guster almost fell out, so he grabbed tightly onto the frame and held fast. Torbjorn was even stronger than he looked.

Storfjell pulled his own sled out from behind the rocks and slid after them. The two sets of runners glided over the flat snow toward the distant mountain, the giants kicking off the ground to push them forward. Torbjorn kicked almost effortlessly now, and they began riding along like sailboats on smooth water. The wind chilled Guster's cheeks.

"Thank you for saving our lives, Torbjorn," said Mom.

"Oh ya! Of course I am happy to do so for you and your younglings," Torbjorn said. "The bears of this island sometimes are having very bad manners!"

That was for certain, thought Guster. If he hadn't come, they would all be bear-breakfast right now, no matter how tough Mom had tried to be.

In another few minutes they rounded the mountain and came to the end of the snow pack. In the middle of a field of bright green clover sat a long rectangular wooden house. Two ornate, carved dragon heads stuck out from either end of the roof like they were watching over the entrances.

"This is our longhouse!" said Storfjell. They parked their sleds and Torbjorn led them through the field of soft, green clover toward the house. It was as green as anything Guster had ever seen.

Even though it was summer the ride was chilling, so Guster couldn't wait to get inside. He thought it was strange that he wasn't more afraid of the two giants, but they'd been so good-natured and charming it was hard not to like them. Besides, they had saved them from the bear, and being in their company was far better than being alone with a creature that wanted to eat you.

They came to the door of the house and Torbjorn gave a tug on the handle. The door opened wide and the most glorious smell of warm, buttery blueberry muffins reached Guster's nose.

Inside, the house was made up of one long room that stretched all the way to the back. Brightly painted shields were strapped to the rafters. A wide, round table with a large hole in the center circled a crackling fire. On the sides of the stone floors, mounds of straw were piled up against the walls.

"These are the pride of our clan," said Storfjell. He pointed to two dozen reddish-brown cows chewing their cud at the far end of the room. An udder the size of a sack of potatoes hung from each one of their bellies.

"You keep your cows inside?" said Zeke.

"Ya! These cows are very delightful to be around," said Torbjorn. "They are always so clever and good company."

"Don't they smell?" asked Zeke. Mariah stomped on his foot. Guster already knew the answer to that. The longhouse was as clean and fresh smelling as the kitchen back at home.

"Ha ha!" laughed Torbjorn. "These cows do not stink! That is silly! They eat the fresh clover of this field, which is watered by the melting glacier! It is a special treat for any animal, and only comes because we live in this spot! There is nothing cleaner and more crispy for these bovines!"

Storfjell leaned down and whispered to Guster, "And they are smart enough to do their business outside." The cows moo-ed. Guster tried to keep from laughing.

"But, we are rude, rude hosts!" said Torbjorn. "Please, take off your rucksacks and sit around our table. We will see if the muffins are ready!" He removed his horned helmet and hung it on a peg.

Guster climbed on to a bench as high as his chest and Storfjell pushed a gigantic wooden paddle inside an earthen oven buried in the middle of the coals. He pulled out an iron tray full of steaming muffins. Their golden brown crowns were studded with dark blueberries that looked like jewels.

"You may have as many as you can eat," said Torbjorn, placing them down on the table. Guster reached for one.

"No wait!" Storfjell said, holding out his massive hand. "I mean excuse me," he said — he seemed embarrassed by his outburst — "but will you have a little fat on your food?"

Torbjorn nodded eagerly. "Ah ya! Of course! The very reason you came here," he said and ran to the back of the room where he lifted a large wooden barrel and carried it over next to the table. He pushed a flat wooden knife down into it, and scooped out a smooth, heaping, creamy pat of pale yellow butter, then smeared it all over Guster's muffin where it melted into every little nook and cranny.

Zeke held out his own muffin, and Torbjorn smothered everyone's in turn. "Now go ahead. Just eat," said Torbjorn.

Guster did. He bit into the top of his muffin. It melted instantly all over his tongue. It wasn't sweet, it was thick, with a tinge of saltiness that added to the flavor. It was more than just a topping — it was a taste worthy of a meal itself. He could feel the strength seeping into his bones.

The muffin, on the other hand, was dry as a dish sponge left in the sun. "More butter?" Guster asked, holding up his muffin. He could tolerate it if he covered the top in butter and licked it off like the frosting on a cupcake. It had been so long since he'd eaten anything.

Torbjorn obliged, smearing a fresh layer over Guster's muffin.

"Thank you very much. This butter is amazing," said Mom between bites. "I absolutely must get your muffin recipe," she said.

"Oh, yes. Eat more if you like it," said Storfjell, pushing a mound full of muffins in her direction.

They ate until they had their fill. Mariah ate three. Zeke seemed to like the muffins more than anyone — he ate ten. Guster only needed the one because Torbjorn smeared a fresh layer of butter over the top every time Guster licked it clean–which was exactly the way he liked it.

He'd had so much of it, that for once, he actually felt full. It had been a long time since that had happened. *If the world knew about this, they'd build a bridge to get here*, he thought.

With warm butter in his belly and the crackling fire in front of him, his eyelids soon grew heavy. They had traveled so far that day.

"Why don't you all spend the night here?" asked Storfjell. "There is no better place to stay on the island, and there is nothing but bears outside who are waiting to eat you."

"But it is still light," said Zeke, his eyelids drooping. "We should wait until it gets dark to go to sleep."

"Ha ha ha!" bellowed the two giants with deep, echoing laughs. Storfjell pounded his brother on the back. "Then you won't sleep until winter!" he said, nearly falling off the bench.

"Zeke, the sun stays up all summer," whispered Mariah. "It's like Alaska." Guster remembered hearing about that in school. In the far north the sun did not go down for months at a time. Bear Island must work the same way.

"Forgive us," said Torbjorn, with tears streaming down his cheeks, his belly jiggling. "But we do not meet outlanders very often here. We have heard of these short days you have in the Warmlands."

"Nevertheless! Let us rest," said Storfjell. "Tomorrow we have many chores to do. We must get up early to joggle the bovines."

Joggle the bovines? That didn't sound like anything they did back in Louisiana. The two giants were strange indeed.

"Joggle the bovines?" asked Mom with a quizzical look. She pronounced it carefully, like it was a foreign language.

"Oh, you know, part of the chores for when you are having cows," said Storfjell matter-of-factly.

"Mr. Storfjell," said Mom, "I don't mean to be rude, but we live down the street from a dairy and I've never in my life heard of such a thing."

"Aha! And that is why never in your life have you had such delicious butter as what you've just eaten!" said Storfjell.

Storfjell had a point. It definitely was the best butter Guster had ever had. But joggling bovines? That sounded like something clowns might do in the circus.

"Tomorrow, we shall show you the secrets of the Buttersmiths' craft! As for now, let us sleep!" said Storfjell. He showed them to a large pile of straw next to the wall. It was covered with thick, brown furs. "You may rest here."

"This is very kind of you to take us in like this," said Mom.

"Oh! It is cozy to have visitors here. Absolutely cozy!" said Storfjell with a bow. He trotted back to the middle of the longhouse where he took off his heavy furs and hung them next to the fire.

Torbjorn did the same. As he removed his furs, a small glass vial of dark liquid swung from a slender rope around his neck. Guster stared. It looked like a potion, which was a very interesting necklace for a giant to wear.

Torbjorn saw Guster looking at the vial and quickly tucked it away under his shirt.

There was something special about that vial. Guster would have to try to get a second glance in the morning.

Mom patted down the straw and made a nest for herself and the children. She placed Henry Junior, who was already sleeping quietly, his thumb stuck in his mouth, on the soft brown fur. He mooed gently. Zeke and Mariah made beds for themselves in the same heap of straw.

"You've all had a very hard day," Mom said.

Guster made a nest for himself on a nearby pile. He'd rather keep his distance than risk some more Mom-talk. *What was I supposed to do? Smell my way here?* Guster thought. Ever since they'd left home it had all been so new and dangerous.

He turned his back to his brothers and sister and pulled a scrap of what looked like grizzly bear fur over his shoulders.

"Before you sleep, let me kiss your faces," said Mom. Guster heard smacking sounds as Mom kissed his brothers and sister on the cheeks. Even Zeke didn't protest. "Your turn Guster," Mom said.

Instead of turning toward her, Guster pretended to be asleep. Mom leaned over him. “I’m glad you got some of that butter today,” she said, running her fingers through his dirty brown hair. He froze at her touch. “Good night my dear children,” she said.

The straw was so soft, Guster was so tired, and the butter in his belly was so warm, it didn’t take long before he really did fall asleep — dreams of cows and giant chickens running through his head.

***

By the time Guster woke the next morning, the butter had worn off. He was hungry again, and felt weak.

Storfjell tiptoed quietly across the stone floor. “Hush!” he said, and motioned for Guster to come and join him. “Your family all looks so tired. Why don’t we let them sleep a little longer?” Guster nodded, picking himself up off the straw. He followed after Storfjell.

“My younger brother is already out on the beach, tending to business,” he said, opening a wide door in the back. Without so much as a grunt, Storfjell scooped up one cow under each arm like they were a pair of kittens.

“Wouldn’t they rather walk?” Guster asked. He was amazed at Storfjell’s strength.

“Oh, no!” laughed Storfjell. “That is not part of good joggling.”

Curious, Guster followed Storfjell out through the field of clover and down a path to a gravelly beach where monstrous waves crashed upon the shore.

When he got there, Storfjell set down the cow under his right arm next to another cow that was already there. Storfjell took the cow under his left arm, slung it over his shoulders and grabbed its legs gently on either side of his neck as if it were a tiny calf.

"Doesn't that hurt?" asked Guster.

"No! She likes it very much," said Storfjell with a grin, as the cow mooed happily. Without another word he took off jogging down the beach, high stepping like a football player at practice. The cow bounced up and down on his shoulders with each step, her head bobbing like a pendulum, her giant udder jostling back and forth like a balloon full of pudding.

Guster had seen farmers carry small pigs like that at the state fair, but he never thought it was possible to run a full-grown cow down the beach with such ease as his friendly giant host did. It was downright astounding.

Torbjorn came running from the far end of the beach, in the opposite direction of Storfjell, a cow also bouncing up and down on his shoulders. "Ya!" the two giants shouted in unison as they passed each other. Torbjorn stopped when he got to Guster, set his cow down, picked up one that had been standing there, and slung her over his shoulders. "Hallo! I hope you are enjoying the fresh morning air," he said, and took off down the beach again, the cow's udder rebounding off his chest the whole way.

They ran several laps with each cow. When they were finished, Storfjell and Torbjorn set the cows in their arms down and crashed their chests together with a loud "Ya!"

A moment later they each had a cow on their shoulders again. This time they started dancing in a circle, kicking up their legs and spinning around, slapping their heels and hitting their knees in unison, all the while shouting some song at the top of their lungs that Guster could not understand.

Mariah and Zeke came up behind Guster, yawning. "What are they doing?" asked Mariah.

"Joggling the bovines," replied Guster with a shrug of his shoulders. He still couldn't fathom why anyone would do such a thing, but at least now he knew what the word meant.

"Does it hurt them?" asked Mariah.

The cows held their mouths open, their eyes shining brightly, almost as if they were laughing. "I think they like it," said Guster.

"I guess they do look happy," said Zeke.

"Ah! Hallo, younglings," said Storfjell. "You are just in time to see Olga do her favorite part of the joggling." He set his cow down and untied a rowboat from a post. "Like our clan in ancient times, Olga very much likes waves, you know." Storfjell heaved a dark red cow into the rowboat and shoved it out to sea. He hopped in just as a wave came crashing down on the boat, nearly capsizing it. "Oh, my!" he said. "The sea will make some very good joggling today!" He shouted as he set two oars from the boat into the sea and rowed, the boat dipping and rising with the waves.

What a strange sight, thought Guster, as the tiny rowboat crested the top of the wave and Olga stood tall, stretching her neck into the wind. Her udder sloshed back and forth with the ocean. She reached down to lick Storfjell on the cheek.

"I think Olga is his favorite," said Torbjorn to Guster. "Though he insists that he likes them all the same."

"If you make so much butter, where are all your butter churns?" asked Mariah.

Guster remembered the butter churn carved into the eggbeater's handle. Mariah was right, there hadn't been a single one in the whole longhouse.

"Oh you mean the old way for making butter!" said Torbjorn. He looked a little taken aback. "We gave that up centuries ago on Bjørnøya."

"But you need to stir the milk and shake it up to turn it into butter. How can you do that without a churn?" said Mariah.

Torbjorn laughed. "That is why we joggle of course! To stir up the milk!"

The rowboat came crashing to the shore with a curling wave. Storfjell hopped out, heaving Olga over the side with him. "You don't pick a strawberry from the vine before it is ripe, yes?" Storfjell said.

Guster nodded. He could understand that. He never ate strawberries that had been picked too early.

"So you do not take the milk out before you've stirred it!" said Storfjell. "It makes the butter so much stronger, like us!" Torbjorn nodded, his horned helmet rocking back and forth on his head.

"This is just too weird," said Zeke. But somehow, it made sense to Guster. Then again, a lot of things were making sense to Guster now that he never would have believed a few days ago.

"Would you like to see one more joggling?" asked Torbjorn. Mariah, Zeke and Guster all nodded eagerly. "Then come with me!" He led them to the foot of a grassy hill, with a cow under his left arm. He stopped at a pile of huge barrels, like the one that he had served the butter out of the night before. He picked up a barrel with his right arm, then started up the hill. Guster, Mariah and Zeke stayed at the bottom.

When he reached the top, Torbjorn set the barrel upright then stuffed the cow inside as if he were packing luggage. Her legs stuck out the top. "Please be careful for where the barrel rolls," he called down to them, then tipped the barrel over and shoved it down the hill. It bounced and tumbled like a shoe in the dryer all the way down to the bottom. Zeke and Mariah dove out of the way. "Guster!"

cried Mariah, and Guster jumped out of the path of the oncoming barrel just in time.

It rolled to a stop in the clover meadow. Torbjorn ran down the hill after it, set his feet on the rim of the barrel and, with both hands, yanked out the cow. She stood up, wobbled, then turned in a few circles with her hooves spread wide, trying to steady herself. "That is very much their favorite!" cried Torbjorn. The cow swished her tail, her udder still quivering.

They spent the rest of the morning and well into the afternoon leading the cows out from the longhouse to the beach and the hill, where Torbjorn and Storfjell continued with their joggling. No matter how many times the two giants ran up and down the beach with the cows on their backs, Guster never tired of watching the sight.

"The afternoon is almost over," said Storfjell, though it was just as bright as it had been that morning. "We must take the cows back to the house. They will be needing milking."

Guster had enjoyed his day so much, he'd almost forgotten how hungry he was. After all that joggling, his knees were wobbly from lack of food, so he was more than happy to head back to the longhouse and get some butter.

When they got there, they stopped outside. Storfjell sat down on a stool next to Olga and placed a bucket under her humongous udder. He started milking her as Guster watched in amazement. Instead of thin white milk, thick, creamy yellow butter squirted out of the cow's nipple like soft serve ice cream out of a machine. It smelled delicious.

"Holy, buttery cow!" said Zeke. Guster never imagined he'd see such a sight. It was indeed the freshest butter anyone could get.

Storfjell and Torbjorn set to work squeezing fresh butter from one cow after another. When they were finished, they sent them out into the field of clover to graze. "Now let us go to eat!" said Storfjell.

Guster still couldn't get over how easy it had been for Torbjorn and Storfjell to joggle so many bovines in such a short amount of time. They were so strong and cheery while doing it, too. Storfjell never seemed to pick on Torbjorn like Zeke picked on Guster while they were doing chores.

Storfjell opened the door to the longhouse. The smell of rancid fish bubbled up out of a pot over the fire. "I used some of your dried salmon to make some fishball soup," said Mom, stirring the pot.

Storfjell and Torbjorn's eyes lit up. Guster felt his stomach turn queasy. The air smelled like a fish market three days after things had putrefied into slime.

Torbjorn grinned at Mom, "Oh this is so wonderful to have a Mom-maiden in our midst."

"Ya! And I can make us some blueberry muffins!" Storfjell said, dusting off his hands.

"Already in the oven," said Mom. She dished out several bowls of light pink slime with a ladle and set them on the table. Zeke and Mariah and the Buttersmiths took a seat. Guster followed reluctantly. It was going to be tough to get out of this one. Mom shoved a bowl of fishball soup in front of his nose. He nearly gagged.

Storfjell fetched the barrel of butter as Torbjorn poured out seven mugs of cider. They slurped down their soup.

"You've made an incredible amount of butter today," said Mom.

"Ya! But this is not very much compared to how much we used to make when the whole clan was here!" said Torbjorn. "Then we had a few hundred head of cattle and made twenty barrels a day." There was a note of pride in his voice.

"What happened to them?" asked Mom, setting down her bowl.

"It doesn't matter," grunted Storfjell from across the table.

Torbjorn looked down at his soup. "They sailed away," he said.

"To where?" asked Mom.

Storfjell slammed his mug of cider down on the table with a thud. "Oh, it is not important!" he said. "Let us talk of happier things!" He stood up and walked to the back of the longhouse to fetch more butter, though the barrel was still quite full.

Torbjorn shook his head. "My older brother has always been the responsible one. He has no time for grieving. Neither of us knows where the clan ended up. They told us they were headed to Vinland to trade butter for grapes."

Mom gasped. "Why would they leave you here?" she asked.

"They were planning on coming back in two months, but it has been at least seventy years."

"Seventy years?" cried Zeke. "That means you're older than Dad!"

Torbjorn chuckled. "Well, I am eighty-two. How old are you, youngling?"

Zeke sunk lower on the bench. "Fifteen," he said under his breath.

"I think that this fresh air does us very good," said Torbjorn. "We live to be very old here on the island. We still have a very long time yet to live. Storfjell is eighty-seven."

"So he was only seventeen when they left you all alone, and you were only twelve," said Mariah, adding up the figures in her head.

"How did you ever manage?" asked Mom.

Torbjorn sighed. "We didn't for a while. It was great at first — no one made us do chores. We could sleep all day, or ski on the glacier. But then we got hungry, and the cows, their udders got full. That is when Storfjell took charge. He made us get up and joggle the bovines and thatch the roof and fish for meat in the ocean, just like we always did when our father and mother were here."

"Imagine!" said Mom, "If my two oldest boys were left all by themselves to tend the farm! I don't know how they would manage all that responsibility. They can barely feed themselves." She shot a look at Guster.

He bit his lip. This was Mom's favorite subject.

"Butter does not come from nowhere, and it wasn't until everyone else was gone away that we realized how much they were giving us," said Torbjorn.

Guster did his best to keep his eyes fixed on the fire, but he was almost certain Mom was staring at the untouched bowl of soup in front of him.

"Ever since they left though, Storfjell refuses to return to the open sea. He won't go beyond the harbor where we take the cows," said Torbjorn.

"Hmph!" Storfjell grunted gruffly as he approached the table again. "I must know something," he said. "In the past, our fathers traded butter with neighboring clans from across the sea where the fjords stretch deep into the land like fingers. After doing business, we always disappeared without a trace. It was good this way, for when their supply ran out, those clans wanted the butter so badly they sailed up and down the coasts, burning and plundering villages in search of us and our butter. But they could never find us here, and we have not had a visitor for five hundred years. When we saw your great silver bird land on our island, we came to see what it was, and

Torbjorn sent away the bear. That is why I wonder, you travelers from far away, how is it that you have come seeking our butter, the golden fortune of our herds?"

Mariah looked at Mom with a pleading expression on her face. "Go ahead dear," said Mom. "You may tell them."

"We're searching for the ingredients in the One Recipe," said Mariah.

Torbjorn looked at her blankly. "Ya well! You outlanders have such funny names for things. What is this 'the One Recipe?'" Mariah unzipped Guster's backpack and showed them the eggbeater. She pointed out the carving of the Bear and explained the coordinates.

Torbjorn scratched his head and took a careful look, his eyes squinting underneath his shaggy red eyebrows. "Ooo," said Torbjorn. "That is a one of our bears! But how did you know about the butter?"

"From the carving of the butter churn. This eggbeater is like a treasure map," said Mariah. "Long ago a great chef named Archedentus must have come to this island and tasted your butter. He left a recipe that described where to find it, and someone carved it into the handle of this eggbeater."

Torbjorn's bushy eyebrows shot up his forehead. "Then the lore is true!" he said. "The Master Mead-Maker said someone would come back, but no one thought it would take this long!"

"Who?" asked Mom.

"The Master Mead-Maker!" boomed Storfjell. "Our legends tell us that he came here, five hundred years ago, and with him he brought a mead that was more delicious than anything we ever drank. It sparkled like sunshine, and a single mug filled our bellies with warmth for days. He saw our butter, and deemed it good. He told us that one day someone would return to claim some of it for a great purpose — one that would change the face of the world. He said that with it, he would silence the roar of the dragons and melt all the violent men's axes into cooking pots."

Archedentus, Guster thought. He'd left a trail, and ever since Peru, they'd been retracing his steps.

"And what is this symbol?" said Storfjell, pointing to the ape and the diamonds.

"The Mighty Apes' Diamonds. We haven't figured out what it means yet," said Mom.

"Hmm," Storfjell said, lost in thought. "Our father once told us of a place deep in the earth, where men dug tiny, white crystals from the rock. They traded butter for the tiny grains, which were delicious, because they tasted like the sea."

"Salt!" said Mariah. "You think that this is salt?"

Storfjell shrugged his shoulders. "I don't know," he said.

Mariah bit her lip in thought. "Mom, what can you make out of eggs, butter, and salt?" she asked.

Mom shook her head. "Hundreds of things. I'm afraid we haven't figured out what enough of the ingredients are to know what they make."

"Interesting —" muttered Torbjorn to himself while he fingered the vial of dark potion. He seemed lost in thought. He stashed it away again before Guster could ask him what it was.

Storfjell finished his fifth bowl of soup as Mom put a tray of steaming muffins on the table. "It was so delicious, thank you. My brother and I are not used to someone making us dinner."

"You are so kind," beamed Mom. Clearly the compliment made her happy. "I do enjoy cooking for people."

Storfjell stroked his long, silvery braids, "How did you come to possess such a token?" he said pointing to the eggbeater again.

Did they have to bring this up now? This was the perfect chance for Mom to tell Torbjorn how Guster had disobeyed, or just how 'picky' she thought Guster was.

Mariah chimed in instead, "Well, Mom went into town because Guster's an Evertaster and he wouldn't eat Mom's casserole."

That did it. "Don't call me that!" Guster said. He shoved the fishball soup aside and reached across the table for the wooden spoon stuck in the butter barrel.

"Guster! Not until after you've finished your soup," Mom snapped. It was like she had been waiting for that.

He cringed. He couldn't eat *that* slime when the butter was right in front of him. He wasn't going to press his burning hand to a hot stove when there was a bucket of cool water nearby. "Don't you like your mother's cooking?" asked Torbjorn.

Guster shook his head. He expected it from Mom, but he couldn't believe that Mariah of all people was calling him Evertaster. She was supposed to back him up. And now Torbjorn was starting in on him too?

"Guster!" said Mom; her voice sounded hurt. "Eat!"

He knocked his bowl of fishball soup into the fire. "I would if you didn't keep making barf-casserole every single day!" He had had enough. He was so hungry it hurt, and it was time the truth came out.

Mom looked at him in surprise, her mouth open, the pain stabbing across her face. Guster shoved back from the table.

"Guster…I didn't mean…" said Mariah, putting a hand on his shoulder. He pulled away. She would never understand.

"What? Do you even know how long it's been since I've had anything — I mean anything — to eat! I'm starving to death, and no one even notices!"

Mom breathed slowly, as if she was trying to concentrate. "They all eat it," she said, holding her arms out as if trying to make it obvious. She looked like she was about to cry.

"I'm not them," said Guster.

Mom's lip trembled. "Even after all this. After we've come so far. For you–" she started out in a whisper, then built momentum. "Cooking day in and day out, without so much as a thank you! Every meal bending over backward just to find something, *anything* you would eat! Zeke eats it! Mariah eats it! But you! You're the only one Guster! And now we're half way across the world and that's still not good enough for you, is it?!"

"I'm not making anyone come along," said Guster, storming from the table.

He did his best to slam the heavy door of the longhouse as he left. It barely budged. He kicked it, madder than ever, the frustration he'd pent up since summer started bursting out. He ran up the hill onto the glacier as fast as he could.

She still didn't get it, did she? Even after tasting the eggs, the butter — everything else they'd encountered ever since that night in the Patisserie. She still couldn't understand what they *could* be eating. How it *should* taste.

What does she want me to do? he thought. He didn't stop running until he came to a pile of snow-covered boulders. When he looked back the longhouse was just a small dot in the distance, far below. "I'm not picky — just careful!" cried Guster aloud. He sat down in the snow, his head steaming with anger.

It wasn't his fault those foods tasted so awful. Even the muffins! Too dry! Why couldn't people just figure out how to make food as good as Renoir's pastries? Guster hugged his knees, fighting back the tears. Why was everyone making things so difficult for him? Didn't they want to make the One Recipe too?

Strangely enough, as soon as he had thought about all those delicious treats, the most wonderful smell wafted into his nose and tickled his nostrils. He turned; there was a single scone, lying on the snow behind him, brown and crisp and still steaming. He crept over to it, bending low to examine its golden, crispy dough. He smelled it — it was perfection. Had he wished it there? It was like something Renoir would have made. He prodded it with his fingertip; it was real enough.

There was no one in sight — just a huge pile of rocks and ice. That was a strange place for a scone. Someone must have left it there. But who? Was it dangerous? Guster shook his head. *Don't be silly*, he told himself, picking it up and drawing it to his face. Something that smelled so wonderful couldn't hurt anyone. He took a bite. It was exquisite! He closed his eyes. The flavor washed down his throat. It was as if he'd been a dry lakebed all his life and now it was raining a sweet pastry rain.

No sooner had he finished it than two strong hands seized him by the arms. A third hand covered his eyes. A fourth hand — with the distinct smell of pickled ginger — clapped over his mouth before he could scream.

"Don't worry, child, all we want is zee One Recipe," someone said.

Chapter 12 — The Cult of Gastronimatii

Pickled Ginger. Guster had smelled it before; and this time — like before — danger was close at hand. The hands lifted from his eyes and he saw him — the Chef in Red from the Patisserie. The chef's red toque was pulled low over his black eyes, masking the top of his face, his pointy teeth bared in a maniacal grin.

Guster struggled to escape when two more chefs — both dressed in flowing red aprons — tied his wrists together. They held him tight by the arms.

"Zee eggbeater, child. Where is it?" said the Chef in Red, his face threateningly close to Guster's.

Guster's heart thumped in his chest. How had they found him here? "What are you talking about?" he was trying to buy some time, but he'd already stolen the eggbeater right out from under the Chef in Red's nose back in the Patisserie.

The Chef in Red sighed. "Do not try my patience, child," he said motioning to one of the other chefs. "Show him how we found 'im!"

The chef on Guster's right arm let go. Guster hadn't noticed it before, but he was shorter than the other two, with tan skin and dark hair sticking out from the toque that masked his face. There were corn designs embroidered in black around the hems of his apron and jacket. He wore a tiny red ear of corn around his neck.

Impossible! thought Guster. He knew that ear of corn. "Estomago!"

"Sí, Señor," he said. "I had you back there in Cusco! But then —" Estomago rubbed the back of his skull. "It seems I owe you a very strong favor." He smiled cruelly. Guster had no doubt he intended a deadly repayment.

Estomago pulled a sealed plastic dish from a large picnic basket covered in a red cloth that he held in the crook of his arm. He opened the dish and showed the contents to Guster. Inside was a piece of molded green Jell-O.

"So?" said Guster.

"It is a mold," said Estomago. "From when your sister foolishly dropped the eggbeater in the mud. It left an imprint. I made this Jell-O in the impression to preserve it after you were gone."

Guster caught his breath. They had the recipe? He strained against the chef still holding his arms to get a closer look at it. There was the shape of the bear and the butter churn as well as the coordinates. Next to that were the very tips of pyramids and the end of a river, but nothing more. No wonder they still needed the eggbeater.

"Naturally we followed the clue, and we know about the butter," said Estomago. "Had I known what you had, I would've killed you and taken the eggbeater back in Peru!"

Which is exactly what the Chef in Red wanted to do. Now he just might do it.

Anger flushed over Guster. He was mad at himself for getting distracted by that scone. He was mad at himself for leaving the longhouse. He was mad that the Chef in Red had caught him. Now he was mad at himself for being so mad, and he wanted to burst. "I know who you are!" he yelled at the Chef in Red.

The Chef in Red smiled wickedly. "Oh you do, do you?" he said. "And who might that be?"

"The Cult of Gastronimatii!" Guster cried.

The Chef in Red scowled. "My, my. Someone 'as been doing 'is homework," he said. "Well, then. Allow me to introduce myself properly: I am Palatus, Arch-Gourmand of zee Ancient Order of Flavor, Sovereign of zee Sect of zee Savorous Societ-ee, Lord-Evertaster of zee Cult of Gastronimatii." He removed the hat masking his face, then bent low to look Guster directly in the eyes. "And you?" he asked with a hiss.

"Guster Stephen Johnsonville," said Guster. He struggled, but the chef still holding him was too strong and the ropes on his wrists too tight. They may kill him, but Guster wasn't going to show weakness. He wasn't going to give away what he knew about the One Recipe. "You were the ones who destroyed those food factories!"

The Chef in Red, Palatus, laughed a cruel, evil laugh. "Of course! It is what zee Gastronimatii do! 'Ave you heard of Marie Antoinette? The one who said 'Let them eat cake!'"

Guster had heard of her. His fifth grade teacher taught them how Marie Antoinette said the starving peasants should eat cake, even though Marie was the only one who had any.

"Zee people were eating bread that tasted like rocks! And in France! Zee Gastronimatii burned as many of those filthy loaves as they could. Only delicious and masterfully made cake remained! Things truly worthy of Paris! And Marie Antoinette was a loyal member of zee Cult! A champion of the sacred flavors!"

"But those people were starving!" said Guster. How could Palatus brag about that?

Palatus lowered his face to Guster's level. "It had to be done. It is zee way history goes — zee Cult of Gastronimatii policing the cuisine of each nation. The French Revolution, zee first World War, and now zee factories. Can't you see? We will stop at nothing to protect the pure flavors from the putrid sewage others would mix with it!"

"You know zee pain that such vile filth causes!" He pointed at his mouth. "Zee way it stabs your tongue like daggers! Zee way it poisons your throat." He coughed, unscrewing the lid of his jar of pickled ginger, his eyes watering. He took a pink slice of the pungent root and slid it into his mouth like it was medicine, then swallowed. "I must cleanse my palette just thinking about it! Those factories made food. Not cuisine. And so they must be eliminated! Wiped off zee map!"

"You can't! People will starve!" said Guster, but even as he said it, even as he feared for his own life, he understood. He knew the pain Palatus felt.

"There are Tasters and there are Scavengers," said Palatus furiously. "Zee ones who simply eat, and zee ones who live for each bite of flavor! It is a war and you would be foolish not to join zee side that will triumph."

"I already have," Guster said, though there was less conviction in his voice than he would have liked.

"Have you?" asked Palatus, his eyebrow raised. "Because, Guster Johnsonville — Evertaster — I see great potential in you. I watched you that night in the Patisserie. I know why Renoir gave the eggbeater to you! The makings of the Gastronimatii are in you!"

A new, different kind of guilt surged over Guster. That wasn't true. He wasn't like them. He was just being careful… wasn't he?

"Estomago! Duodenum! Go to zee house. Tell them we 'ave zee boy, and that they will only get 'im back when they give us zee eggbeater!" shouted Palatus as he took the picnic basket from Estomago.

Estomago took one malicious look at Guster, then hiked downhill. The other chef — the one Palatus called Duodenum — turned and bore a set of pointy fangs at Guster before he too took off down the glacier toward Guster's family.

Palatus yanked the ropes around Guster's wrists, pulling him further up the ice. "Where are we going?" asked Guster. He dreaded how it would all end, but he had to know.

"To have a meal," said Palatus, trudging through the crusty snow. It was a strange answer, but there was nothing Guster could do. His wrists were bound too tightly. Palatus could end it all right then if he wanted to and Guster knew it.

They trudged on. Guster sank up to his knees with each step, the sweat trickling down his forehead. The going got more difficult the higher they went. Pulling his legs out of the deep snow over and over was hard work.

Eventually they came to a vertical shelf of ice that blocked their path. Just to his right, a narrow ice bridge spanned a crevasse so deep, Guster could not see the bottom.

Palatus forced Guster across the bridge. Guster stepped gingerly. If the ice broke, he'd plummet to his death. It trembled beneath him. He took a few more shaky steps. Miraculously, it held until they got to the other side.

Palatus threw Guster down in the snow. Tiny chunks of ice got down Guster's jacket and froze to his back. He propped himself up on his hands. "You are just a selfish, picky eater!" he cried. He wasn't going to let Palatus kill him before he'd said the truth.

Palatus shook his head. "You misunderstand me, boy. Indeed, zee mere sludge you call food pains me. Indeed, I want to taste zee One Recipe more than anything. I 'ave given my life in pursuit of it — as have the rest of the Gastronimatii — but I am not like my colleagues. Where they are insatiable monsters, I alone have taken steps to understand zee full power of the Gastronomy of Peace. It is not meant merely to be consumed. It has a purpose."

"The One Recipe is supposed to bring world peace!" shouted Guster.

"Indeed," said Palatus. A smile formed on his lips. He untied Guster's wrists. "And that is why there is no reason for men of like minds to quarrel. Not when there is joy to be had." Palatus set down the picnic basket and spread the red table cloth out on the snow. He set a plate on it, then pulled a steaming bowl of French onion soup, a baguette, and a cut of filet mignon out of the basket and placed it on the table cloth.

It was startling how good the soup smelled — the true opposite of Mom's. The aroma pulled on Guster like a magnet. He wanted to dive in, to consume it all. Something to finally fill his stomach! He *needed* it.

"Come, enjoy all that the Gastronimatii have to offer," said Palatus. He held out a fork and a spoon.

As if Guster could trust him! But Guster was so hungry. He folded his hands close to his body to keep them from reaching out. He had to resist. He had to —

He snatched the utensils and dove toward the meal, slurping the soup greedily, tearing tender strips of meat off with this teeth. He was no longer in control. He needed those foods. The flavors burst across his tongue like an explosion. They did not just consume his mouth — they flooded his body.

"There is so much the world could be," said Palatus tenderly. "Zee Gastronimatii know the Octaves of Taste, frequencies of flavor that when used properly can make astounding cree-ations! Zee symmetry in a simple baguette, or the beauty of mixing soup ingredients in the golden ratio. These things move people — more than music, more than theatre. It is zee ultimate art — for cuisine is humankind's lifeblood! Why shouldn't I want that for humanity?"

I see now, thought Guster, as he bathed in the flavor. He was the meat and this was the marinade. If only food always tasted like this. His pain would be over.

Perhaps he had judged them too harshly. If this is what the Gastronimatii wanted for everyone, maybe it was the right thing to do. Who was he to stand in the way of such progress?

"You need not go back," said Palatus, removing his mask. His hair was so blonde, it was nearly white. "Come with us."

And if he did? He may never see the farmhouse again. Would that be so bad? *Don't be an idiot*, thought Guster. He was in danger, and he wasn't going to let his guard down.

"They are coming," said Estomago as he and Duodenum came charging back up the hill. They stopped at the shelf of ice on the other side of the chasm. "And they have two giants with them!"

Palatus touched his fingertips together. "Good. Prepare the ambush," he said.

An evil grin twisted across Estomago's face. He took a cooking torch from his belt, lit it, then pressed the flame close to the bottom of the frozen ice shelf. "It's like roasting a ham," he laughed. "You have to know which parts to make tender." The ice cracked and groaned, on the verge of breaking free. Estomago stepped to the side and waited.

Moments later, Mom, Zeke, Mariah, Torbjorn and Storfjell came hiking up the hill. Guster's mouth was too full to cry out a warning.

"Stop there!" shouted Palatus, his voice echoing across the chasm.

Mom stopped in her tracks. Henry Junior clung to her back. Torbjorn and Storfjell stood ready, round wooden shields strapped to their arms, battle-axes in hand.

"Give us the eggbeater!" said Palatus.

"Give us Guster first!" shouted Mom, her hands on her hips, her eyes blazing with such fury that Guster could hardly believe she was his own mother.

"Do you really think that you are able to make dee-mands when you face zee strength of zee Gastronimatii?" said Palatus. His metal cleaver sang as he pulled it from his belt. Estomago and Duodenum pulled wickedly long, pointy blades from their belts too.

"Yes we do," said Mom. "Torbjorn, Storfjell, do your worst."

"Gladly!" said Torbjorn, and the two giants thundered up the mountain like bulls, their beards waving behind them, Torbjorn's head lowered so that his horned helmet was aimed at Estomago.

Palatus hurled his cleaver through the air just as his two minions did the same. The knives flew, spinning straight for Mariah and Zeke. Torbjorn saw the first cleaver and pushed off one foot, throwing himself in front of the flying blade. He extended his shield; the cleaver struck it with a thud. Storfjell blocked a second knife with his shield. The third sailed dangerously close to Zeke's head.

Seeing his chance, Estomago lit his torch and held it to the cliff side. The ice creaked dangerously. With a horrible cry, Duodenum turned up the dial on his torch and spewed a huge ball of fire at Torbjorn.

The Buttersmiths ducked just as the wall of ice broke free. Duodenum and Estomago leapt out of the way as it came crashing down on Torbjorn and Storfjell. They were buried in an instant.

Horrified, Guster searched for a sign that they were still alive. The ice was silent. Duodenum laughed.

Mom gasped. Guster's heroes had fallen. Now no one could rescue him, even if he wanted them to. Duodenum and Estomago seized Mom, Zeke and Mariah easily by the arms.

"Ha!" said Palatus. "You see what happens when you dare to dee-fy us! Now, give us zee eggbeater."

"We'll copy the recipe! Then we can both have it," she called across the chasm. Guster could hear fear in her voice. They were trapped and he could tell she knew it.

Palatus laughed. "And share zee Gastronomy of Peace with lowly Scavengers like yourselves? Never! That recipe has a destin-ee!"

"But the world needs it!" said Mom. *Yes*, thought Guster. And Palatus wants to be the one to give it to them.

"If only you understood!" cried Palatus. "We will blow up a thousand more factories, or burn a thousand more farms if that's what it takes to get that eggbeater. We'll sink this island if we 'ave to! Or simply," Palatus' eyes narrowed, "You will never see zee boy again."

Mom closed her eyes, sighed, then took the eggbeater from Mariah's backpack. Estomago ran up to her and wrenched it from her fingers.

He crossed the snow bridge and kneeled before Palatus, presenting him with the eggbeater. Palatus grasped it like a scepter and smiled cruelly. “Ah, the One Recipe.”

“Let Guster go!” said Mom.

“That is for ’im to decide,” said Palatus. He motioned with his head. “Estomago, the Dreamless Gravy!” he said.

Estomago pulled a steaming silver gravy boat from the picnic basket and crossed the snow bridge once more to where Duodenum held Mom tightly by the arms. Estomago drew a ladle from his belt, filled it with a meaty, steaming brown liquid and put it to her lips. She kept them sealed.

“You ever see a man fall asleep in his chair after a turkey dinner?” said Palatus to Guster. “This gravy is one million times more potent! There is enough turkey juice in it to knock out an elephant. One mouthful, and your mother will sleep for a full decade.” Mom struggled; it was no use.

Could Palatus really do that? Could he really put Mom to sleep?

“Do not worry. It won’t hurt her — she will sleep soundly,” said Palatus, the hatred pouring from his eyes. “You are an Evertaster, Guster Johnsonville. Consider my offer. She tastes the gravy and you get ten years of freedom.”

There was no reason to doubt the gravy could do that. Guster had seen enough damage done by the Gastronimatii to believe it.

“Imagine, ten years of this,” Palatus pointed to the meal at his feet.

Ten years without anyone telling him what to do. No chores, no nagging, no casseroles. No more burnt or rubbery food that tasted like damp carpet. He’d be grown by the time it was over. She would never be able to tell him what to do again. How many times had he wished for this! “And if I refuse?”

"No one can be forced to go the way of the Gastronimatii," said Palatus. He breathed in the remnants of the filet mignon and held it in his nostrils. Guster could smell it too. "You must make the choice between taste and hunger."

If only the Gastronimatii had made this offer eleven years ago. If only he could have skipped his time at home. If only he could erase it. It was just one sip. It wasn't going to hurt her.

"Gusser!" cried Henry Junior. Guster couldn't meet Mom's eyes. It was Mariah's he saw instead. They were pleading, but brave.

What if he hadn't grown up on the farmhouse? What if he hadn't had those wrestling matches with Zeke, or heard all those facts from Mariah, or been there when Henry Junior mimicked the rooster's morning call? Could he give up that? Palatus clutched the eggbeater tightly in his hand.

"What shall we do, boy?" Duodenum forced Mom's jaw open and raised the ladle. Guster imagined an empty kitchen with no Mom banging pots and pans.

"Eat yourself!" cried Guster, stabbing his fork into Palatus' thigh. The chef stumbled, losing his grip on Guster's arm. Guster broke free and darted for the snow bridge. Chunks of ice broke from the edges and fell into the crevasse below as he ran. He was terrified to think it might collapse now. Halfway across, he dove for the other side like a football player diving for the end zone. He landed chest-first on packed snow.

There was a cry, then a gurgle as he looked up to see Duodenum forcing the gravy down Mom's throat. "No!" Guster screamed. Zeke kicked at the chef's legs, knocking him over. Mom swallowed. Her eyelids fluttered, then fell shut like the lead doors on a bunker. She swayed, then slumped down in the snow, asleep. Estomago grabbed Guster by the hair before he could reach her.

"You've had this coming!" hissed Estomago. He lifted his cleaver. Guster braced himself, dreading the worst. Suddenly, the mound of fallen ice next to Guster's feet rumbled and a huge fist smashed out from below. Shards of ice sprayed Estomago in the face. Torbjorn leapt out, his head shaking in rage and his horned helmet pointed skyward.

Estomago dashed for the snow bridge, but it was too late. With a roar, Torbjorn grabbed him by the back of his neck and lifted him off the ground. He flailed; his cleaver fell to the snow.

"Insolent Scavengers," Palatus cried, pulling the fork from his leg and tossing it aside casually. He drew another cleaver and started deliberately toward them. Torbjorn saw him coming and hurled Estomago like a missile at the Lord-Evertaster. Palatus stepped aside, dodging the projectile body.

"Torbjorn, the bridge!" cried Guster. Before Palatus could get any closer, Torbjorn smashed both fists down onto the ice bridge. It crumbled and broke into huge chunks of snow that plummeted into the crevasse. Palatus stepped backward, firmly planting himself on the ground as the bridge fell away, his eyes never leaving Guster.

"You will come back to us, Guster," Palatus said. Duodenum drew another knife, but Torbjorn caught him by the apron and hoisted him high before he could attack.

"Be gone, swine!" Torbjorn bellowed, his nostrils flaring with anger. He swung the screaming Duodenum by the apron around his head like a lasso, then tossed him over the crevasse where he smashed into an ice shelf just above Palatus. It rumbled; the entire shelf broke free and crumbled down all around Palatus and Estomago. Palatus stood unflinching, staring coldly at Guster as chunks of ice plummeted down around him.

"Everywhere you go, you will remember what it is you 'ave tasted!" said Palatus as a huge pillar of ice toppled over, cutting him and the other two Gastronimatii from view.

"Mom!" cried Zeke. Guster scooped her up from the snow and cradled her limp body in his lap. Zeke slapped her gently on the cheek. She was breathing, but there was no response. Her body was there, but she was in a sleep so deep, her mind was far away. "Mom! Mom!" Zeke slapped her again. She lay still.

Torbjorn dropped to his knees on the mound of ice and began to dig. "Brother!" he cried. "Can you hear me?" The sound of Storfjell's voice was barely audible through the ice.

"Oh ya! Mine brother!" said Storfjell as his face appeared under the snow. "Did you vanquish the foes?"

"Ya! But there is loss," Torbjorn said, a frown coming to his face "The Mom-Maiden — she has fallen," he said, looking to Mom as he dug more furiously.

Guster held his hands to her face, trying to warm her cheeks. This was worse than when Dad fell asleep after eating a big Thanksgiving dinner. What had he done? Pangs of guilt stabbed at him. He had gotten Mom into this.

"Come, we haven't much time," said Torbjorn as Storfjell climbed out of the ice, his lips blue and shaking. "We must get you back upon your silver bird so you can find help for her before the Wicked Ones return."

Guster couldn't lift her, so he took Henry Junior from Mom's back and strapped him to his own. He was heavy, even for a little guy, and he squirmed and pounded on Guster's neck. It was a small price to pay — one that in no way could make up for his crime.

Torbjorn gingerly plucked Mom's sleeping body out of the snow. They raced back down the hill toward the longhouse, the burden Mom had always carried now weighing heavily on Guster's back, because she could no longer carry it herself.

Chapter 13 — The Castaways

They made their way quickly down the glacier to the longhouse, where they mounted the sleds. Torbjorn placed Mom down carefully on a blanket in the middle, then fetched a barrel of butter.

"Feed her some of the butter-gold. It can cure wounds," he said, putting the barrel in Guster's lap. He and Storfjell kicked off toward the airstrip. The sleds sped along the crusty snowfield toward the mountain, even faster than they had come the first time.

Guster had to try. He popped the lid off the barrel, scooped up a spoonful of butter in a wooden spoon, and held Mom's jaw with his other hand. He forced the butter to the back of her throat until she swallowed.

He counted the seconds, hopeful. There was no reaction to the crisp breeze, no notice of Henry Junior howling in her ear. Mom's eyes were shut fast.

"It didn't work," Guster said, the panic building inside him. He looked to Torbjorn for help.

"Then I do not know what can save her," Torbjorn said.

Ten years. It was a long time. She would sleep through family vacations, the first day of school, even Christmas. He needed her. He had done this to her, and now he had to fix it. "We have to get help," said Guster.

"From who?" asked Mariah .

"I don't know. Maybe a doctor. Maybe someone like the Master Pastry Chef," though he knew Renoir was dead. The thought popped into his mind: *maybe Archedentus*, but he knew that was impossible too.

If not the butter, then maybe another ingredient would help. If they stayed on the trail of the One Recipe, maybe, somewhere along the way, there would be a chef or someone or something that could cure Mom. It was their only option.

"We've got to follow the Gastronimatii," said Guster.

"Are you crazy!" Zeke said. "Mom is practically a zombie and all you can think about is getting your taste buds tingled!"

He couldn't blame Zeke for thinking that. This was his fault and he knew it. He felt sick with himself.

"Guster is right, Zeke," said Mariah. "Going home isn't going to do us any good. It was the Gastronimatii's gravy that did this to Mom and only some food just as rich will be able to undo it. We've got to keep going."

Just then it hit Guster. He'd been so worried about Mom he hadn't realized it until now. *It's gone*, he thought as the sled zipped along the snow. Palatus had gotten what he wanted. "I lost it," he said. "The eggbeater is gone." He started to shake. After all he'd done to hold on to it, it had been wrenched out of his fingers.

Mariah put a hand on his shoulder. "Doesn't matter," said Mariah.

"Of course it matters. Without the One Recipe the trail is cold!" shouted Guster angrily. *Didn't they understand?*

“After all that time you spent studying the symbols, don’t you remember any of them?” she asked.

Guster shook his head, “Vaguely. But there are so many details. And there’s no way I can remember all the measurements and mixing instructions,” he said.

Mariah smiled. “You don’t have to. I wrote it all down,” she said. “There’s a copy on the plane, for safe-keeping.”

So it wasn’t over. His brilliant, brilliant sister had done it again. Guster could have hugged her.

There was still a chance. They would have to race the Gastronimatii every step of the way now, but it wasn’t impossible. Maybe they could save Mom and make up for everything he’d done. They just had to get to the plane.

It came into view as they rounded the mountain. It was good to see its sleek silver lines. It meant comfort — their one constant throughout a journey full of so many surprises.

Torbjorn kicked the sled on furiously. When they reached the gravel, Guster leapt from the sled, and jogged as fast as he could toward the airstrip, his younger brother bouncing on his back.

He hadn’t gone more than a few yards when he saw a faint wisp of smoke rising from the plane into the air. Braxton ran toward them, something under one arm. A moment later, there was an enormous crack. The plane exploded in a gigantic burst of red flames.

“No!” shouted Guster. The rushing wind and the deafening noise hit at the same time. It was searing hot on his cheeks for just a moment, then it was gone.

An orange and black fireball floated skyward from the wreckage in a mushroom cloud; the charred wings of the plane broke loose from its now hollow fuselage. *This can’t be happening*, Guster thought.

He ran in a daze toward the wreckage, ignoring Henry Junior's weight. The rest of the family was right on his heels. Braxton lay on the ground face-down, knocked over by the force of the blast. The old pilot groaned and pushed himself up, his chauffer suit singed.

"Braxton! Are you alright?" shouted Mariah.

He nodded, then slumped back down in the gravel. "I need a rest," he said.

A sick feeling welled up inside Guster's gut. Where was the egg? He scanned the ground until he found it, half-buried in gravel a few feet away from Braxton's outstretched arm.

He rushed to inspect it, wiping away the gravel with his arm. There was no yolk or crack. The shell must've been made of stone, after all it had been through.

Mariah turned Braxton over to check for wounds. He groaned. "I'm fine little lady. Nothin' I haven't been through before."

"Did you get my notes?" asked Mariah.

The old man's smile faded. "Sorry darlin'. Didn't know you had any. I smelled smoke and only had the sense to grab the egg from the fridge on the way out. Somebody must've sabotaged the fuel tank."

Guster smelled a faint hint of caramel mingled with the burning aircraft fuel. The Gastronimatii must have stuck it to the fuel tank sometime before they found Guster on the glacier. Just like a plastic explosive. "Palatus!" he cried. He hated that man.

"Boom boom?" asked Henry Junior, apparently unaware just how bad things had gotten.

"Sadly, yes," said Mariah, smoothing his hair.

A whirring noise from the mountain caught Guster's attention. A blood-red zeppelin rose from behind the peak and set coarse straight out to sea. The Gastronimatii were headed back to the mainland with the eggbeater.

Hope drained out of Guster's toes. Mariah's copy of the recipe was the only chance they had. Without a plane, their only means of escape was gone.

"We're stranded," said Mariah as she watched the zeppelin make its way toward the mainland.

Guster stared at his hands. If only he hadn't been so greedy, he never would have been caught by Palatus. It was his fault they lost the eggbeater. It was his fault Mom had fallen asleep for good.

"Stranded?" cried Zeke. He charged toward Guster when Mariah caught him by the shirt. "You fancy-mouth! If you didn't always have to eat so-and-so and such-and-such, none of this would have happened!" he yelled. "Every one of us is here because of you!"

Guster felt hot embarrassment rise in the back of his neck. Zeke was right. He had been all along. The days of frustration and years of guilt finally boiled over.

"You — ," Zeke started again.

"I'm sorry!" Guster cried, cutting Zeke off. "I'm sorry for almost getting us killed. I'm sorry for doing this to Mom! I'm sorry for being such a… such a…," Guster stuttered. He had to say it before Zeke could, and because he knew it was true, "such a… picky eater!" As soon as he'd said the words, he felt like he'd snapped a net that had been tying him down.

"Like I said," said Zeke, but he wasn't gloating this time.

A picky eater. Guster kicked the dirt. It felt good to kick something. "I didn't mean for all this to happen, Mom," he said, looking into her sleeping face.

Guster could almost imagine the advice she'd give him. This time, he wouldn't mind the lecture. "I don't want to be an Evertaster," Guster said glumly.

If she could hear him, she would have told him to be brave. He wished she was awake to say it. He wished he knew how to do what she asked. "The Gastronimatii have the eggbeater. Mariah's notes are all burned up and we have no airplane. We'll be lucky if we ever see Louisiana again," he said. Even if Mom were awake, there was no way she — or anybody — could fix this one.

Storfjell began pacing back and forth furiously. Torbjorn hung his head. No one said anything for a long while. Would this be there life from now on? No Mom? Joggling bovines on Bear Island? Guster was sure to starve to death if it was. They were stuck, and they knew it.

Finally, the fuming Storfjell stopped in his tracks and beat his chest, his eyes on Guster. "At times, the sun shines even when it is midnight!" he announced. "Come with me. There is hope yet!" He turned and started back toward the longhouse.

What's the use? thought Guster. No matter how big and strong the giant was, he couldn't get them back to the mainland by brute force alone.

Zeke trudged after him. Torbjorn, who looked just as confused as Guster felt, picked up Mom and followed his older brother.

"I say, who exactly are these large fellas?" asked Braxton, picking himself up off the ground.

"Meet the Buttersmiths of Bear Island," said Mariah as she helped Braxton up. He started toward the longhouse. "We'll explain everything on the way."

"Come on Guster," said Mariah. She held out her hand. He couldn't stay here. He couldn't go to the plane. He picked up the egg, cradling it in both arms. There was nothing else to do but follow.

Chapter 14 — The Return of the Sea Dragon

Torbjorn and Storfjell argued the entire way back to the longhouse. They didn't stop when they got there.

"Du verden! Er du helt gal?" exclaimed Torbjorn melodically.

"Nei, men du — !" burst Storfjell back, his words striking a high note.

Guster couldn't tell what they were saying, though it was obvious they were fighting about something by the way they threw up their hands and pounded their fists at each other.

Storfjell turned to Zeke, "You, take those and harness the bovines on their heads," he ordered, pointing to a row of leather straps hanging on hooks. "And you two," he said to Mariah and Guster, "Please be stacking as many muffins and dried fish as you can in those barrels." He clapped Braxton on the shoulder. "You can bring the ropes," he said, and had Braxton coil lengths of thick brown rope and strap them around the cows' mid-sections.

The work didn't bother Guster, since it was a welcome distraction from their predicament. In a matter of hours they had each cow saddled with a load of rope, barrels, and blankets.

"It has been decades! You don't even know if it is still working!" said Torbjorn in English. "And your skills may not be as sharp as you remember!"

Storfjell grunted, "Then we will perish," he said. He opened the longhouse door and led the cargo-laden cows out through the field of clover. Guster followed. He trusted both giants, though it was hard to decide which one to believe — especially without knowing what they were arguing about.

They hiked across rocky beaches that led them around the far side of the island. They came to a sheer cliff that plunged straight into the ocean, blocking their path. Storfjell turned toward the island interior and led the herd up a faint trail of winding switchbacks. It was hard going for Guster, especially with Henry Junior in the backpack on his back — how had Mom carried him all this time? — and the egg in his arms. Eventually, they made it to the top of the cliff. From there Guster could see the sea fade off into the distant horizon. They were so very, very far from anywhere.

They carefully picked their way down a steep face on the other side of the cliff to a narrow beach tucked between sheer rock walls. It took hours, until finally the entire herd of cows, Mariah, Zeke and Braxton all stood on a small sandy beach surrounded by cliffs with nowhere to go. It was a dead end.

"Wait here," said Storfjell. He led the herd into the mouth of a wide cave and disappeared into the darkness. Torbjorn set Mom down carefully on the beach and followed him inside. Guster sat next to her.

"Mom sleep?" asked Henry Junior, tugging on Mom's baby blue apron. She let a tiny snore flutter from her lips.

"That's right," said Guster sadly. "But we'll get her back," he said. That's what Mom would want him to say.

Zeke skipped rocks from the banked beach into the waves. After almost an hour, he stopped. “This is boring. I’m going to see what they’re up to,” he said. He wandered up toward the mouth of the cavern.

Suddenly, the sound of groaning wood echoed out from the cave. Torbjorn came running from the mouth, the entire herd behind him, each cow pulling at a rope that led back into the darkness.

The cows were halfway to the water when the ropes went taut. They heaved against them, mooing in unison, straining at some unseen object inside the hole. “Hi-ya!” cried Torbjorn, and together they gave one more great tug.

A bow of a ship shaped like a dragon’s head emerged from the darkness with Storfjell standing proudly and magnificently on the deck beside it.

Torbjorn cried “Hi-ya!” again. The herd pulled, and an entire wooden vessel spilled out of the cave on a bed of rolling logs. It tumbled down the slope and splashed into the sea.

Storfjell hoisted a thick wooden mast straight up into the air and drove it down into the deck, then unfurled a billowing red and white sail. “Behold, the *Sea Dragon*!” he cried.

“You have a ship!” cried Mariah.

“Ya,” nodded Torbjorn. “It’s been so long since our last visit to the cave. I was not believing that it might work, but my brother is right: the vessel is seaworthy.”

Zeke pounded on the side of the ship. “Dude, this thing is solid. Are we taking a trip around the island?” he asked.

Storfjell laughed. “Nay! We are taking you back to the Warmlands, of course.”

“Sweetness!” said Zeke.

Storfjell threw a gangplank from the dry shore to the side of the boat and led the entire herd onto the deck. Torbjorn carried Mom aboard, then Zeke, Braxton, Mariah and Guster boarded the ship. Henry Junior made a low mooing noise in Guster's ear.

Storfjell and Torbjorn fixed a dozen oars on each side to the gunwales, while Braxton watched the whole process in disbelief. "Who's going to do the paddling?" he asked. He hadn't been able to stop gawking at the two Buttersmiths and their strange appearance since he'd met them.

Storfjell smiled. He barked a command in his melodic language and the herd lined up in two rows, one on each side of the ship. "The bovines, of course," he said, and one by one, fastened each oar to a harness on the back of a cow.

"Well I never seen the likes of that," said Braxton as Storfjell pulled up the ramp. Torbjorn began to beat a big skin drum next to the mast and the cows began to move, leaning forward, then back in time with the beats, dipping the oars in the water as they did so. The ship pushed slowly against the waves, then gathered speed, rocking up and down as it sailed toward the open ocean.

Chapter 15 — The Sky Demons

Two nights later Guster sat next to Mom, staring out to sea. She showed no signs of stirring. Her face seemed blank–like she'd forgotten how to dream.

They were much further south now, so the sun dropped closer toward the horizon than before. For as far as Guster could see, there was nothing but open water.

Torbjorn leaned on the ship railing next to him. "You will find a way to cure your mother," he said.

"I will," said Guster. He wouldn't rest until he had.

"I think that the Master Mead Maker would be proud for you to finish his quest," said Torbjorn.

Guster hoped so. It was funny, but he realized right then that he actually cared what Archedentus would think, even though the chef had lived so long ago. It was as if Archedentus were watching over his shoulder, waiting for him to make the right moves.

"I also am sure that he would want you to have our creamy gold," said Torbjorn, nodding toward the stacks of butter barrels scattered across the deck. "When we get to the Warmlands, you may take as much as you like, of course."

"Thank you," said Guster. The two Buttersmiths had been so kind to him, even after all the danger Guster had put them in.

"Also, there is another thing," said Torbjorn. He took the glass vial of dark liquid from around his neck. Guster had almost forgotten about it. The sight of it renewed his curiosity.

"Some drops of these we like to use in our muffins — but only on special occasions. When the Master Mead-Maker came to us long ago he gave them to our people and said that someday, like the butter, they would be needed. So my fathers handed them down to their sons, and they gave them to their sons, until my father gave them to me. Storfjell and I are the last ones left. We have no brides, and so have no sons." Torbjorn dangled the vial in front of Guster. "Will you take them, Guster Johnsonville?"

Guster closed his hand around the bottle. It was smooth to his touch. If Torbjorn's ancestors had gotten it from Archedentus, it had to be one of the ingredients. Guster uncorked the bottle and smelled it. It was spicy and sweet, with flavors so deep and complex, it would take blissful hours to absorb them all. *Seven drops of Sweet, Black Tears*, thought Guster.

"Yes, Torbjorn. I will protect them," he said, hanging the bottle around his neck. He would see to it that they found their way into the Gastronomy of Peace, no matter where that would take him.

"Now let us rest," said Torbjorn. Guster nodded. They took Mom and made their way past the lines of cows to the low roof where the rest of the family slept.

Guster made himself comfortable, and after much worrying, finally fell into a light sleep.

He woke a few hours later to the sound of helicopter blades beating the air. He turned over, got up and staggered onto the deck. The wind beat down on him and salt water sprayed his face in sheets, jolting him to consciousness. Two large, armored green helicopters hovered over the ship in the grayish night. The cows strained against their harnesses.

Storfjell stood at the back of the ship with his battle-axe raised, yelling something to Braxton over the deafening clamor.

Torbjorn circled the mast and grabbed Guster by the shoulders. "There is no telling what these sky demons are," he said, opening a hatch in the deck. "Your mother is below; you must go there until we are sure of your safety," he said. Before Guster could explain what a helicopter was, there was a hissing noise and Torbjorn winced. A small, metal dart stuck out from the back of his neck. He grunted, then turned and looked upward.

A man in dark military fatigues with a long sniper rifle leaned out of the closest chopper and took aim. Panic caught hold of Guster. Someone was shooting at them!

"Watch out!" he cried.

Torbjorn raised his shield. Guster ducked behind the mast. Two darts zipped past Guster's ear, hitting Torbjorn in the thigh. He winced in pain. "Go!" he cried.

Henry Junior was safe down below; Guster had to make sure Zeke and Mariah were too. Frantic, he scanned the ship. He spotted them crouched beneath a pair of cows on the far side of the deck. He had to get them below.

"Zeke!" shouted Guster. He didn't respond. The helicopters were too loud.

If he stayed low, he might be able to make it to them; he was a smaller target than Torbjorn. He darted to the nearest cow, when a rope dropped onto the deck. A mercenary in dark fatigues zipped down the line toward him. Guster put on the brakes. Two more ropes hit the deck — one behind and the other to his right – cutting off his route to Zeke. The first mercenary hit the wood in front of Guster and grabbed for his jacket. Guster dodged, then a strong hand clamped onto his arm from behind.

Torbjorn smashed into that mercenary with his shoulder and sent him flying. Freed, Guster dove under the nearest cow's belly. *No one is a match for our giant*, he thought.

Another rifle cracked twice. Two more darts lodged in Torbjorn's shoulder. Guster rolled under a second cow. Tranquilizers. They were trying to take down Torbjorn. When he looked up, Mariah and Zeke were gone. *Where are they?* he thought, as two more mercenaries landed hard on the deck. Torbjorn was surrounded.

More rifle cracks. There were so many of them. He had to think of something fast.

Then, a half-dozen cows charged from the front of the ship toward the four mercenaries. The stampede plowed into the mercenaries, knocking all but one of them to the ground.

The last mercenary jumped nimbly up on the mast and out of the way. Torbjorn was riddled with darts. He staggered, then fell forward like an overturned refrigerator, unconscious.

Guster screamed. His faithful protector had fallen. There was nothing he could do. *Where was Storfjell?* An arm caught Guster by the middle and strapped a harness around his chest. He struggled to break free, but the mercenary was too strong. With a clip and a whir, he was hoisted into the air like a marionette, his feet kicking desperately, the rope reeling him upward fast.

The ship below him was in chaos. Another half-dozen mercenaries were closing in on Storfjell. There were a few – no doubt bludgeoned by his shield – lying unconscious on the deck.

Storfjell was fighting valiantly, but slowing down with each rifle crack.

A second group of mercenaries broke into the hatch and swarmed below.

Out of the corner of his eye Guster saw Zeke reeling up to the chopper, just below him. A pair of hands grabbed Guster from above and yanked him onto a warm, humming metal floor. He landed face-down in front of a pair of boots. A second later, Zeke landed with a thump right beside him. Two hands shoved Guster to the back of the helicopter, took off the harness, and strapped him to a seat. He struggled against the restraints, trying to unbuckle himself, but it was no use. He was locked into place.

The mercenary who pushed him into the seat strapped Zeke down, while another tended the ropes. Their helmets, goggles, and vests did not look like the uniforms of the Gastronimatii. So who were they?

"Are you okay, Capital P?" whispered Zeke. He looked scared.

"I think so," said Guster. There was still a chance Mariah had escaped. And where was Braxton? No matter how wily the old pilot was, he was no match for armed men who had felled two giants.

Two more mercenaries climbed into the helicopter. A moment later, they pulled Mom's limp body up after them. A third mercenary forced Mom into a seat and buckled her down, while a fourth hoisted Henry Junior up in a net. "Gusser!" he cried, reaching out to Guster as the men pulled a sobbing Mariah, a barrel of butter, and the giant egg onto the helicopter deck.

The last mercenary spoke into a headset attached to his helmet. "Targets acquired. Chopper two has the rest of the team," he said. "We're clear to exit." The chopper surged forward.

Guster noticed a patch stitched to the mercenary's left arm. It was the letters 'FC' shaped like a house with a white picket fence in front of it. *Who are these people?* If they were after ingredients that was one thing, but to kidnap the entire family? It didn't make sense.

"Ten-hut!" shouted a polished voice from the cockpit. The mercenaries snapped to attention on either side of the helicopter deck. A middle-aged woman with blond hair that framed her face like a masterpiece painting, teeth that shined like porcelain toilet bowls, and tiny grenade earrings that dangled from each ear turned to face them.

"I hardly expected to find you way out here," said Felicity Casa.

Chapter 16 — The Harbinger of Peace

This didn't make sense. Felicity Casa was supposed to be in prison. He'd seen her there. Capturing a bunch of kids and their sleeping Mom in the middle of the arctic sea was hardly something a celebrity-homemaker-prisoner ought to do.

"We've been kidnapped by a TV star!" cried Zeke.

"She's not a star anymore!" Mariah shouted. "She's supposed to be behind bars!"

Felicity smiled smugly. "I respectfully disagree."

"Then why are you here?" shouted Guster. "We don't have the eggbeater! The Cult of Gastronimatii stole it!" He was boiling mad at her; Felicity had tranquilized Torbjorn and Storfjell and left them and Braxton to drift in the middle of the ocean!

Felicity's perfectly aged face darkened, but only for a moment. "There is more than a list of ingredients at stake here," she said, removing one of her grenade-shaped earrings and sticking Mom in the neck with the sharp end. Mom flinched, then kept right on snoozing.

"Hey!" cried Guster. Mom couldn't defend herself; Felicity was taking advantage of that. He tried to break free from his harness. It was no use.

"I see the Cult has left its calling card," Felicity said, lifting one of Mom's closed lids, "I recognize their work."

"If you don't care about the eggbeater, then what do you want with us?" said Guster.

"Don't assume you know what I care about," said Felicity, "but since you asked, I've come to ask your opinion." She turned to a small cabinet and pulled out a jar of wriggling, slimy worms. Guster shivered at the sight of them. She unscrewed the lid and dumped the entire contents into a blender bolted onto the helicopter wall, then pressed a button. The blades whirred, chopping the stringy worms into a thick paste that looked like mashed up spaghetti soaked in stale rainwater. She poured the mixture into a glass and pushed it at Guster's face. "Have a taste," she said.

Guster threw up a little in his mouth.

"You ought to be a more gracious guest. This is a delicacy in some countries," said Felicity. "And if you can tell me what these worms were fed before I prepared them, I'll wake your mom up for you."

Mariah looked pleadingly at Guster. He'd already decided he would do anything for Mom. Did it have to be that? He wasn't sure he could. "Give me the drink," he whispered. Hot sweat dripped down his neck.

She put the glass to his mouth. Guster smushed the worm-slime to his teeth with his lips. It was warm and salty, like squishy raw beef seasoned in dirt. He spat. His stomach turned dry.

"Wilted spinach," he said, trying to breathe. "Probably grown somewhere dry," He felt like he was going to pass out.

Felicity clapped her hands slowly, "Arizona to be exact." She allowed herself a triumphant grin. "Renoir was right. You are an Evertaster."

"What about my mom?" Guster demanded.

"All in due time."

"Let us go!" yelled Zeke, his face flushing pink as his pimples.

Felicity shook her head. "And let you miss out on all this?" She asked, glancing around the helicopter. "Guster, isn't it?" she said to Guster, extending a manicured hand. He did not respond.

She dropped her hand. "My men had been keeping a close watch on New Orleans. Apparently, one of them followed you all the way to Key West."

The chopper pilot turned and waved. He had a thick neck and wore aviator sunglasses. "The man in the cream Cadillac!" said Zeke.

"After you came to the prison, I made arrangements for my escape. I can read French, naturally, so I made sure to memorize as much of the handle as possible. We were on our way to Bear Island when we detected your ship on radar."

"Then you know where the ingredients are. You don't need the eggbeater," Guster said angrily.

Felicity laughed. "If only. It was just a glance, Guster. The One Recipe contains infinite subtleties. One can memorize the location of Bear Island and the symbols, but to make the Gastronomy of Peace without clear mixing instructions — it would be foolish to attempt such a feat."

So she didn't get all of it. She needs the eggbeater back just as much as we do. "You attacked us for nothing?" Guster cried.

She raised a well-plucked eyebrow. "No. You have my ingredients, for one thing," she said, waving her hand at the giant egg and the butter barrel.

"Those ingredients aren't yours to claim!" he shouted. He'd never talked to anyone like that before, least of all a celebrity, but she'd torn them from their friends, made him eat worms, lied about waking up Mom, and now she had nothing to offer. He would have kicked her if he could, but he was strapped too tightly to his seat. He wanted to get her back; he wanted her to pay. "The Gastronimatii might have backtracked and found more ingredients. For all you know, they've already made the One Recipe!" he said.

Felicity's eyes settled on Guster. "No, I am quite certain they have not." She looked him over from head to foot. She'd said it with such conviction, it made Guster uneasy. It meant she knew something. He remembered the vial of Sweet Black Tears around his neck. Instinctively, he reached for it. It was well hidden under his shirt.

"You don't have any idea who you are, do you Mr. Johnsonville?" she asked.

It was a puzzling question. What was she talking about? She'd already told him he was an Evertaster. He folded his arms and glared at her; he had to pretend like he didn't care.

"Not interested?" said Felicity, cocking an eyebrow. "You will be." She was so sure of herself, it was aggravating.

"Long ago, Archedentus left France and set out with conquistadors on an ocean voyage to the New World," Felicity said, "While the Conquistadors sought to plunder the land for its gold, Archedentus sought a treasure of a different sort. The King of France had commanded Archedentus to bring back something new and exotic, something never before tasted in Europe.

"That's when Archedentus discovered the eggs you found in Peru," she nodded to the giant egg cradled by one of her mercenaries.

"When Archedentus found the egg, I think that's when he began to imagine the possibilities; the first inklings of the One Recipe stirred in his mind."

"The Conquistadors set sail back to Europe, but the great chef wasn't done exploring. He jumped ship and — to the fury of the King — didn't return to France for years. The exact details of his journey after that are cloudy; some evidence indicates he made his way to North America with Ponce de León."

"The one who discovered the Fountain of Youth," Mariah whispered to herself. However upset she might have been about their capture, she could not resist stating the facts.

"If you believe in that sort of drivel," said Felicity, smirking. "The next few years Archedentus spent stowing away on ships as the Age of Explorers opened up an uncharted world. Who knows how far his journey took him? Some think he sailed around Africa with Vasco da Gama. Others say he made it as far as the Orient. I think he was gathering ingredients, piecing it all together in his mind, fitting together the parts that could make the whole like only he knew how.

"When he finally returned to France he spent a year in isolation. Archedentus had made so many promises about the recipe, there were many in Paris anticipating its completion.

"That's when he took the understudy. No one knows why, but the apprentice had no training or skill as a cook. Most people criticized Archedentus' choice of apprentice. Some were jealous — they could not understand why Archedentus had rejected the best and brightest chefs of the time in favor of someone so inept. They wanted Archedentus to pass his knowledge on to them."

That made sense to Guster. Perhaps the recipe wouldn't have been lost if Archedentus had given it to a skilled chef. "That was stupid," Guster said.

Felicity crossed her arms. "Maybe. But maybe not," she said. "I think Archedentus found his first Evertaster."

At least an Evertaster would care, thought Guster.

"The strangest part is this: Archedentus passed the One Recipe on to his apprentice, without ever making it even once."

"He couldn't gather all the ingredients in one place," said Mariah.

"Doubtful. A genius like Archedentus would have found a way, even with the limited technology of the age. There must have been another reason he didn't make it."

Guster tried to comprehend what she was saying. The thing they were searching for — and they didn't even know what it was — had never been made. No one had ever tasted it. "Then why didn't he make it?" Guster demanded.

"Ah! Nobody knows! Maybe he didn't want anyone else to have it. In the end, he just wandered away one day, never to be seen again."

Guster felt panic seize hold of him. What she was saying was preposterous. "Then he couldn't know how it would turn out!" he cried. It just didn't make sense, having something at your fingertips, then letting it go. How did they even know it was real?

Felicity shook her head, "I think he *did* know. It's like a composer who composes a symphony on paper, before he ever hears it. He knows how it will sound."

"Like Beethoven," said Mariah under her breath. "He was deaf near the end of his life, and he never heard some of his greatest works." That made a little bit of sense — just the egg, the butter and the Sweet Black Tears together were certain to be delicious indeed. Guster didn't have to taste the combination to know that. Still, it was like hunting for a treasure chest that may or may not be full of real gold.

"And Leonardo da Vinci drew plans for a helicopter hundreds of years before the Wright brothers ever actually made an airplane," said Mariah.

"It was the master blueprint. Archedentus knew it would redefine eating forever," Felicity said.

That made Guster feel a little better, but still — it was all such a gamble!

"Before he left, Archedentus told his apprentice that he would be a guardian and a messenger, and that the apprentice would be the one to bring the Gastronomy of Peace to the world.

"The chefs of Paris were infuriated. They couldn't tolerate some bungling fool holding the most promising recipe of all time. It's only because the apprentice smuggled the chef's diary out of the palace that he was able to keep it for himself.

"Other gourmets around Paris, the ones who trusted Archedentus, began calling the assistant the Harbinger of Peace; they began waiting for him to bring the One Recipe to light."

The Harbinger of Peace, Guster thought. It sounded so royal.

"And they're still waiting," said Mariah.

Felicity nodded. "Before the first Harbinger of Peace died, he secretly passed the diary on to *his* trusted assistant, who in turn passed it on again. About a hundred years ago, one of the Harbingers built the eggbeater and carved the symbols into it as an added measure of security.

"Each Harbinger of Peace has had to take special care to conceal himself and the One Recipe from the Cult of Gastronimatii. It's been an epic game of hide and seek ever since Archedentus disappeared."

“So Renoir was the last Harbinger of Peace,” said Guster.

“Possible,” said Felicity. She fixed a lock of her hair that was already in place, as if deep in thought, then settled her eyes on Guster. “And he would have been, but he passed on the recipe, just as they’ve always done.” Suddenly, everyone, Mariah, Zeke and all the mercenaries were staring at Guster.

“That’s right, Mr. Guster Johnsonville,” said Felicity. “When Renoir gave you the eggbeater, he dubbed you the new Harbinger of Peace.”

***

Harbinger of Peace. What did that even mean? Two seconds ago he was just Guster Johnsonville, and now Felicity Casa, Celebrity Homemaker, all her mercenaries, his brothers and sister were staring at him like he’d just come back from the dead. All his life he’d been a kid. No one had ever given him a briefcase full of cash or the keys to a car. He didn’t even get his own room. And now he was in charge of a recipe that was supposed to bring peace to mankind?

“Renoir believed in you as an Evertaster,” said Felicity. “Which is why I think he gave you the eggbeater.”

“It makes sense that Guster should do it,” said Mariah. “He’s the one who unlocked the carvings in the first place.” Whoever he was, Guster couldn’t get mad about being called ‘Evertaster’ anymore. He knew it was true. Harbinger or not, he’d already decided that he would see this through to the end. He would see that the One Recipe got made. He could not expect anyone else to do that for him now.

"The Harbinger of Peace has managed, for the most part, to keep his identity concealed from the Gastronimatii, but they have always been searching for him, getting closer. They got so close to Renoir, they poisoned him. That is why things are so critical now. They've stolen the eggbeater from you," said Felicity.

A familiar pang of guilt stabbed him. He'd lost the very thing Renoir entrusted to him. No wonder Felicity doubted him. "We have the egg and the butter," he said. He could take some hope in that.

Felicity pressed a button on the wall and a cabinet opened, revealing a rack of spices and bottles of liquid. "Now let's see what we can do about your mother," she said. She opened the lids of a few bottles and mixed and stirred their contents together until a peculiar ammonia smell filled the chopper. She dashed a few more drops into the mixture, until it finally smelled a little like a cough drop, then waved it under Mom's nose.

Mom yawned a yawn the size of a saber tooth tiger, scrunched up her eyes, then opened them. "You!" she cried, looking straight into Felicity's face. She kicked at her shins. Felicity dodged just in time.

"Mom!" cried Guster.

She looked frantically around. "Where am I?" she said.

"On a helicopter, heading toward the mainland," said Guster. Suddenly, she was back in his life. His future with Mom came rushing back to him, and he realized how much he needed that.

"Did they hurt you?" she asked, looking for a way out of her harness as she tried to inspect her children.

Zeke nodded, holding up his arm. "Rope burn," he said. Relief washed across Mom's face.

"I'm sorry about all this," said Guster.

She looked at him kindly. "It wasn't your fault, Guster."

"No Mom, it was. I got us into this," he said. "We're here because of me." He had to tell her. He had to say it out loud.

"We chose to come with you," she said. If she really meant it, if he didn't have to do this all alone — then that made all the difference.

Mom turned to Felicity. "Are we guests, or are we captives?" she asked, fire in her eyes.

Felicity motioned to her mercenaries who unlocked Guster's, Mariah's, Mom's and Zeke's straps. Guster jumped up and stretched his back, finally able to move. Mom rushed to Henry Junior and took him from the mercenary who held him awkwardly. He buried his face in her neck.

"Do you really want to try to make the One Recipe on your own?" Felicity asked.

She was right. They needed her resources. Mom stared back at Felicity, but didn't answer.

"We have something in common, Mrs. Johnsonville. You want the Gastronomy of Peace, and so do I. The difference is that it has been my life's quest to make it. Every homemade birdfeeder, every hand-antiqued flower pot — they were all stepping stones — vehicles to build an empire. Every good thing was intended to lead to something better, and now it's right in front of us — the best thing of all!

"It's the culmination of the Felicity Casa Homemaking Empire. This chopper, these men, the endless informants tapped into every nook and cranny of the gourmet world. They won't allow me to miss a single sentence, not a single word spoken anywhere about the One Recipe.

"I suspected all along that Renoir had the eggbeater in New Orleans, though no one knew for sure. He kept it secret. The

Gastronimatii must have been suspicious though, just like I was. They must have been watching him — waiting for a chance to snatch it away."

Whatever Felicity's motives for finding the Gastronomy of Peace, they needed her to get back to the mainland. They needed her for her knowledge. They needed her to be the one to make it. "If you know so much, then you'll be able to tell us where to find the Mighty Apes' Diamonds," said Guster. He couldn't let on how helpless they were without her.

"I have my theories," said Felicity. "The carvings indicated pyramids. The only place we'll find those is in Egypt."

"But there were also apes, and those live in the jungles of Africa," said Mariah. "The details showed a river that flowed from a lake. I'm willing to bet my Atlas that river is the Nile, and we'll find the diamonds at its source."

Felicity pursed her lips. Guster could tell she wasn't used to being challenged. "Very well. Let the Harbinger decide," she said.

Guster scanned the faces in the chopper. Him? They were going to leave the decision to him? He didn't feel qualified to make that choice. Now that Mom was back, shouldn't she do it? He looked to her for help.

Mom closed her lips tight. Apparently, she wasn't going to tell him what to do.

"The Gastronimatii have a head start. We can't afford to make a mistake," said Felicity.

There was a sudden pressure inside the chopper that felt very real. *The deserts of Egypt or the jungles of Africa? Pyramids or Gorillas?* Guster thought. Both seemed likely, and without the eggbeater, it was impossible to look for more clues in the carving. Felicity was the Celebrity Homemaker. But Mariah was Mariah. He would have to go with his gut. And his gut told him to go after those apes.

"Africa," he finally said. "Find us the source of the Nile."

Chapter 17 — Felicity's Quest

The Johnsonvilles and Felicity's crew landed in Tromso, Norway a few hours later, where they boarded one of Felicity's private cargo planes to Africa.

The flight was comfortable, but all they had were a couple of reheated, Casa Brand instant dinners. Guster was dying. Besides the butter, it had been days since he'd eaten something he could tolerate. If they didn't make the Gastronomy of Peace soon, he didn't know how much longer he could last.

Zeke, on the other hand, didn't seem to notice anything wrong as sauce dripped all over his shirt.

Mom still seemed a little groggy; she grew more alert as the flight took them further south. Guster had never seen her look so rested. Mariah explained in detail everything that had happened since Bear Island. When she got to the part about Renoir dubbing Guster the Harbinger of Peace, Mom smiled. "Then it is up to you now," she said to Guster. That was a lot of pressure. Suddenly, he felt older than Zeke.

"As full of herself as she is," said Mom, looking at Guster thoughtfully, "I could never do the One Recipe justice like Felicity could."

Maybe Mom was right, but something about Felicity's involvement bothered Guster. She seemed irritated by their presence. So why didn't she just take the ingredients and go? She hadn't explained what he was supposed to do as Harbinger of Peace, especially since he'd already lost the eggbeater. Was there something she wasn't telling them? How much could they actually trust her? For now, they would just have to play along.

And then there was Africa. They had no time to spare in the race against the Gastronimatii. Guster had made the decision; he couldn't afford to be wrong.

***

After what seemed like a whole day, Felicity's thick-necked, dark-browed Lieutenant with the aviator sunglasses brought the plane to a landing on the runway at the Kilimanjaro Airport in the middle of Africa. Guster was the first to climb down the huge ramp that came out of the tail and into the sweltering heat. He had watched plenty of nature shows about Africa with Zeke, and now they were actually there — the home of hippos, crocodiles and lions.

A crowd had gathered on the other side of the chain link fence outside the airport to watch the landing. An African man in a pair of green rain pants and a dirty pink T-shirt ran up to Guster. "Can I interest you in some authentic African jewelry?" he said, shouting every third syllable. He held up a board with dozens of carved wooden necklaces and bracelets hanging from pegs.

Guster shook his head. "We'd like to do some sightseeing," he said.

"Excellent choice! This country is beautiful! My name is Riziki and I want to welcome you here! Would you like a safari? Or to climb the mountain?"

"We'd like to see gorillas," he said.

"Oh," said Riziki. He hesitated, "And you came here for this, of all places?"

"Yes. We would like to see the ones on the shores of Lake Victoria, please," said Guster.

"Lake Victoria?" Riziki asked. He looked confused for a minute, as if considering. Then he smiled. "Oh yes! I can show you the most wonderful gorillas there — and it will be for a very good price! How many of you will be coming?"

Mom, the rest of the kids, and several armed mercenaries marched out of the plane. "All of us," Mom said.

Felicity was right behind them. "Lieutenant, bring the jeeps," she called back into the cargo bay of the plane. She'd changed her earrings to a pair of miniature elephant tusks, and wore a bandoleer strapped across her slender hips.

A moment later, the Lieutenant drove the first jeep down the ramp and onto the runway. Three more followed.

"Guster, you'll ride with me," said Felicity.

"With my permission of course," said Mom curtly.

Felicity gave her a look. "It's okay Mom," said Guster. Ever since Felicity's helicopter had picked them up, he'd been turning the list of ingredients over and over in his head. He'd been too preoccupied with other clues to remember where he had heard the name Arrivederci before. The man with the pencil-thin tie on the newscast about Felicity's arrest was the connection. That meant the Dark Milk Bricks from Arrivederci's Bean could only be one thing, and he was going to call Felicity out on it.

"Go ahead then, honey," Mom said. Maybe his role as Harbinger meant something to Mom. She'd already left the decision between Egypt and Africa up to him, and now she was letting him out of her sight, just because he asked. It was like his opinions were worth something — like they mattered. He climbed into the back seat of the jeep right behind the thick-necked Lieutenant.

"What about him?" asked the Lieutenant pointing to Riziki.

"Guster wants him along, so bring him," said Felicity.

Riziki loaded his peg board of jewelry into the back of the jeep then hopped in. "Thank you so much, madam. I promise you, you will not be disappointed!" he said. "I can guarantee you the best in touring services, without any of the funny business that comes with other guides. For you, I will give a very good price!"

Mom and the rest of the kids got in the other three jeeps and the entire convoy rolled across the runway, through a gate, and out onto a street.

The Lieutenant sped up, and soon they were zipping along, the wind whistling in Guster's ears. The road leading away from the airport was long and straight, cutting right through a wide plain covered in short, brown grass. Tall, skinny Tanzanians with extra-long earlobes walked along the side of the road. Some of them wore bright red or blue blankets over their shoulders and sandals made from old rubber tires. Bicyclists pedaled alongside the road, with dozens of large, empty yellow water jugs strapped to their bike frames so awkwardly, it looked like they'd fall over at any moment. Guster wondered how often people from America visited there, if ever.

"We must travel all day to get to the shore of Lake Victoria," said Riziki. "It is many, many miles in the west."

"Lieutenant, follow this man's instructions," said Felicity. "When we get near the lake, we'll camp for the night. In the morning, he'll show us how to find the gorillas."

"Roger, Ms. Casa," said the Lieutenant.

Guster let them ride in silence for a minute before he took the chance. "You know what the Dark Milk Bricks from Arrivederci's Bean are, don't you?" he said.

Felicity turned in her seat, anger in her eyes. "All too well," she said. He thought that might strike a chord. He never guessed it would be that bad.

"Why do you think I was in prison?" she asked clutching the seat. That confirmed it: she'd been arrested for stealing the famous Arrivederci Chocolate — Dark Milk Bricks that came from Arrivederci's cocoa bean.

"Why'd you do it?" he asked.

"Would you believe me if I told you I was innocent?"

Guster paused. He didn't know what he could believe anymore.

"That's what I thought," said Felicity settling into her seat again. "Luckily, there are members of the Casa Homemaking Empire who I can still count on to get me out of any scrape," she smiled over at the Lieutenant.

"Always, ma'am," he said, his face still pointed straight ahead, his jaw square. He allowed himself a grin. "There's nothing like fast-acting bread dough rising, prison walls crumbling, and the sound of heavy shrapnel exploding as you airlift an innocent prisoner out of Maximum Security Prison under heavy gunfire… Not that I would know anything about that, though," he said.

So that's how she'd escaped. She had baked her way out.

"What's so special about the Arrivederci's chocolate?" Guster asked. He had to know every detail.

"They've been making it for centuries," said Felicity. "The Arrivederci's are the greatest chocolate makers in the world."

So that was it. The chocolate was so old, Archedentus could've known about it back in his time. What was even more important — and this was the good part — if chocolate was one of the ingredients, the Gastronomy of Peace was likely to be a dessert. Now *that* was good news. Guster watched a lone tree in the middle of the dusty plain pass by. He wondered just how much Felicity knew.

Felicity turned in her seat to face Guster again. "I hope you are sufficiently afraid, Guster Johnsonville," she said seriously.

"Of Palatus?" he asked. He did not want to admit that to himself.

"You have good reason to fear him," Felicity said. Her voice went dark. "The Arch-Gourmand of the Sect of the Savorous Society has been searching for the Gastronomy of Peace his entire life, as his predecessors did. Many good chefs have fallen by his hand — perhaps many more will before he has achieved his end."

The way she said it — it was almost like Felicity was jealous of the Gastronimatii's power. "But there are worse things to fear," she said.

"Like?" said Guster.

"Tasting the One Recipe."

Guster shrugged. Tasting the One Recipe was the thing he wanted most in the world. What was there to be scared of? "Can't wait to try," he said. He wasn't going to let her bully him.

Felicity locked her eyes on him for a moment in an icy stare. "Good," she said, then turned back around in her seat.

Guster shivered despite the heat. What wasn't she telling him?

They drove for hours, passing small villages and long stretches of green jungle as they went. The Lieutenant stopped the car in a tiny village where they used the bathroom and bought supplies and gas.

The Lieutenant bought a bunch of bananas and gave one to Guster. It was no larger than his hand. He nibbled on the end and found it particularly sweet — almost like a little white candy bar wrapped in a peel. It felt good to put something in his tiny stomach.

"You like our bananas?" said Riziki. Guster nodded since his mouth was full. "We have forty-six varieties in this country, but you will find that there are none so sugary as the ones that come from the shores of the lake itself!" Guster decided to keep an eye out for more.

When they came to the open plains again, there were zebra galloping along in the distance, their fat bottoms bouncing up and down as they ran.

Riziki tapped Guster on the shoulder as they passed a herd of gazelle, "I do not know about all the crazy things you tourists say, but you see those little brown creatures?" he asked. Guster nodded. They were like miniature deer, no larger than big dogs, but much, much skinnier. "When the lion or the cheetah is hungry, the gazelle is easy to catch, so they make a tasty treat. Snatch!" Riziki trapped his fist in his hand. "We call them the lunchbox of the Serengeti!" he laughed.

Guster didn't quite understand. "They are tasty," Riziki said shrugging his shoulders. Guster doubted it was true.

As the sun set, they turned off the main highway onto a dirt road that wound through the jungle. When they came to a clearing in the trees, Felicity told the Lieutenant to stop for the night. "We'll make camp, then start again at first light tomorrow," she said.

The Lieutenant parked on a flat spot as he spoke into the microphone in his helmet. "Set up a perimeter," he ordered. The other jeeps followed the Lieutenant off the road and parked, each one forming one side of a square on the edge of the trees.

Guster caught a glimpse of himself in the rearview mirror as he climbed out of the jeep. His face was covered in dirt from the long, dusty journey, except for a mask of white around his eyes.

"Did you see that hyena, Guster?" exclaimed Zeke, trotting up to him. "It was so ferocious, it bit this guy's motorcycle in two!"

Mariah rolled her eyes behind him. "It wasn't a hyena, Zeke. It was some stray dog. Hyenas are much bigger and they hunt in packs. Besides, it was only barking at the guy's heels. It didn't even get close to the motorcycle's tailpipe," she said.

Guster could tell that Zeke was starting to feel comfortable in Africa, since he was exaggerating again. Now that he had the chance, he told Mariah, Zeke and Mom what he'd found out about the Arrivederci Chocolate, as well as his guess that the Gastronomy of Peace was something sweet. Even Zeke started to get excited at the mention of dessert. Mom pinched her chin and stared off into space, like she was trying to add up numbers in her head.

Felicity's men started to set up a camp. They worked like clockwork, pounding in stakes, lighting a fire, pitching tents, unfolding a table, and hanging lanterns and mosquito netting.

Felicity took a machete from the jeep and disappeared into the thick tangle of trees.

Odd, thought Guster. Just then, the Lieutenant dumped a rolled up tent into his arms. "This is for your family," he said.

Guster and Zeke spent the next half hour setting up the tent. Felicity returned a short while later with a snake the size of an elephant's trunk slung over her shoulder. It was dead.

"Eeee!" Mariah screamed. Mom pulled her into a hug.

"That's slimy-slitherin' sicko," said Zeke. Felicity paid them no heed. She flopped the tube onto the table and slit it up the center with a chef's knife. She yanked out the intestines and threw them over her shoulder into the jungle, then started to peel back its skin. The Lieutenant opened up a wooden box full of plates, cookware and spices and placed it on the table for her. Felicity's hands worked so fast they blurred, first filleting the snake and then spicing the meat. In a minute, it was frying in a pan over the fire.

Guster almost heaved at the sight of it. "You can't expect anyone to eat that!" said Zeke.

"No one is forcing you but the sauce," said Felicity. She flipped the snake fillets deftly, then removed them from the pan. In another minute she had a brownish sauce simmering in the leftover juices.

Zeke wandered toward the fire. His face seemed to lighten as the smoke touched his nose. "Never seen anyone do that…before," he said, his bottom lip quavering. Felicity poured the sauce onto individual plates next to the filets. The mercenaries rushed to attention on either side of the table. "I don't suppose they can eat all of it —" said Zeke and joined them.

Mom and Mariah stood at the table too. Guster never would have believed it if his own nose hadn't told him, but it smelled delicious. "Hmph," muttered Mom, shaking her head. "Using strong sauce to cover up bad meat."

"One more thing," said Felicity. She lopped off a few branches of what looked like palm leaves with the machete. In a flash, she wove the individual leaves together until they were a slender, canoe shaped basket. The Lieutenant placed a bunch of bananas he had just chopped off a nearby tree into her centerpiece.

"There. You have to make a house a home," Felicity said. "Dinner is served."

The mercenaries and Zeke dug into their food without hesitation. Riziki gobbled it down like a lion. Even Mom gave in and ate some. Guster tested it with the edge of his tongue. It was actually quite good. He ate three mouthfuls.

"Tomorrow we break camp at dawn. I want us to find those gorillas before midday is through," Felicity said. She turned to Riziki. "Is that going to be a problem, tour guide?"

He looked up from his food, his lips smeared with stew, a surprised expression on his face. "Most certainly. I mean, most certainly not. I mean… of course. You will be very happy with your visit, I assure you," said Riziki with a forced grin. He looked nervous. Guster sniffed the air. Riziki did not smell of spices. As eccentric as he was, he was certainly no Gastronimatii.

"Good," said Felicity.

"If it's that easy," Mom replied.

Felicity cocked her head sideways in surprise. "What do you mean?" she asked. "There is no way the Gastronimatii followed us here. We're hundreds of miles from civilization."

Mom laughed. "The Gastronimatii are only half the danger," she said. "Do you have any idea what horrors were guarding the first ingredient?"

Felicity looked like she didn't know what to say. "No, Mrs. Johnsonville, I suppose I do not."

"Let's just say we should keep your mercenaries close," said Mom.

Felicity's eyes narrowed, and the two women locked gazes.

"While we're on the subject of undiscovered secrets —" said Felicity. She pulled a small pad of paper and a pen from the

Lieutenant's front shirt pocket. She scrawled something on it, then slid it across the table to Guster. "It's a line from Archedentus' original diary, commonly recited by those who were in his inner circle." Guster read it:

That with a single taste,
The strong and mighty shall cease,
To lay their waste,
Consumed by the Gastronomy of Peace.

It was a cryptic poem. Who were the strong and mighty? How could a dessert consume anyone? If that's what it could do, was he sure he wanted it? It was supposed to make whoever ate it feel peaceful, not destroy them. "Quite a recipe, then," said Guster, trying to hide his anxiety.

"Perhaps Archedentus never made the One Recipe because he was afraid it would kill him," Felicity said gravely.

"How could dessert kill anybody?" mumbled Zeke with his mouth full. He'd loaded his plate with a second mountain of snake meat.

"Gluttony comes to mind," she said in Zeke's direction.

"Like it's so good, Guster couldn't stop eating it, and his stomach would blow up and squirt out everywhere like you'd stomped on a sausage?"

Felicity did not answer. She merely cleared her plate.

Guster shivered. Whatever appeal the snake meat had was lost. Why did Felicity want the Gastronomy of Peace? She did not seem like the kind of person who cared about peace.

Riziki began to laugh uncontrollably. "You tourists! You tell such strange stories! I don't know what kind of animal this

'Gastromatter' is, but if it is your liking we can avoid it altogether. We give good service here. That is why it is customary in my country to receive payment at the earliest moment possible," he said, holding out his hand.

Felicity continued to clear the plates. "We'll pay you when we see the gorillas," she said.

Riziki shook his head. "Oh I am very sorry to say then that I will not be going a step further until payment is received and the transaction is complete," he said, emphasizing the last word.

Felicity stood up, her face motionless. "Very well." She snapped her fingers, and the Lieutenant handed her a wad of bills. "Here's twenty-five percent of your payment, in US dollars," she said, tossing the wad of bills on the table. "You get the other seventy-five percent when we reach the gorillas."

Guster had never seen so much money in one place. Riziki snatched it up and counted it eagerly. He slid a bill out of the stack and held it up so he could examine it. "This one is ten years old," he said, shaking his head and clicking his tongue disapprovingly.

"I can take it back," said Felicity holding out her hand.

Riziki clutched the wad of cash close. "No, this is fine, thank you," he said. He forced a smile.

"Dessert," said the Lieutenant. He took candy bars from his backpack and handed one to everyone sitting at the table. Guster sniffed his, but it smelled too waxy, so he gave it to Zeke who stuffed it in his pocket.

He snatched one of the bananas from the basket centerpiece. They tasted even sweeter than the ones back in the village, so he wolfed it down. The snake meat had turned on him and now it felt like it was crawling around in his stomach. He was hungry, and he didn't know how much longer he could survive on bananas alone.

How many more days before he starved to death? He really, really hoped the Gastronomy of Peace could cure him — if they could find it at all.

The mercenaries cleared the rest of the plates, then Guster, Zeke, Mariah, Mom and Henry Junior — who had mushed banana all over his face — bedded down in one of the tents on the far side of the clearing. Guster squished toward the center of the tent to keep away from the outside where there might be bugs or snakes. Mom switched off a lantern that hung from the tent's roof. "Good night, my dear children," she said.

"Good night," said Guster.

"Wait till Betsy hears about this," said Zeke.

"Yeah. Thanks for the best vacation ever Mom," said Mariah.

"You are welcome," chuckled Mom nervously.

Guster thought it was funny that Mariah and Zeke would say such things, considering that they might not make it back to tell Betsy about their vacation at all.

Grunts and growls followed by the occasional roar came from the jungle on the other side of the tent.

It was quiet for a long time when Zeke turned to Guster and whispered, "Capital P, let's make a promise that if a hyena attacks one of us, the other one will jump in and help fight it off."

"What are you scared for? You're the one who totally KO'ed those giant chickens. Hyenas don't even have razor-sharp beaks," Guster whispered back. Guster thought about how brave Zeke had been when he'd saved him. It got quiet.

"Zeke?" Guster said.

"Yeah?"

"I promise," said Guster. He fell asleep, his dreams filled with the sounds of the jungle.

***

Hunger pangs woke Guster a few hours later. He stared at the ceiling of the tent, trying to fight it. It was getting worse.

He threw off his sleeping bag, quietly unzipped the tent door, and went outside. He half expected some hyena or rhinoceros to come charging out of the tangled wall of thick, black trees. The leaves and branches rustled and scraped together, though there was no wind. There was no telling what was in there.

He crossed the camp toward the table where the mercenaries had stored the food. He might even have some more of the sauce — without the meat of course. He especially wanted more bananas.

He crawled underneath the table where he'd seen the Lieutenant store the leftover rations in a metal cabinet. He felt in the dark for the latch, opened the door and began rummaging around inside. His hand passed over some plastic pouches and a few candy bars before he finally found a small package of mints.

"You told me that it was a rescue, not a kidnapping!" said a voice from the other side of the clearing. Guster froze. It was the Lieutenant. He and Felicity were facing the other way, staring off into the darkness.

"We adapted to the situation," said Felicity.

"The way they tell it, they were on that ship by choice," he said.

"Maybe. But if that boy really is the Harbinger of Peace, we need him more than he knows. He is responsible for a lot more than guarding the eggbeater. He, as the chosen Evertaster, will have to confirm the dish's validity once it is made. He will be the first person in the history of the world to taste the Gastronomy of Peace."

"Isn't that what he wants?" asked the Lieutenant calmly.

"Yes. But the Gastronomy of Peace is still a mystery. No one knows what will happen to the person who eats it."

"I thought you said it was his cure."

"It is, if it doesn't kill him first."

"Then let's take him home! Let's keep him safe!"

Felicity laughed. "He's an Evertaster, Lieutenant. If he's got it as bad as I think he does, he'll either join the Gastronimatii, or starve to death by his thirteenth birthday."

They were quiet.

"You think it will really kill him?" asked the Lieutenant.

"Perhaps," said Felicity. "It's a bitter pill. I just don't know."

The jungle slithered all around them. First Felicity told Guster that the Gastronomy of Peace would cure him. Now she was saying it might kill him in the process. It was all an age-old experiment, and from the sound of it, Guster was the guinea pig.

"What about Mrs. Johnsonville?" asked the Lieutenant.

"She will have to do the thing which I cannot. I only hope she is ready for it."

"Do they know?"

"I don't think so. They never finished translating the recipe."

"You're not going to tell them, are you?"

Felicity shook her head. "I can't take that chance. I can't let them go on their own."

The Lieutenant sighed. "I'm going to protect them," he said.

"I would expect nothing less," she said.

The two of them turned and walked toward their tents, right past the table. Guster lay down on the ground as flat as he could and held his breath. When they were gone, he let out a huge breath.

He didn't understand. Was this recipe his cure or his death sentence? He was going to die if he didn't eat it, but what if he did?

If only they still had the eggbeater, then maybe Mariah could translate the rest and find answers.

He took a pair of bananas, snuck back to the tent and slipped inside. He shoved a few in his mouth, then settled down on his sleeping bag again, but it was no use — after what he'd heard, the best he could do was toss and turn the rest of the night.

Chapter 18 — The Sweetest Way

Guster awoke the next day to the sound of the troops speaking to Felicity. "Gone," said the Lieutenant. "He vanished in the night."

"Lions?" asked Felicity.

"Not likely Ma'am. We traced his tracks. He left on foot."

Felicity pounded her fist into her hand. "I should never have trusted such an eager tour operator," she said.

Guster unzipped the tent and stepped out. The morning was already hot. "Riziki?" he said.

"He tricked us!" said Felicity with a glare. Guster wanted to kick himself. He was the one who'd decided to bring Riziki along. Now what? They were deep in the jungle without a single clue to lead them to the gorillas.

Mom and the rest of the kids emerged from the tent as one of the jeeps zoomed off the dirt path from the north and came to a halt. "Ms. Casa, the settlements are few and far between," said the driver of the jeep. "The villagers report that there are no gorillas in the area. In order to see them, we have to go all the way to Rwanda or Uganda."

"Is that so?" said Felicity. She shot another glance at Guster. No wonder Riziki had been so hesitant back at the airport. He'd known all along he was leading them on a wild goose chase.

Felicity looked Guster squarely in the eye. "You chose this route Guster. The diamonds aren't here."

She turned to the jeep driver who had born the bad news. "Pack up camp, Private. We should have gone to Egypt in the first place," she said. The men started to take down the tents.

Guster couldn't believe this. Just like the camp, his hope of finding the Mighty Apes' Diamonds was being dismantled all around him. One of the diamonds in the carving had been on the shores of the lake. He was sure of that. Felicity couldn't blame Riziki's lies on Guster. He couldn't have known Riziki was a thief. "They're here!" he pleaded. "We just have to look in the right place!"

Felicity ignored him. It wasn't long before the equipment was packed and the clearing was empty. Felicity mounted the jeep and turned to the Lieutenant. "We've got to start over."

"How far back?" the Lieutenant asked.

"Square one. We have to find a new Evertaster to be the Harbinger of Peace."

The mercenaries secured the last of the tents then mounted the jeeps. One of them shook his head at Guster. Guster didn't care what he thought. It wasn't his job to impress Felicity or anyone else.

"You're making a mistake," said Mom to Felicity. "We haven't even seen the lake yet."

"The locals know it's a fruitless search. Why can't you see that?" Felicity said, waving Mom away with her hand. "Start the jeep Lieutenant." The Lieutenant did so, and turned slowly back down the dirt road in the direction of the airport.

Guster felt his temper rising. He had to think. He couldn't let Felicity do this to them — he couldn't let her take control like this.

Mom pulled Guster, Zeke and Mariah close. "Maybe we were wrong about the diamonds being in Africa," she said. "Either way, we can't keep going on foot."

She climbed into the jeep and Zeke and Mariah followed. Guster rooted himself to the spot. He shook his head.

"Guster, there's nothing more we can do right here," Mariah called back to him as their jeep pulled away after Felicity's. "You can't stay here by yourself."

The last jeep in the convoy started its engine and drove after them. Wandering on foot alone in the jungle wasn't going to help, so Guster ran and jumped onto the back bumper before it picked up speed. Mariah wasn't entirely correct. There had to be something more they could do here. He just didn't know exactly what yet.

He climbed into the back seat without even acknowledging the Private or the other mercenaries riding with him. He had to think. Had he really been wrong to come here? His gut told him no, but everyone else was convinced otherwise. Maybe they would have to go to Egypt.

A gloom fell over him as they drove back onto familiar roads. Something about this place had seemed right. It was like it was on the tip of his tongue, but he just couldn't say what. Felicity confirmed that the One Recipe called for chocolate, which meant it had to be a dessert, and it had to be sweet.

They drove for another hour, winding back and forth through the jungle. They had lost valuable time. Who knew? The Gastronimatii could be in Egypt; they could have the diamonds already.

"It'll be nice to finally get away from all this humidity," said the Private, wiping his brow. The mercenary next to him groaned in agreement. Guster watched the jungle trees zip by like fence posts.

The Private slowed the jeep as they rounded a tight turn. There was a banana tree on the right side of the road. Suddenly, it clicked. "Stop the car!" Guster shouted.

The Private slowed the jeep for just a second. That was all the time Guster needed. He leapt out, the jeep still in motion, and hit the ground running. He didn't stop until he was at the base of the tree.

The Private honked the horn, and the three jeeps in front of them all came to a stop. "He just jumped out!" said the Private. The mercenaries looked at Guster like he was crazy, but he didn't care. He needed one of those bananas.

The ones they'd eaten the night before at camp in the deep jungle were remarkably sweeter than the ones back on the main road. So maybe, just maybe —

"Can't you wait for us to get back to the village?" shouted Zeke from his jeep.

Guster reached up and plucked a banana from the tree, peeled it, and took a bite. He mashed it up against the roof of his mouth. It was almost imperceptible, but for Guster, there was a difference. It was definitely sweeter than the ones from the village, but not as sweet as the ones from camp the night before.

Felicity stormed from her jeep back to the banana tree. Mom wasn't far behind. "We've wasted enough time already. I will not let you waste more of it," Felicity said, pointing a finger at Guster.

Guster didn't care if she was angry. He was too busy considering the possibilities. If the banana back at the village was sweet, and this one was sweeter, and the one deepest in the jungle was sweetest of all — it marked a nearly obvious trail of progression. The further they went, the sweeter they got. As if they were pointing to something —

"We've got to go back," he said.

Felicity put her hands stubbornly on her slender hips. "We've already been down that road Mr. Johnsonville. Get back in the jeep. It's useless."

"No it is not," he said. It was only a hunch, but it was one worth risking. "The diamonds are that way," he said, pointing back to the camp.

Felicity folded her arms. "What makes you so sure?" she asked, her eyes boring into him like two drills.

Guster held steady. He couldn't let her intimidate him like that. He knew what he knew. "I can taste it," he said, holding the half-eaten banana up at her face.

For a fraction of a second, Guster thought he saw a real smile flash across Felicity's face before the hardened lines returned.

"Do you want the advice of an Evertaster or not?" Mom chimed in.

Felicity did not answer. "Men, turn the jeeps around," she said. "We're going back into the jungle."

She leapt into her jeep. Mom followed her, and Guster got in with the Private again. He knew better than to question Felicity's sudden change of heart out loud. She was the one who'd called Guster an Evertaster in the first place. Maybe she was willing to bet on it now.

"Which way Ms. Casa?" asked the Lieutenant as he started the ignition.

"North," she said. The Lieutenant hit the gas and to Guster's satisfaction, the convoy turned up the dirt path. They were actually listening to him.

It didn't seem to take nearly as long to get to the camp the second time. They drove right past it, the undergrowth squeezing at the jeeps the further they went. They passed a few empty huts.

As the miles passed, the trees got taller and taller until he could barely see the sky. They hadn't passed any huts for a very long time when they came to a fork in the road at the base of a small hill. The Lieutenant brought the jeep to a stop and idled the engine. "Right or left?" he asked. The path to the left was even more overgrown than the one they were on. The one to the right went up the hill.

Guster answered before Felicity could, "Both," he said. "We need bananas from both ways." Zeke looked at him like he was crazy. The Lieutenant waited for an answer.

"Private, take your jeep up the hill and bring me back the first banana you see. Sergeant," Felicity said, addressing the driver of the third jeep in the convoy, "head down the other path and do the same. Be back here in fifteen minutes." The Sergeant and the Private drove off in opposite directions until they were swallowed by the foliage. "You'd better be right about this," she said to Guster.

There was no way to tell until he had more of those bananas. "Why not just go back to the main road if you want more bananas?" asked Zeke.

"Because I'm guessing we can find some that taste even better," said Guster.

A half hour later, both jeeps returned. The Private handed a few bananas to Felicity, and the Sergeant did the same. "Had to chase off a snake to get these," he said.

Felicity broke off a banana from the bunch and handed it to Guster. "From the right," she said. He peeled it and took a bite. It was good, but not as sweet as the one back in camp. "And from the left," said Felicity and handed him one from the Sergeant's bunch. Guster bit into it too.

The difference was obvious. He was sure of it now. The one from the left was so much sweeter than the rest. They were getting sweeter by the mile.

"That way," he said, pointing down the narrow path.

Mariah let out a small gasp. "You're tasting your way there," she said. Guster smiled. He knew he could count on her to understand.

"That's my boy," Mom said, absolutely beaming at him.

Felicity motioned to the convoy, and ordered the four jeeps down the path and into the brush. This was it; they were finding the sweetest way.

The road got rougher and the jungle more tangled until it became more and more difficult for the jeeps to make any progress. The Lieutenant stopped the jeep in front of a banana tree that had grown in the middle of what was left of the path. He turned off the engine. "It looks like we may need to go on foot from here," he said. He got out and pulled a machete from his backpack. He picked a banana and handed it to Guster, who took a bite.

"Even better than before," he said with his mouth full.

The Lieutenant hacked his way into the jungle. Guster, Felicity and the Johnsonvilles followed him in, the rest of the mercenaries bringing up the rear. They hiked for hours, stopping whenever they found a banana tree so Guster could have a taste. Occasionally, the fruit was blander, so Guster made them backtrack to the tree before and try a new direction.

"I think my legs are going to fall off," grumbled Zeke around noontime. They came to the top of a sheer cliff overlooking a deep chasm.

"Look there," said Mariah pointing to a banana tree on the other side. A thick log had fallen across, forming a flimsy bridge.

The Lieutenant motioned for everyone to stay back. He tested the log with his foot, then carefully balanced out onto it. When he got to the middle, it wobbled beneath him for a second. It looked like he might fall until he quick-stepped to the other side and leapt onto firm ground. He picked the banana and tossed it back across to the Sergeant, who caught it and gave it to Guster. He took a bite.

It was the best one yet. It was so full of sugar it was almost like candy. He hated to make them do it, but they were all going to have to cross the chasm. "That's the way," he said.

The Sergeant took a step out onto the log when the Lieutenant stopped him. "Wait, use this," he said, tossing a rope from his backpack to the other side. "Tie it off over there." The Sergeant did as he was told, and the Lieutenant tied his end off to a tree on his side, forming a taut line in between. The Sergeant then balanced his way across, using the rope as a handrail.

"Your turn," said Felicity. Guster grabbed hold of the line and stepped out onto the log. Without even seeing it, he could imagine the terrified look on Mom's face behind him.

When he reached the middle, the log sagged under his weight, throwing him off balance. Panicking, he grabbed the rope with both hands. He put his weight on the line, and was able to steady himself enough to get to the other side. His hands were shaking when he finally let go.

Felicity went next, crossing with the grace of a dancer. Mom and Henry Junior, then Mariah, Zeke, and the rest of the mercenaries all balanced over to the other side before the Lieutenant started hacking into the brush again.

The forest was brighter here. Yellow, red, and orange flowers grew from vines that wrapped around the trees, giving off the sweet scent of honeysuckle. The further they went, the more flowers there were, each one more vibrant than the last until even the green leaves of the undergrowth were crowded out by their splendor.

"It smells like fresh, honey-flavored rain," said Mariah though, from what they could see under the heavy foliage, there wasn't a cloud in the sky.

"It's the flowers," said Felicity. "The soil must be extra rich."

"Almost like everything that grows here is sweeter," Mariah said. Then she whispered to Guster, "Maybe Archedentus knew something that Riziki didn't."

"Maybe," said Guster. He was sure about the bananas, but ever since finding out that Archedentus had never made the Gastronomy of Peace he had to wonder — perhaps the chef never found any diamonds at all. Who knows, maybe he'd sent one of his apprentices along this very path and they were torn apart by lions, never to return.

The Lieutenant led them into a narrow, foliage-covered gorge, both sides of which were overgrown with flowers. The rustling of jungle creatures and chirping of birds in the trees overhead echoed through the gap from the cliffs above. The walls narrowed so much as they hiked, Guster had to fall in line single-file behind the Lieutenant in order to squeeze between them.

Sunlight barely leaked through the tangled treetops, making it difficult to see clearly through the shifting jungle. What looked like a shadow leapt overhead. Guster dismissed it as his imagination — there were too many weeds and vines to be sure of anything.

The gorge widened a little ahead, where a giant boulder blocked the way. "Dead end," said the Lieutenant. "Looks like we'll have to turn back." Just then, the birds stopped chirping and the jungle went deadly silent. The muscles on the back of Guster's neck tensed. They were being watched.

Another shadow leapt across the top of the gorge, then two more. He was sure of it this time. There was something up there.

"What's going on?" stammered Zeke. He looked nervous too.

Then, almost as quickly as the chirping had ceased, a whooping and hollering sound exploded from the trees above. Four gigantic gorillas with dark, matted fur dropped from the cliff above onto the boulder like falling pianos.

"Run!" cried the Lieutenant, drawing his gun. He fired a tranquilizer at the closest gorilla. It lodged in its chest. Before Guster could move, seven more gorillas climbed down vines from the top of the cliff and charged them from behind. A gray-faced gorilla rushed at Guster from the front, the ground thundering as he pounded across it on all fours.

Guster shoved Mariah out of the way, just as the beast lunged past her and snatched up Zeke with one arm. "No!" yelled Guster, but before he'd finished crying out, two more gorillas plucked up Mom and Henry Junior and the Lieutenant and began scrambling up the side of the cliff. Henry Junior screamed. Guster looked for a way to escape when two palms the size of catcher's mitts snatched him up from behind, wrenched his feet out from under him and, before he could tell Mariah to run, covered his face. With another lurching motion the gorilla wrapped his furry arms around Guster's middle and shot up the face of the cliff, Guster's limbs flailing like a rag doll as the ground fell away beneath him.

Chapter 19 — The Mighty Sugarback's Treasure

Guster did not know which to be more afraid of: the gorilla squeezing him to death, or the gorilla letting go. It was a long way to the rocks below — long enough to shatter Guster's bones if the beast decided to drop him.

In two more upward lunges the gorilla reached flat ground. *This is where he rips my arms off,* thought Guster.

But the beast did not stop. Instead, it charged into the jungle undergrowth, branches lashing Guster's bare arms like whips.

He craned his neck to see if he could catch a glimpse of Mom or Mariah when a huge leaf whacked him in the face. It stung, so he pressed his face against the ape's smelly black fur to shield his eyes and almost gagged from the stench. It was like riding a bulldozer, the way the big smelly ape snapped vines and twigs into little pieces as he smashed through the jungle.

On and on the gorilla pounded, shaking Guster's bones as it charged. Guster's neck hurt. His head was on the verge of falling off from all the lurching when the big smelly gorilla broke into a clearing and stopped.

Big Smelly tossed Guster on the ground. Guster got up on his knees, gasping for air now that his ribs were free. He had to find the others. Before he could get his bearings another pair of dirty hands grabbed his wrists and pulled him out flat. A second pair grabbed his ankles, lifting him off the ground. He caught a glimpse of the large gray-faced gorilla entering the clearing, the Lieutenant slung across its shoulder like a sack of potatoes. Where was Mom? And Mariah?

More apes grabbed hold of him; they were pulling him somewhere. He saw hundreds of thousands of bright red, blue, and yellow flowers surrounding the clearing; he was too dizzy from all the jolting and turning to get a clear picture of where he was.

Do gorillas eat people? he wondered, when he saw five more apes burst into the clearing carrying their human cargo — it looked like Mom and Mariah. A dose of adrenaline squirted out of his pounding heart and shot to his toes.

Then there were more of them. Gorillas swung down from the trees, hooting and hollering as they herded Mom and the mercenaries toward Guster, pressing him in from all sides. Guster tried to struggle free. There was a crack and a thud. The Private was there — he had freed his gun from its holster and shot a dart into one of the beasts. It fell. Two more took its place, wrenching the weapon from the Private's hand.

It all made sense now. This is why Archedentus never made the recipe — he was killed by the Mighty Apes. A smooth hand grabbed Guster's arm. It was Zeke. At least they would die together.

Suddenly, the beasts dropped Guster in a heap onto the ground. He landed on something soft: Mariah. Zeke rolled over next to him as he was tossed into the pile. Henry Junior wailed.

Then, from the far end of the clearing came a ferocious, deafening roar. The gorillas backed away. Everything went silent, and the jungle trembled as the apes shrunk away, bowing their heads and huddling behind each other in fear.

"What was that?" stammered Zeke. In front of an enormously wide tree at the edge of the clearing, stood the most humongous gorilla of all. He was the size of a bulldozer. His fur stood on end like porcupine quills; his head was as big as a baby bear, his arms as thick as telephone poles. His eyes burned like coals; his nostrils flared, spewing steam like two exhaust pipes over a set of long, brownish fangs that protruded from his open mouth.

He charged like a herd of rhinos. The ground shook. Guster grabbed hold of Mom's apron as Zeke whimpered. They could not outrun him; they could not fight him.

In less than a second, the giant ape was on them, his shadow covering them in blackness, his full animal force coming to destroy them. Guster saw Zeke stretch out his hand. The beast shifted midstride. It smashed into the ground in front of them, the earth shaking with the impact.

Guster clamped his eyes shut, cringing, waiting to be torn in two, waiting for the blow that would end it all.

But it was silent. He could feel the giant's hot, steamy breath beating him with stinking air. Slowly, Guster peeked — one eye at a time. The ape was crouched only inches in front of them.

Guster was alive — for the moment. Mom and Mariah and everyone else were still as statues. Only Zeke had moved. Zeke's arm was extended toward the giant ape, his hand trembling, a single, partially unwrapped chocolate bar sticking out of his fist at the ape like a flat brown thumb.

Guster kept frozen in place. He wasn't sure he could move if he'd wanted to, he was so afraid. Why did the beast hesitate? The giant ape slowly gathered his feet under him, cocked his head to one side and gingerly plucked the chocolate bar from Zeke's hand between his thumb and forefinger. He sniffed it.

They waited.

The ape nibbled the end, his big jaw rolling like a horse's as he chewed, his eyes turned upward in consideration.

He's really eating it, thought Guster. Had the giant ape really just taken Zeke's offer? If only they'd had some Arrivederci Chocolate to give him.

Slowly, the gorilla's lips peeled back over his teeth in a grin so ridiculous, it squeezed his eyes shut. He hooted a happy hoot.

The clearing burst into chirps, hoots, and roars of applause. Guster had forgotten to breathe.

The giant gorilla smashed the rest of the chocolate bar into his mouth, then whacked Zeke on the shoulder, knocking him off his feet. He turned back across the clearing, apparently unconcerned now with the matter of the intruders.

Zeke had saved them all. "How did you know to give him the candy bar?" Mariah asked.

"I don't know!" Zeke muttered, exasperated. "I was just trying to get him to eat something besides me!"

Guster was just happy — and surprised — to be alive.

One by one, the apes scrambled down from their trees and returned to the clearing. As if on cue from the biggest ape, they didn't seem concerned anymore about the humans in their midst.

"Keep your weapons ready," said Felicity to her men. "They may have forgiven us for now, but wild animals have short memories."

The great beast himself climbed back up the enormously wide tree at the far edge of the clearing. The fur on his back lit up bright and crystal-white, sparkling all over like glass in the sunlight. It was beautiful.

"Look at him," said Mariah. "He must be the leader. They're called the Silverback because of all that silvery fur on him."

"More like the Sugarback," said Zeke. "It looks like he rolled around in candy!" Zeke was right. The fur on the giant gorilla's back glistened like sugar.

The big smelly gorilla that caught Guster in the first place emerged from the jungle with a pineapple in one hand. He broke it open, then made his way over to another, smaller gorilla that was clutching a log hollowed out at the top like a crude bucket. Big Smelly snatched the bucket from her. She screamed and batted at him, but it was useless — Big Smelly was much too strong. As soon as Big Smelly got it to himself, he dumped the bucket upside down, pouring sugar granules all over his two pineapple halves.

"It's sugar!" said Mariah. The gorilla was actually sweetening his lunch.

Big Smelly seemed to understand he was being talked about, because he smiled a big, wide grin with a set of brown, rotting teeth that made Guster feel like worms were crawling between his toes.

"Gross-aholic!" said Zeke. "It looks like he's got cavities!"

"There are no dentists in the jungle, Zeke," said Mom. "Let that be a lesson to you on proper brushing."

Now that Zeke mentioned it, all the gorillas in the clearing had bad teeth. And most of them were crowded around one barrel-log or another, all fighting for their turn to sweeten their fruit. It was remarkable just how much they all looked like Zeke — only with more hair — pouring mounds of sugar over his cold cereal on a Saturday morning.

"There must be a sugarcane field nearby," said Felicity. "Look around for some tall stalks — kind of like bamboo."

As the Sergeant and the Lieutenant scanned the edges of the clearing, Guster watched the Sugarback lounge on a branch of the enormously wide tree. Two gorillas emerged from a hole in the trunk, each carrying a barrel-log under one arm. At the sight of them the clearing erupted in hooting; gorillas charged in from all sides, trouncing over to the fresh barrels of sugar, fruit in hand, shoving and cutting in front of each other to get first crack at the prize.

One grunt from the Sugarback and the unruly apes fell silent, cowering back from the entrance. The two gorillas that had brought the sugar out poured it into one ape's hollow log after another, until each had his fill. Then the apes were back out in the clearing, frolicking, tumbling, and hoarding their sugar-caches.

"I'm guessing we'll find the sugarcane over there," said Guster, pointing to the hole in the trunk.

"Underground?" said Felicity.

"Yes," said Guster. They had found the source of the sugar, and he'd led them to it. Even Felicity couldn't deny that. He felt a sense of pride at being right.

"Lieutenant, flashlights," she said. They picked their way through the herd toward the hole in the tree.

When they were only a few feet from the trunk, the Sugarback leapt from his perch above, all five hundred pounds or more of muscle smashing into the ground in front of them like a cement slab blocking their path. There was fire in his eyes. The Lieutenant stepped back, and the Sugarback put the tip of his forefinger and thumb to his lips.

"I think he wants more candy," said Zeke.

"How many more bars do we have in our rations?" Felicity asked. The three mercenaries rummaged through their packs.

"Two," said the Lieutenant.

"And I've got three more," said the Sergeant.

"Good. Unwrap as many of them as you can. We want to be gracious guests," said Felicity. Zeke handed two more bars to her.

Felicity knelt on one knee and bowed her head, spreading the chocolate across the ground in front of the gorilla like he was a king. Guster and the rest did the same.

The Sugarback reached down, scooped up all the candy bars in his arm, and shoved them all into his mouth at once. He smiled as he chewed. His teeth were the worst of all the apes in the clearing.

The Sugarback reached one catcher mitt hand out to Zeke, and grabbing him by the forearm, led him down into the hole.

"Zeke, are you okay?" asked Mom.

"I think so," he said, looking scared. The Sugarback smoothed Zeke's hair out with one hand. Zeke's knees almost buckled under the force. Apparently the Sugarback had taken a liking to him.

"It looks like he has accepted our gift," said Felicity. "Lights on." The Lieutenant switched his flashlight on and followed Zeke and the Sugarback into the hole.

Guster grabbed Mariah's hand and they all picked their way carefully over the rocks into the darkness. He tried to stick close to the Lieutenant so he could follow the beam of his flashlight in the narrow tunnel. He had to duck here and there to keep from hitting his head on roots that stuck out of the ceiling.

"Can you see?" said Mom.

"N..no," whimpered Zeke, "He's sniffing his way."

There was a flash of brilliance under the Lieutenant's flashlight. "What was that?" Mariah asked. He shined his beam back over the wall, where a glistening line of clear white mineral shined under it. A thin vein of crystal rock wound through the side of the cave and up into the ceiling.

"It looks like quartz," said Felicity.

"It certainly is beautiful," said Mom.

They continued on. They wound up and down until Guster's back got tired from bending so low for so long. They turned one more corner in the passage and came to a cavern where, to his relief, he could finally stand.

The chamber was littered with piles of crumbling rock. A stack of sharpened, wedge-shaped stones lined one wall. More of the same crystal veins spread out like spider webs all over the ceiling.

The Sugarback smacked his lips while he waited for everyone to catch up, then took one of the sharpened stones and drove it with both hands into the closest crystal vein. After a few more blows, a thin sheet of clear rock, no thicker than a piece of window glass, broke loose. He pulled it free with his fingernails, then handed it to Zeke.

Zeke looked like he was going to cry. The Sugarback grunted softly, pushing it at him until he finally took it. It broke in Zeke's hands.

"He wants you to eat it," said Mom.

Reluctantly, Zeke licked the crystal. A smile slowly came to his face. "It tastes like candy," he said. He handed one of the shards to Guster. "You try," he said.

Guster knew before it touched his lips that it wasn't rock. It was sweet; it was succulent; it tasted like frozen air mixed with a hint of honey. No — it was like someone had squeezed the sweetness from a hundred syrup bottles and turned it to glass. "Sugar!" cried Guster.

"From a mine?" asked Felicity.

"It's Archedentus' sugar," Mom said, smiling smugly. "You'll get used to it."

"Look," said Mariah, grabbing the Sergeant's flashlight and shining it on the opposite wall. There was some writing scrawled across it above a hole near the floor. "It looks like it's French," she said.

"Eat not..." Felicity translated out loud. "No, Taste not," she said. "Taste not for Fortune nor Fame, but Taste to set Earth right again."

"And it's signed below," said Mariah. A large flowing 'A' was scrawled right above the hole. It was his signature. The great chef had made it here.

Felicity crossed the room and nearly touched the letters with her fingertips. "Archedentus," she said, her hand hovering over the rock. "To think, he walked this same path."

She looked at Guster, and for the first time, he saw a hint of genuine admiration in her eyes. "You found it," she said. "You truly are the Harbinger of Peace." Was this some kind of test? Guster didn't care if he'd passed it or not. He knew who he was.

All that mattered was that Archedentus *had* gotten this far, and whatever he'd wanted them to find was inside. There was no reason to wait.

The hole below the inscription was just big enough for Guster to crawl through. "I'm going in," he said, grabbing the flashlight from Mariah.

"Take this," said Felicity. She pulled a glass container with a screw-on lid from the Lieutenant's backpack and handed it to Guster. He held it in his armpit and crawled into the tunnel.

"I'm coming with you," said Mariah, scrambling on all fours behind him.

"Good," said Guster. He couldn't begin to guess what was inside and he did not want to go alone.

The ground was rough and he had to keep his head low so he didn't bump it on the ceiling as he crawled. The passage twisted a few times until Mom and Felicity were completely out of earshot.

The deeper they went, the narrower it got. Guster had heard about spelunkers who got trapped for days or weeks until they starved to death — he couldn't let that happen to them. After a few minutes of crawling, the tunnel turned upward sharply, and a faint glow seeped into the darkness. "It looks like there's light ahead," said Mariah.

"Let's find out," said Guster. The passage widened enough to let them walk in a crouch. A few more yards, and the tunnel opened into a cavern as tall and grand as a baseball stadium. Pencil-thin rays of sunlight streamed through small holes in the ceiling and slanted across the room, bouncing off dozens of giant towers made up of millions of sparkling crystals. A clear, shimmering lake covered the cavern floor.

It was like a city of crooked crystal sugar towers, all glistening like clear icicles or a necklace of precious jewels. It was a sacred place — the very place Archedentus had found. "The Mighty Ape's Diamonds," Guster whispered.

"It's spectacular," breathed Mariah. Almost too spectacular for humans to enter.

The two of them staggered down the slope toward the sugar towers. Guster sloshed straight into the lake without stopping. The water came up to his knees.

"No wonder there were so many fruit trees and flowers the closer we got to these sugar mines," said Mariah as they neared the pillars. "There is a higher concentration of sugar in the ground here, almost like sweetened fertilizer."

It made sense. That's exactly why the bananas tasted better too. And now Guster was going to taste the source. He picked out an especially shiny pillar. He took a rock from the water to use as a chisel, and hammered it against the pillar's surface. A sugar crystal the size of his fist broke free. He caught it in his hand. "It's practically a 100 karat diamond," he said.

He bit into it, the sugar breaking easily in his teeth. It tasted clear and clean — a thousand times more extraordinary than the shard the Sugarback had given them.

Then something happened: His head swirled and his body surged. It was without compare. All he could think about was the taste in his mouth. Nothing else mattered. Mariah's chatter began to fade away, and it seemed like Guster was alone in the cave — just him and his gigantic, pure pillar of taste.

He would have to lick the whole thing. It would take years — years of untold bliss. And he had just begun. After that he could have more.

To taste them all! Diamond after diamond, as long as they left him alone.

He broke loose another chunk and ate it.

Time slowed. Then he had another.

And another.

The cavern was the only place that mattered. It was the world.

He could stay there a hundred years.

It was like a dream.

He was made for this place, and it for him —

Mariah shook him. "Guster!" she said. "What are you doing?"

"Wha?" he asked, his mouth locked to the pillar so he could barely speak. Why did she have to bother him now? It was so wonderful —

She took him by the shoulders and yanked him backward off the pillar. He stumbled, his legs splashing through the water, the hard rocks beneath him jarring him back to reality as the sugar fell from his open mouth.

"I've been trying to get your attention. Where have you been?" she said, yanking a sugar crystal from his hand.

Guster rubbed his eyes. He felt like he was waking from a dream. "Right here," he said. She wasn't making sense. It had only seemed like a moment.

"I think the sugar was doing something to you, like putting you in a trance."

"Couldn't be," said Guster; he hadn't felt any time pass at all.

"You shouldn't have any more right now," she said.

He wiped the sugar from his mouth. "Okay." If that's what it took to make her feel better. He'd sneak some more when her back was turned.

"Let's just grab some crystals. Mom will be waiting," said Mariah.

And leave this beautiful place so soon? thought Guster. But he could spend years there!

Mariah took the glass jar from him and unscrewed the lid. Guster gladly helped her break off more chunks of crystal until the jar was full. Mariah tightened the lid down as Guster reached for the jar. "Why don't I carry it?" she said, eyeing Guster suspiciously and snatching it away.

Guster pretended not to care. He shrugged his shoulders. "Suit yourself," he said, but really, he could hardly stand it, letting her have even one jar-full of the cavern's sugar. That was one less jar-full for him. Maybe he should tell Mariah to go on ahead, and he would catch up.

Before he could protest, she grabbed him by the hand and pulled him back up toward the narrow tunnel. An instant later, she screamed.

They hadn't seen it on the way in, but there, on the edge of the lake, with his arms wrapped around a pillar of sugar, was a bleached white human skeleton. His jawbone was locked on the pillar like he was gnawing on it with his old, rotting teeth. Whoever that skeleton had been, he was trying to get one more taste up until his very last breath.

Mariah let out a sob. "He must have been with Archedentus' crew when they discovered the place," said Mariah. "It looks like he never wanted to leave."

Guster gulped. So he wasn't the only one. There were no monsters or bottomless pits guarding the sugar — just the sugar itself — powerful diamonds that if given their way, would keep him there to rot.

They had to get out of there. Mariah grabbed Guster by the hand and crawled back into the tunnel. He followed, forcing himself into the passage before he could reconsider.

When they came out the other side, Mom was in the corner, shining a flashlight into the dirt where she wrote with a stick. The Sugarback sat cross-legged behind Zeke, picking through his hair.

Felicity rushed to meet them. "Did you get it?" she said eagerly. Mariah took the jar from her backpack, the diamonds sparkling under the flashlight beams. They were even more beautiful in the darkness.

Felicity reached out like she was going to kiss the glass. Mariah pulled the jar back.

"They're remarkable," said Felicity, giving Mariah her space. She seemed to sense that this was not worth a fight. "Truly worthy to take their place in the Gastronomy of Peace. Sugar, eggs, butter, chocolate — and then, just one more," she said.

"Sweet Black Tears," said Mariah. "Which could change the recipe entirely."

"Possible. But unlikely," said Felicity confidently.

Mom looked up from her scratching in the dirt. "You know what it makes, don't you?" she said. Her eyes locked on Felicity.

Felicity nodded. "I had it narrowed down to a few prime suspects for years now. As soon as I saw the sugar, I knew what it was."

"Even without having the Sweet Black Tears?" asked Mom.

"It's obvious when you put the other ingredients together." Felicity scowled, "But without the eggbeater, we have no way to find the Sweet Black Tears."

Guster felt the glass vial pressed against his chest. It was his last secret. Felicity was their captor. She couldn't prove that she hadn't stolen the Arrivederci Chocolate, but innocent or guilty, she could help them get it. She'd made it possible to get this far. There was no other way. He would have to take a chance. They would have to trust her.

He took the vial from around his neck and tossed it to Mom. "Finding them may not be as difficult as you think," he said.

Mom uncorked it and sniffed the contents. "Vanilla," she said. "Guster, where did you get this?"

"Torbjorn gave it to me," he said.

Mom's face brightened. She scratched a final line in the dirt, then looked Guster in the eyes. "It's soufflé," she said.

Guster felt chills run up his spine.

"The very recipe to end all recipes," whispered Felicity reverently.

So that was it. Out of all the dishes in the world, The Gastronomy of Peace — the one dish that would leave its taster never wanting again — was a chocolate soufflé. It was something Guster had never tried, in any form.

"Big deal," said Zeke. "I've tasted soufflé before." The Sugarback hooted in agreement.

"Not this soufflé," said Felicity.

Mom wrung her hands. "You just did a show on this. It was right under our noses," she said.

"And now it's at our fingertips," said Felicity. She pulled a tranquilizer gun from a holster on the Sergeant's hip and fired it into the Sugarback. The dart whizzed past Zeke's head and hit the gorilla in the chest. He slumped over, unconscious.

"What did you do that for?" yelled Zeke.

"He showed us his treasure, now we can't have him interfering with our escape," she said. "Sergeant, dynamite," she snapped. The Sergeant took a red stick from his backpack and gave it to her. She lit a match and touched it to the fuse, then threw it into the tunnel that led to the sugar pillars. A second later, it blew up in a blinding red flash. The blast shook the cavern, spraying rock everywhere in a burst of dust and debris, and knocking Guster into the wall. The walls quaked, as if trying to decide whether to collapse, then settled back on themselves.

By the time the dust finally cleared, everyone had picked themselves up off the ground. The crawlspace was blocked with rubble.

"You've blocked the passage!" cried Guster. He was cut off from his precious sugar-diamonds.

"Exactly," said Felicity. "Now no one else can get it — least of all the Gastronimatii."

Guster wanted to kick himself, he was so angry. How could she do something like that?

"They'll never give up the Arrivederci Chocolate, if they really do have it," said Mom. She looked as angry as Guster felt.

"I have no doubt in my mind that they do. And they'll have to share it if they want the rest of the ingredients. We've got four to one. They'll bargain."

"What do you propose?" said Mom.

"That we get to France. I have a castle there where we can stand our ground, lure the Gastronimatii to us, and then — once we have the chocolate — make the Gastronomy of Peace."

Felicity's plan was madness, but Guster knew there was no other way. They would have to come face to face with Palatus and the Gastronimatii once again.

Chapter 20 — Chateau de Dîner

Thirty-six hours later, the Lieutenant slowed the engines and brought Felicity's private jet to a landing on a runway north of Paris. The few mercenaries who'd escaped the gorillas were waiting back at the jeeps, all too eager to take the dusty, bumpy roads from the sugar mines back to the airport at Kilimanjaro.

Once they were onboard, Guster asked Zeke what chocolate soufflé tasted like. "It's like a brownie, but lighter," Zeke said. "No wait, more like pudding, but firmer. Or chocolate soup that's really a cake."

Guster tried to picture it. It sounded good, but somehow, now that he knew what it was, the Gastronomy of Peace seemed further away than ever before.

Mom found some recordings of Felicity's program in the jet's video library. She turned on a television and watched the soufflé episode over and over, rewinding one part twenty times: "To make the perfect soufflé is to capture a cloud," sounded Felicity's smooth, recorded voice. "The complexity lies in the simplicity of it. You must remove it from the oven at the precise moment of perfection. If you bake it too long, it will deflate and be ruined. If you don't bake it long enough, you will get the same result: disaster! It inspires fear in the inexperienced and awe in the master — the final challenge for any homemaker!" Mom cracked her knuckles nervously. It was a good thing Felicity was there to make it.

All things considered, Guster should have been ecstatic. They'd made it out of Africa without getting torn into bite-size bits by gorillas, and now they were headed to Felicity's castle where — if everything went according to plan — he was finally going to get a taste of that soufflé. It should have been like waiting for Christmas morning.

Instead, Guster was filled with dread.

It wasn't the cleavers and poisons and flame that worried him — he was used to that by now. This was more personal. It was the fact that maybe Palatus was right — maybe Guster did have the makings of the Gastronimatii. If all they wanted to do was share it with the world, maybe the Gastronimatii *should* have the soufflé.

The whine of the engines died and the Sergeant opened the hatch so they could descend the stairs onto the runway in Paris. The journey seemed like it was over before it started.

A long, sleek cream-colored limousine pulled to a stop beside the plane. Two little flags with the 'FC' logo stitched on them waved from each corner of the hood. Felicity stepped out of the back of the plane. She had changed into a fitted cream-colored business suit trimmed to precision, with lace at the cuffs and a red rose pinned to her lapel. A tiny wooden spoon hung from each ear.

"Welcome to Paris," she said to Guster and Mom. "I radioed ahead to have most of the arrangements taken care of. All of you will be riding with me to the castle. My men are waiting outside the gates to provide an escort. We'll discuss more of the details on the way." She snapped her fingers and the limo driver pulled a silver ice chest from the trunk.

"Sergeant, the ingredients," said Felicity.

"Mariah and I will get them," said Guster before the Sergeant could move. This was his responsibility — besides, he still didn't want anyone but his immediate family handling them — not after they'd fought so hard to get them. He ran up the steps and was back in a minute, the egg under his arm. Mariah brought the butter.

Felicity opened the lid to the ice chest and Guster and Mariah set the egg and butter inside. She closed the lid and moved to put the ingredients in the trunk. "I'd rather they ride up front with me," said Guster.

Felicity looked like she was about to protest, then thought better of it. "Very well," she said giving the ice chest to the limo driver. He put it on the back seat.

"And the vanilla," said Felicity.

Mom patted the front pocket of her baby blue apron. "It's taken care of," she said.

A big white delivery truck came speeding across the runway toward the plane and screeched to a halt. A chef in a puffy white hat frantically jumped out of the driver's seat and opened up a pair of doors at the back. He yanked out a tray of cupcakes, scrambled up to Felicity, and presented them to her.

There must have been at least fifty of them, all still warm. A fresh-from-the-oven aroma tickling Guster's nostrils. They were taller than most cupcakes, with a thick layer of dark frosting, and an extra layer of pink flowers winding around the edges. In the middle, written in pink frosting in looping letters, were these words: "Felicity has the rest and is willing to bargain."

"The Gastronimatii keep a careful eye on anything baked, stewed or roasted in this city," said Felicity. "They will be watching the Patisseries with extra care." She pulled the jar of sugar from the back seat of the limo, unscrewed it, then placed it on the closed trunk of the limo. She took a small porcelain bowl and grinder from the back seat and broke off a sugar nugget from the jar. She ground it up in the bowl and sprinkled the glistening sugar grains across the tray of cupcakes. It sparkled.

"That should get their attention," she said. "They'll be able to smell sugar like that from a mile away. It will be like reading a billboard to them." She turned to the chef with the puffy hat. "Put one of these in every Casa-owned Patisserie in Paris," she told him. He saluted, took the cupcake tray and slid it in the back of his truck, then drove away.

"And how will they find us?" asked Mom curtly. Guster was wondering the same thing.

"Oh, believe me, they'll know where to look," she said. It made their meeting sound so inevitable. Guster had to wonder how she knew them so well. Had she worked with them before?

Felicity slipped into the back seat of the limo. There were two long benches running down the length of it. Zeke and Mariah slid all the way to the front. Guster scrambled in behind and planted himself protectively next to the ice chest.

"This is how movie stars get places," Zeke told Henry Junior smugly after Mom climbed in. The tiny boy tried to bite Zeke's plump finger.

The driver drove across the runway through the security gates at the airport and out onto the streets of France. The same four jeeps that had taken them across Africa drove up alongside them, the Lieutenant steering the jeep in front, each seat filled with one of Felicity's mercenaries. Guster waved, but the limo's windows were probably too dark for anyone to see inside.

"In addition to this escort, I have a troop of more than twenty men hidden at the castle. Once we lure the Gastronimatii inside, that should be enough to help us subdue them and secure the chocolate."

Having reinforcements waiting for them was reassuring. At least the plan sounded reasonable, and Felicity's men would be there to keep Guster from doing anything stupid. If this wasn't all just a ploy to make Felicity look innocent, that is.

"Right now, we're about seven miles northeast of Paris," said Felicity. "My castle is southeast of the city. It will take us more than an hour to get there."

"And then what?" asked Mom.

"Then, we wait," said Felicity.

Guster stared out the window as they drove through the countryside. It was lush, green and dotted with the occasional lake or pond. They passed a small village or castle here and there, which made the whole place feel old as if they were slowly going back in time as they drove.

Felicity held the jar of sugar diamonds in her lap. It was the one ingredient Guster hadn't managed to place under his personal protection. She hadn't let go of it since she'd taken it from Mariah in Africa.

If it weren't for Mariah, I'd still be in the cave, he thought. *Still clutching the sugar column, still licking it until I rotted into a pile of bones*. How would that sugar taste once it was combined with eggs that tasted like the sun, butter that tasted like gold, sweet black tears of vanilla and the world-famous Arrivederci Chocolate? What kind of effect would it have on him then?

He hadn't told anyone the extent of Palatus' offer on Bear Island. He couldn't even tell Mariah that.

And yet — he couldn't wait to get his hands on it — the most delicious dessert in the history of the world.

At dusk the convoy rounded a lake and turned off the main road onto a narrow private drive that cut through a forest like a tunnel in the wood. Gray shadows under the branches overhead made it hard to see, even with the jeeps' headlights.

The convoy halted when the drive turned the corner and came to a spiked, wrought iron gate blocking the way. The gate was held up by two stone pillars, each topped with a polished marble stuffed turkey that looked like it had come fresh from the oven on Thanksgiving Day. The letters 'CDD' were spelled out in curling iron in the center of the gate's arch. The Lieutenant punched in some numbers into a keypad on a small black box and the gate swung slowly open.

"Welcome to the Chateau de Dîner," said Felicity as they drove through the gates.

The forest opened onto a wide lawn with a river running through it. At the far end was a huge, gleaming white stone castle with a blue roof. It was enormous, with arched windows, dozens of chimneys and several imposing round towers capped in blue shingled cones. Between the two widest towers in the center, there was a small arched opening with an open wooden drawbridge.

"It's like a princess's castle," said Mariah dreamily.

"The place where you keep your state-of-the-art kitchen," Mom added.

"One and the same," said Felicity.

They drove up the long driveway through the spacious grounds. They were exquisite, even in the dark, with shrubbery trimmed to look like dinner forks, knives and spoons. A fountain sculpture of a milk-maid holding a pot of soup under one arm adorned the center of the lawn. Water poured out of a ladle she held in her other hand.

About a half mile from the house, Felicity suddenly grew tense. "Stop the car," she said.

"What is it Madam?" asked the driver.

"Something's wrong. Kill the lights."

The driver shut off the headlights. Felicity stared out the window into the night. She pushed an intercom button in the back seat and whispered into a speaker, "Lieutenant, stealth mode." All four jeeps in the convoy shut off their headlights too, and the lawn went dark.

"What's wrong?" asked Mom.

"The drawbridge is down," said Felicity. "That's not the way I ordered it. My men know that we always leave the drawbridge up. It's a standing order." She pressed the button on the intercom again. "Lieutenant, recon!"

The Lieutenant hopped out of the jeep and fished a pair of clunky black goggles from his bag. He slid them over his head, turned a few dials, then snuck up toward the house on foot. The darkness swallowed him.

Guster didn't dare make a sound. If whatever was going on was enough to cause Felicity concern, it had to be something important. Everyone else must have felt it too, because nobody said a word.

A few tense minutes later the Lieutenant returned. He pressed a button on his helmet and his voice crackled through the speaker inside the limo, "Ms. Casa, Chateau de Dîner security has been compromised. Usual guard detail is not present. No signs of forced entry. Lights on inside the west wing indicate that it is inhabited."

"Impossible!" cried Felicity slamming her fist on the limo wall. "I've got twenty highly-trained mercenaries in there!"

The intercom crackled again, "Ms. Casa, there's something else."

"Yes?" said Felicity.

"There were two huge brutes in hoods standing watch in the shadows by the drawbridge. I think — I think the Budless are guarding the entrance," said the Lieutenant.

Felicity got quiet. Whatever the Budless was, it sounded bad. She reached for the intercom and pressed the button again. "Lieutenant, turn the convoy around. Take us back toward the road."

"What's going on?" said Mom. Guster was wondering the same thing.

"The Gastronimatii — they're here," said Felicity.

Guster felt his throat dry up. What about the plan? It wasn't supposed to happen like this. Felicity's armed guard was supposed to be waiting inside — what about them?

"How can you tell?" asked Zeke, his voice shrill. Guster wasn't the only one who was afraid.

"Because the Budless are the minions of the Gastronimatii. They're gigantic men raised from birth to serve the purposes of the Arch-Gourmand and obey his every whim. The Gastronimatii burn their mouths when they're very young, killing off their taste buds. They even sear their nostrils, giving them almost no sense of taste or smell."

"But why?" asked Zeke. He was starting to tremble.

"To make them their slaves and their enforcement squad. They are the exact opposite of the Gastronimatii — they know nothing of taste or cuisine. They have no desire for flavor. They don't know what it is. It's like having a guard at your bank who doesn't care about money — you know he'll never try to steal it. They're the perfect protectors for the Gastronimatii treasury."

"Which means they've got something to protect," said Mariah. "The chocolate is already here," she whispered.

Felicity looked smug. If Mariah was right, and the Gastronimatii had brought it, it would prove her innocence. But that also meant that all the ingredients were in one place. Guster felt his mouth tingle again, like it wasn't his own.

They rolled down the driveway, past the gate and back out onto the private drive. The limo driver switched his headlights back on and sped along, the jeeps following behind. No one made a sound, as if talking would alert the Gastronimatii to their presence. Why did Guster feel like he was waiting in line for a roller coaster that would fly off the track?

Felicity stared out the window, counting quietly to herself as they drove past tree after tree. After more than fifty, she spoke, "Stop."

The driver slammed on the brakes. Felicity got out of the back. A tall row of wild-growing hedges filled the gaps between trees forming a solid wall on either side of the drive that looked completely impassible. Felicity paced up and down the length of it, inspecting the ground.

It didn't make sense. She was the Queen Bee of the American Household, but was she really concerned about gardening at a time like this?

She bent down and pushed on the trunk of one of the shrubs. The whole wall of bushes shook and moved slightly. "Lieutenant, a little help, please?" she said. The Lieutenant jumped from his jeep and pushed on the nearest bush until the entire wall of shrubbery swung away like a tangled green gate.

Guster pressed his face up against the limo window so he could see better. The roots were connected at the bottom. There must have been a set of hidden hinges mounting the entire assembly onto the trunk of a nearby tree. On the other side of the secret gate was a steep dirt road that veered off through the forest. It was all very clever: a road hidden in the trees for emergencies.

Felicity and the Lieutenant pushed the shrub gate open until it was wide enough to drive through. She motioned the limo driver and the four jeeps through, the Lieutenant's copilot driving the first jeep while the Lieutenant took a dead branch and wiped away the tire tracks in the dirt. He swung the bushes closed again.

They jumped back into their vehicles, and the line of cars drove down the bumpy dirt road into the forest. Bare branches from the bushes reached out from the forest, scraping at the limo like skeletons' fingers. It looked haunted, like it belonged in a Halloween movie, or had something dangerous to hide. Zeke looked scared.

"Kill the lights again. We're getting close to the house," said Felicity into the intercom after another minute of driving. The beams illuminating the forest disappeared, and all was dark. Guster's eyes raced back and forth anxiously across the woods. He couldn't pick out the trees from the shadows. It was uncomfortable, knowing that anything could sneak up on them now.

A half mile later they came to a small clearing. There was a stone well in the middle. "Park here," said Felicity. The convoy stopped.

"The Chateau de Dîner was built seven hundred years ago," she said clicking off the intercom. "The nobility who lived here never knew when they might have to escape from a jealous king or rebellious peasants, so they built a passage into the well as a means of getting out undetected. Now we're going to use it for the opposite reason — getting in without being seen."

"And once we're inside?" asked Mom.

"Fortunately for us, the whole castle is riddled with secret passageways. We should be able to move around freely and observe our unwanted guests without them knowing."

"Cool," squeaked Zeke. Guster could tell he was nervous. Guster was too. It would have been different if they weren't trying to sneak into a place where people were waiting to kill them.

Jar of sugar in hand, Felicity climbed out of the limo. Guster and Mariah hauled the ice chest out between them. The mercenaries followed Felicity to the well. "Sergeant, fetch the harnesses," she ordered. The Sergeant fetched a tangled armful of webbing from the back of the closest jeep.

His hand still on the handle of the ice chest, Guster peered over the ancient stone brim of the well. A rope hanging from a small wooden roof on top descended into the darkness until it disappeared far below. "Lieutenant, the cable," said Felicity. The Lieutenant pressed a button on a winch on the front bumper of his jeep, unwinding several feet of cable. He hooked the looped end of the cable around a metal carabineer. Mom's eyebrows bent her soft face with worry.

"You don't have to go in there," said Felicity.

"Excuse me?" said Mom, straightening her face. She looked like she'd been challenged.

"I'm doing this because this is my life's quest, and because there is nothing else. You are a housewife. You've got obligations to your children. This may not be a place you want to take them."

Mom forced a chuckle at Felicity. "After all the places we've been! I believe you when you say that this won't be a picnic, Felicity Casa, but the Johnsonvilles started out this journey together, and about two and half continents ago, it became clear to me that this family needs to stick together like cinnamon rolls fresh from the oven." She looked sympathetically at Guster. He knew why she was doing this: she was thinking of his cure — a cure he needed worse than ever. "So we're going inside that castle," Mom said folding her arms over her apron, "And we're going to see to it that that One Recipe gets made, no matter what."

"Good," said Felicity. She looked pleased, like she knew what Mom would say before she said it. Had she been taunting her? She had to have known that Mom wouldn't turn back.

"Put these on," said the Lieutenant taking the harnesses from the Sergeant and handing them out. He helped Guster step through the straps and cinch up the waist, then put one on Mariah, then Zeke, and finally strapped one on himself. Felicity cinched one around her waist too. Mom put Henry Junior on Mariah's back while Mom strapped on her own harness.

"We'll lower you down, one by one," said the Lieutenant.

Just then there was a roar of something mechanical and a burst of heat as the entire clearing lit up bright orange. Two huge flames shot out of the bushes, straight for the Sergeant's head.

The Lieutenant was lightning quick. He leapt out of the way, throwing Guster and Mariah to the ground. The Sergeant wasn't so lucky. His uniform caught fire, the flames spreading wildly across his back. He rolled to the ground, screaming in pain.

Too many things happened at once for Guster to process it all. His ribs hurt from being thrown down. He heard a gunshot. The mercenaries spread out, some taking cover behind the jeeps, others diving for safety behind the well. Guster tried to find Mom in all the commotion. There were more shots.

The Lieutenant was on the ground, blasting his handgun into the bushes. It wasn't the hissing of tranquilizer darts this time, but the crack of live ammunition. There was a thump and a rustle in the foliage. Two chefs in red aprons leapt into the clearing, blasting thirty foot spurts of fire from flame throwers strapped to their backs.

"Gastronimatii!" screamed the Private.

Guster thought of one thing: the silver ice chest. He had to get back to the well where he'd left it. His eyes darted frantically between the jeeps looking for an opening in the crossfire. Felicity had taken cover behind one of wheels.

He ran for it, staying low as fire blazed overhead, when two more Gastronimatii burst out of the bushes, cleavers in hand. The one on Guster's right threw his knife. It spun until it struck the jeep's tire, inches from the Lieutenant's head. The Lieutenant turned and fired, dropping the chef to the ground. Six more stormed out of the bushes after him.

The Lieutenant grabbed Guster by the waist and yanked him back. *Not now*, thought Guster as the Lieutenant clipped a loose cable to Guster's harness.

"Go," he shouted, shoving Guster back toward the well. Another flame shot between them, blocking his way. There was no time to argue. He threw his leg over the stone lip of the well and dropped over the edge. The cable caught him. He floundered, scrambling with his arms to gain some kind of control. He tried to grab the ice chest. His fingers brushed it, then the Lieutenant lunged for the button on the winch and smashed it down.

Guster dropped into the darkness. Ten. Twenty. Thirty feet. Then whump. He hit the ground feet first and fell back onto his rear, jarring his back hard. The cable had slowed his fall just enough.

The ingredients were still up above — too far to reach.

There was another zipping noise, and the dark blue spot of sky far above filled with black for a second. Something slammed into the ground beside him. "Ouch," said Mariah.

"Mom!" cried Guster. There was a whine of cable scraping against rock. Mariah grabbed his arm.

"Help me!" she said. "They're pulling me up! Get this cable off." Guster fumbled to find it in the dark. The Gastronimatii must have engaged the winch. He couldn't lose Mariah now too. He didn't want to be alone. He snatched the cable. "It's caught. It's too tight," she said.

Guster got down on one knee. "Step on me," he said. Mariah stood on his leg and the cable loosened. He unclipped it, and it whipped upward. Mariah fell back. Then there was crying.

Guster felt panic well up inside him. It sounded like a tiny boy. "That's not — Henry Junior is it?" he said. The last thing he wanted was for his baby brother to be stranded in a dark tunnel.

"Better down here than up there," said Mariah. Guster reached out. Sure enough, there was Henry Junior, strapped to Mariah's back. It only made their predicament worse. How was he going to get himself out of there, let alone his sister and baby brother?

There were shouts above. It sounded French, which could only mean that the Gastronimatii were winning. They had to get moving before they came down the well after them.

The black outline of a head with a bun on top thrust over the lip of the well. "Run!" echoed Mom's voice. Her shadow was yanked backward. A flame shot across the opening.

"Let's go," said Guster, grabbing Mariah's hand and stumbling into the dark. He could only hope that flame hadn't hit her. He hated to leave Mom and Zeke, but there was nothing else they could do.

Mariah switched on a flashlight. Trusty Mariah. She was always prepared.

The beam shone on a tunnel as wide as a doorway, the sides supported by rectangular, rough-hewn stone bricks. As soon as Guster could see, he started to run.

He could hear Mariah's panting and Henry Junior's crying right behind him as the tunnel rose slightly, their feet splashing through a trickling stream. It would only take moments for the Gastronimatii to drop down the well and be on their heels. He had to put as much space between them and the well's opening as possible.

The tunnel forked; Guster took the right path. It was only a guess, but there was no time to weigh the options.

The tunnel forked again. This time they went left. If they were lucky, they could throw the Gastronimatii off their trail.

Henry Junior started to wail louder than ever as they ran, dashing Guster's hopes of evading anyone as the eerie echo of his screams bounced across the tunnel walls. The crying was a dead giveaway. How was it that Mom had always managed to keep him so quiet?

There was no time to console his baby brother now. They had to keep moving.

Water dripped on his head as he ran. The tunnel had a musty smell about it, like it was very old. They came to a hole in the floor where the stream flowed from underneath a rocky outcropping. After that there was dry earth under their pounding feet.

"Guster," gasped Mariah, "I need to rest."

"Okay, but only for a second," he said, reluctantly slowing his pace. There was no way to tell how far they'd come.

The ground sloped upward, steeper than before, until they turned a corner and the tunnel dead ended at an old, heavy wooden door.

A rat scurried across the floor and under a gap beneath the door. Henry Junior stopped crying, apparently distracted from their grim predicament. "Mow mow," he said, pointing.

Grateful for the quiet, Guster grasped a thick iron ring that hung in the center of the wood and pulled. "Help me," he said. Mariah grabbed hold and yanked with him, until the door, groaning, opened slowly on its rusty hinges.

On the other side was a narrow stone staircase that spiraled upward into a tower. "We must be under the castle," said Mariah.

Guster had no idea where to go from here. What were they going to do once they were inside anyway? All he knew was that they couldn't allow themselves to be followed. He yanked on the door until it closed, then stopped to listen. The slow, rhythmic drip of water plinked on the rocks on the other side. If they were behind them, the Gastronimatii were being very sneaky about it.

He and Mariah mounted the stair and climbed upward. *If only Zeke were here*, thought Guster. *And Mom*. She always knew what to do. But they weren't. They'd been attacked by the Gastronimatii, and as far as he knew, only he and Mariah had escaped. Mom could be hurt — or worse.

Guster shook his head; he couldn't think about that right now. He had to concentrate on the moment. He had to find a way out of this, if not for him and Mariah, at least for Henry Junior.

He guided himself along the cold stone wall of the spiral stair with his hand. The next twenty steps took them upward almost two full turns inside the tower. A straight narrow hallway branched off from the staircase. Mariah shined her light inside. It was uninviting — cobwebs strewn across the narrow gap waited like wispy nets to trap them.

Guster urged her up the steps. They passed three more hallways as they ascended the stair. The staircase dead ended at the fifth one. With nowhere else to go, Guster turned and squeezed himself into the passage, his back up against the wall.

"Guster, wait," whispered Mariah, handing Guster the flashlight. She took Henry Junior off her back and held him on her hip so she could shimmy her way in too. Henry Junior buried his face in her neck.

The passage curved, like it was going around the perimeter of a larger tower. There was a faint slit of light up ahead on the left wall no thicker than a dime. As Guster got closer, he could see a tiny door only one inch tall and six inches wide mounted on the wall just above his head. If there was light coming through, maybe it could help them find a way out.

Guster pulled on the knob and swung the tiny door open. There were two remarkable things about the other side: the first was a set of holes, one for each eye, that let light stream through into the tunnel; the second was a pair of eyes painted on the inside of the wood.

Guster clicked off the flashlight — he didn't want it shining out — and put one finger over his lips so Mariah would keep Henry Junior quiet — if that were possible. They'd been lucky so far.

Guster stood on his tiptoes and peered through the eyeholes. On the other side of the stone wall was a wide hallway with a blue throw rug running down its length, several golden tapestries hanging on the walls, and electric chandeliers lighting up the otherwise dim interior. They were definitely inside now.

He felt around for a lever or switch. If there was a way to see into the castle hallway, there had to be a way to get out of the secret passage too. He fumbled with a wooden beam hanging from the ceiling, but nothing happened.

"Try this," whispered Mariah. She pushed on a brick protruding from the wall only a few feet from the eyeholes. It groaned, and a column of bricks barely wide enough to fit through swung slowly inward, grinding across the floor beside them.

Mariah's eyes brightened. Guster shut the tiny eyehole door and squeezed stealthily through the opening into the hall.

He turned off the flashlight and gave it back to Mariah. On this side of the wall where the eyeholes would have been was a life-size portrait of a man holding an old hunting musket, his face painted exactly at eye-level. *That's what those eyes on the inside of the door are for*, he thought. He looked closer, and sure enough, there was a thin, almost invisible line around the man's eyes where the painting had been cut.

If Zeke was there, he would definitely think that was cool. The thought pained Guster. He tried to shove it out of his mind.

He helped Mariah put Henry Junior back in the toddler backpack then led them left. Walking was easier now that they were inside the castle, but it made Guster feel exposed; they no longer had the advantage of secrecy.

They passed tapestry after tapestry. The hallway finally ended at a large stone archway that opened into a spacious banquet hall. "Let me go! I'll pay my own ransom!" whined a voice inside.

Guster motioned for Mariah to stay close to the wall. He recognized the voice. It sounded like Aunt Priscilla. He crouched low and peered into the room.

Sure enough, Aunt Priscilla was tied to a chair at the end of a massive oak table on the far side of the hall. She was blindfolded, her nose still as red as a tomato, though slightly less swollen. "They must have taken her after we left Key West," Guster said.

Two Gastronimatii came through an open archway behind her. They were both dressed in their red chefs' garb. "We should've gagged her," said one Gastronimatii to the other.

Guster grabbed Mariah's hand and doubled back into the hallway. They couldn't risk being seen. They were just short of the painting of the hunter when there was a scuffling of feet and a low voice from behind. The two Gastronimatii were coming down the corridor from the banquet hall.

There was no way to make it back to the secret passageway in time, even if they ran their hardest. He looked frantically around for a chair or a vase they could hide behind, but the hallway was bare.

The voices were getting closer when Mariah pulled Guster by the arm over to one of the tapestries. She slid behind it, pulling him in with her. It was dark, and his feet were probably showing, but it was better than nothing.

The footsteps got louder as the Gastronimatii began to run. Guster held his breath. They couldn't be discovered now. The footsteps came a few feet from the tapestry, then the chefs passed right by, their voices eager. Guster sighed.

"Ba!" said Henry Junior, tapping Guster on the shoulder. Guster shot a glance out into the hall, certain that the noise had been enough to give them away. The two Gastronimatii were running, their backs to Guster, apparently in such a hurry they hadn't even noticed the toddler's cry. He felt a wave of relief.

"They must be going somewhere important," whispered Guster.

"Maybe they know where Mom is," said Mariah. Guster nodded. *If Mom's alive*, he thought.

"What should we do about Aunt Priscilla?"

Guster shook his head. "Nothing right now. We've got to find a way out of this first."

He grabbed Mariah's hand and tiptoed after the Gastronimatii. They passed the portrait of the hunter again and followed the voices until the hallway came to a T. Guster peeked carefully around the left corner, waited until the two chefs descended a set of stairs, then followed after them.

They never reached the stair. Something far more important caught Guster's attention: dancing firelight and shouts pouring in from a balcony on the left. Something was happening in the courtyard below — something big.

Guster motioned to Mariah. "Stay here," he said and crept onto the balcony so he could peer over the edge of the stone railing without being seen.

The balcony gave an excellent view of the castle's inner courtyard. He felt his throat tighten again — it was a view he did not want to see: down below were more than a hundred members of the Cult of Gastronimatii, all dressed in red, holding shining knives and burning torches above their heads and shouting into the night.

Chapter 21 — The Rites of the Gastronimatii

Guster could hardly believe it — he never suspected the Cult was so large. They were a sea of frightening, surging crimson. Their blood-red aprons trailed on the ground like snakes. Their tall hats were pulled low like robbers' masks — more than a hundred red reasons Guster and Mariah should never have snuck into the castle that night.

The Gastronimatii were lined up in rows across the enclosed courtyard, facing a raised stone platform, their backs toward Guster and Mariah. The castle at the far end wrapped around behind them, closing off the courtyard around the shouting chefs.

Palatus stood atop the platform, "Soon, it will be zee day that we have waited for!" he cried. "Our time is coming!"

Guster clenched his teeth. He hated that chef. He was evil; he was dangerous; and he was doing the very thing Guster wanted to do but hadn't: taste the good and rid himself of the bad.

"Let us cleanse ourselves!" cried Palatus. On cue, the chefs wailed as they poured tiny bags of powder over their heads and rubbed the powder under their armpits. A pungent smell of mustard, cumin, and cinnamon floated up into the air.

"Centuries 'ave waited for this, and now you, zee Ancient Order of Flavor, will purge zee earth!" Images flashed on the castle wall behind him like a movie screen. Chefs in red, hard at work, chopped and stirred ingredients. The scene changed. They marched in rows, silver platters topped with succulent cuisine raised above their heads. Then there were flames.

The crowd exploded with excitement, cheering on the destruction.

Guster forced himself to look away. The film was hypnotic, enticing.

Palatus held up his arms and motioned for silence. The Arch-Gourmand placed his hand on a large piece of red canvas draped over a lumpy mound as high as his chin. "Zee earth is polluted!" he said. "Behold, zee filth!" he shouted, and yanked the canvas away.

Underneath was a pile of colorful boxes and bags: macaroni & cheese, microwave dinners, frozen burritos, plastic bags of hot dogs, loaves of factory-made white bread.

The Gastronimatii screamed, clutching their throats and spitting like cats thrown into water. They backed away from the putrid garbage. "It's like acid!" hissed one near the pile as he stabbed his knife through a box of mac & cheese.

"No longer will this painful, vile slop sting our palettes!" Palatus said, holding both arms out straight toward the pile of manufactured food. "You've spent your lives fighting back vile filth with your delicacies. You've suffered from the way it pollutes our soil, our water, our air and ultimately mixes with zee few pure ingredients left. Tonight, destiny turns in our favor!" He wrenched a torch from the hand of a nearby Gastronimatii and touched it to the pile. It went up in flames.

The Gastronimatii hissed and jeered. They pulled boxes and bags from their jackets and cast them like sacks of vomit into the fire, which coughed sparks and debris as it swallowed more and more of their rejected meals. The flames rose higher into the night — ten, fifteen, then twenty feet as they danced, casting eerie shadows across the castle walls. The fire lit up the bottom of Palatus' nose and chin in a ghostly glow.

"Purge! Purge! Purge!" The Gastronimatii chanted, raising their torches up and down in unison.

An image of a food processing plant flashed on the wall. The plant exploded into a fireball. Then there was another factory reduced to a pile of rubble and ruin. Guster recognized it instantly — the Foodco Instant Dinners Factory. Then there was another, and another. Some collapsed, some burned. This time he couldn't look away.

Then a map of the world appeared. Forks flashed on the screen, stabbing the map in London, New York, Boston, Rome, then across the world. "This is our work!" cried Palatus.

So many destroyed! thought Guster.

"War!" cried one of the Gastronimatii. The crowd roared their approval. They were rabid, untamed, ready to spill out over the castle walls and ravage the world.

Palatus held up his hands to stop them. "No." he said, pulling the eggbeater from under his apron. He held it in the air like a scepter, forcing the crowd into awed silence.

Guster nearly leapt from the balcony. *It's mine*! he thought. *I never should have lost it*. Mariah's gentle tug pulled him back to the ground.

Palatus spoke calmly. "Not war," he chuckled, "Peace! Nation by nation, man by man, they will choose zee thing that they want most: zee delicate, flawless fruits of your kitchens!" he said. "Yours will be the ruling cuisine on zee earth! No more will filth pollute the purity of your work! Zee earth will be purged! Your genius will be recognized! They will not reject the marvelous cuisine of your making ever again!"

"Give us the soufflé, Lord-Evertaster!" screamed one of the Cult. A murmur of agreement rustled through the crowd.

"When will we taste it?" cried another.

Before Palatus could answer, a man with a pencil-thin tie emerged from the shadows behind Palatus and whispered in his ear. Guster recognized him instantly — it was Felicity's public relations spokesman. The same one he'd seen on TV.

Felicity's own employee, here with the Gastronimatii! She was a traitor! Guster had taken a chance on her and lost. He had been foolish to trust her.

Recognition, then a sinister smile came to the Arch-Gourmand's lips as the man with the pencil-thin tie continued to whisper. "Sooner than any of us could have hoped," hissed Palatus.

He turned to the shadows and beckoned something toward himself. Two huge brutes with bare chests and pot bellies marched side by side up to the platform. They wore loose, wooly gray pants over their legs and gray executioner's hoods over their faces. In between them they carried the metal ice chest with the objects Guster wanted most: the ingredients.

"That must be them," whispered Mariah.

Guster shot a confused look at her.

"The Budless," she said. "Gigantic men. Immune to the taste or smell. Just like Felicity described."

She was probably right; they were enormous. But where was Mom?

"Masks!" said Palatus, pulling a gray bandana from his pocket and tying it around his mouth and nose. The Budless set the ice chest on the ground in front of Palatus, then stood at attention by his side.

He lifted the lid and examined the contents. Slowly, almost reverently, he removed the red cylindrical hat from his head and set it down, exposing his eyes and whitish-blonde hair. His fingers trembled as he reached toward the ingredients. Then he pulled back his hand, hesitating, wonder in his eyes. He spread his arms wide. "Behold, the ingredients in the One Recipe!" he cried.

The crowd roared. A Gastronimatii pushed his way through the crowd and leapt onto the stage. His gray bandana dangled around his neck, his tongue hanging from his wide-open mouth. Even from the balcony Guster could see that his eyes were wild, like a wolverine's. "Just one bite!" he cried and lunged for the ice chest, fingers outstretched like claws. A meaty hand caught him by the neck in midair. One of the Budless held the chef aloft then slammed him to the ground. The maddened Gastronimatii screamed as the Budless kicked him back into the crowd.

Palatus spat at the fallen Gastronimatii. "Impatience is the very reason we have not obtained our victory! Zee time will come when our own self-control will be zee only thing that ensures our triumph. The One Recipe is 'ere, after all these years! Will you wait so that you can taste it?"

The crowd raised their knives in the air and hissed like a den of snakes in approval.

Something rustled in the shadows behind Palatus. A dozen Gastronimatii marched the Lieutenant, half a dozen mercenaries, Felicity, Mom and Zeke, all tied at the wrists, into the back of the courtyard. A glimmer of hope lit in Guster's chest. Mom's blue apron was dirty and charred, but she and Zeke had survived the battle; they were okay — for the moment.

But if Felicity was tied, did that mean she was innocent?

"Let us make it!" cried the Gastronimatii. There was a murmur of agreement.

"I'll do it!" shouted one of them.

"No, it should be Uvula! He makes the finest soufflés in all of Paris!" shouted another. A very short, thin chef standing next to the speaker folded his arms and stuck out his lip.

Felicity slammed her elbow into the gut of the Gastronimatii guarding her. He doubled over. "No!" she shouted stepping out of the shadows. "Certainly you've read the entire Recipe by now! You know the rules," she managed to say before the guards pulled her back.

Palatus' eyes narrowed. "I do," he said, then jerked his head back toward Mom. The Gastronimatii guards cut the ropes from her wrists and pushed her toward him. He unsheathed the eggbeater and thrust it at her.

Mom caught it. She looked confused. Palatus had been trying to get that eggbeater ever since they met him in New Orleans. Why was he giving it back?

"MA MA!" Henry Junior cried out, reaching toward her. Mariah jumped back from the balcony into the shadows. "Not now," she pleaded. His face scrunched up and turned red as he began to cry.

The man with the pencil-thin tie shot a glance upward. Guster ducked into the hall, hoping he wasn't seen.

"A housewife?" jeered another chef. "What does she know of our craft? Give it to Uvula! Or Sophagus!" There were cries of approval.

Mom? thought Guster. He'd always assumed someone like Felicity, a celebrity homemaker, would make it; or now that the Gastronimatii had the eggbeater, Palatus would want to be the one.

Mom's casseroles were wretched at best. How could *she* make the Gastronomy of Peace?

"Will you make me a heretic?" Palatus shouted, enraged. His icy stare swept over the crowd. There was an immediate but reluctant silence. "The instructions of Archedentus stand," he said. The debate was over.

"Prepare the kitchen," he said, jerking his head at the guards again. "And take the soldiers to the dungeon." He stormed from the platform, the crowd parting before him. The guards followed, shoving Mom in front of them, the eggbeater still in her hand. Felicity, Zeke, and the mercenaries went next. The Budless brought up the rear, the ice chest hoisted on their shoulders. The Gastronimatii kept a healthy distance, hissing at them as they passed.

Guster and Mariah had to get out of there.

"There's got to be another passage around here," said Mariah. She was running her fingers along the frame of a painting of a dog on the wall. Guster had been so fixated on the courtyard, he hadn't noticed it. Sure enough, the dog's eyeballs were painted at face level and ringed with thin, almost invisible cuts.

Henry Junior's cries had turned to low sobs by the time Mariah stopped her hand, held her palm up against the wall and pressed hard. A stack of stones in the wall ground slowly inward.

"You're a genius, Mariah," said Guster.

"Little good that will do you now," said a man's low, silky voice behind Guster. Guster whirled around to see the man with the pencil-thin tie standing there, more than a dozen Gastronimatii at his side.

"Guster, save Mom!" cried Mariah, jumping between him and the chefs. They lunged at her. She tripped one, sending him smashing to the ground.

Guster darted for the secret passage, jumping over the felled Gastronimatii and narrowly missing the other. It was close. The others closed in as he catapulted his skinny body through the narrow opening. He made it just as an arm reached through and grabbed him by the back of the shirt. He struggled to get free, but the arm wouldn't let go. Any second now they would pull him out or come in after him. He kicked out and missed.

Then he saw it: a protruding stone just like the switch that had opened the first passage door. He jammed it with his elbow, ignoring the pain. The door started to grind closed behind him.

The Gastronimatii shouted. There was a scuffle, then he yanked his arm out and the stones sealed shut.

Guster was in the dark narrow passage, completely alone.

Chapter 22 — Fate's Kitchen

Guster ran through the dark, unable to see even the ground beneath his feet. He thought he heard banging behind him, so he ran and ran and kept on running. He tripped over something he couldn't see, bruising his shoulder as he fell. If only he'd brought the flashlight.

He listened. Whatever had been making the noise was gone. *They must not be able to find the brick that opens the passageway.* Which was good; it would buy him some time.

It also meant he was separated from Mariah and Henry Junior. Who knew what the Gastronimatii would do with them now that they were captured?

He'd never meant for it to happen like this. He'd never meant to force his family into the middle of such a dangerous fight. And now there was no one else who could help.

He didn't care anymore about eating some stupid soufflé. He didn't care if they never made it, if they went home and he was never able to swallow another edible morsel of food again. He would starve to death if he had to, as long as he got his brothers, sister and mom out of there safely.

He wandered down the passage looking for something, *anything* to inspire a plan.

It branched left so he followed it. His only hope was to find his way to the dungeon, where he might be able to free the Lieutenant and the rest of the mercenaries. Without a flashlight it was nearly impossible. He was lost in the dark.

He stumbled on a bit of uneven ground, and felt around with his cowboy boot to see if he could figure out what was ahead. The floor dropped a few inches into a stair, so he picked his way down it, then found another, and another. He guessed he'd gone two, then three, then four floors.

He felt the floor even out and followed the wall with his hand to the left. There was a passage. Guster followed it. *I must be on the outer edge of the castle again*, he thought. His face collided with a tangled sheet of cobwebs that wrapped around his head. He spat and brushed at the cobweb until it unraveled. It was going to take hours if not days to find the dungeon.

Then he smelled it — a luxurious, chocolate aroma. It hit him suddenly, like it had just burst open the box it was sealed in. It came from behind. He turned back and felt around with his hands until he found a second passage at the foot of the staircase. He followed it. The smell got stronger. Thankfully, there was a wide line of light streaming through a gap in the stonework up ahead. There were voices.

"The proof of my innocence!" came a muffled cry from the other side of the wall. Guster pressed his face up to the gap. It was just wide enough to see through. Instead of a hallway, he was looking out onto a spacious sitting room. There were couches and tapestries of blue and gold. A bright chandelier hung from the ceiling, an elegant grand piano sat in one corner, and a fire burned in a fireplace on the opposite wall.

Palatus was there, flanked by two Budless. Felicity and Mom were at the back of the room, guarded by two Gastronimatii. It was Felicity who had spoken; she strained against the ropes, trying to get at the source of the smell that had lured Guster there: a silver platter full of thick, dark, chocolate bricks.

The Arrivederci Chocolate. The final ingredient. Guster wanted to reach out, to touch it with his own hands. He'd never smelled anything so strong. It had been so long since he had anything to eat. If only he could break down these stones!

Guster slid his shirt over his nose. *I mustn't think like that. I have to concentrate*. The Gastronomy of Peace was so close. The cure that was supposed to save him. It was strange how it didn't matter now. He would give it all up in a second if he could just take Mariah, Zeke, Henry Junior and Mom home safely with him right now.

The man with the pencil-thin tie entered the room from an open corridor. Two Gastronimatii held Mariah and Henry Junior captive behind him. All the Gastronimatii were masked.

"Mariah!" shouted Mom, straining against the ropes that held her.

"Hello Benjamin," Felicity said coolly to the man.

"Hello Felicity," he said.

"I never picked you for a traitor."

"You know this man?" asked Mom.

"Of course. I give you Benjamin Arnold, former Chief Public Relations Officer for Casa Brand Industries."

"I beg to differ," said Benjamin, "I still hold my position. You, on the other hand, are the one who is no longer president there. The board overruled you as soon as they heard of your arrest, remember?"

"You planted that chocolate in my office, didn't you?"

Benjamin gave an innocent shrug, "Me?"

"You alone would be foolish enough to store chocolate in a refrigerator instead of a cool, dark place! That ruins it! When the SWAT team came crashing through my office window, they knew right where to look. Haven't you learned anything from my shows?"

"Never watched a one."

Felicity scoffed. "And you think this is all worth it, to fraternize with this murderous cult!"

"Be their agenda what it may," yawned Benjamin. "I never understood the nature of these silly games. They offered me the right price: power and riches — something you never would have given me. All so I'd frame you to get their chief competitor for this recipe thing out of the way."

Guster shifted himself to see if he could get a better look at Felicity's face. So she *was* innocent. The Arrivederci Chocolate in the hands of the Gastronimatii was proof enough of that.

Palatus turned to the short skinny chef from the courtyard. "Uvula!" he said, "Yours are the most disciplined chefs. When zee housewife has completed zee One Recipe, I need your men to study it carefully. Then you'll get your chance."

Benjamin Arnold shook his head. "I'll never understand the great lengths you go to, just for some dessert. It all seems like a bunch of snobbery, if you ask me."

Palatus sneered. "You don't need to understand. You've been compensated enough." He motioned toward Mariah. "Throw the girl and the baby into the dungeon with the rest of the prisoners."

The Gastronimatii closest to Mariah yanked her by the arm back out of the room. Henry Junior wailed like an ambulance's siren that faded as they forced him down the hall. Mom stiffened her lip. Guster could tell she was trying to be brave.

"And the boy?" asked Benjamin.

"He cannot resist the lure of perfection," said Palatus. "There are guards scouring the castle as we speak. They will either capture him, or he'll surrender from desire. The Harbinger of Peace will fulfill his duty."

That's what he thinks, thought Guster. He wasn't going to give in to Palatus. He'd eat mud first if he had to. And yet, Palatus seemed so certain of what Guster would do.

"No," said Mom. She folded her arms across her chest.

Palatus looked taken aback. "No, what?" asked the Arch-Gourmand.

"I will not make it," said Mom defiantly.

It was hard to tell who looked more shocked, Palatus or Felicity. Then Palatus began to boil inside, like he'd never even considered the possibility of being disobeyed. He lowered his eyebrows in a poisonous stare.

Mom stared back, her round face hardened. He seemed like he was waiting for her to break. She did not flinch.

"You would let the wars of the earth continue to rage? You would deny humanity its peace?" said Palatus. Mom clenched her teeth. She did not budge.

"And what about your son? How long do you think he can bear to live without it?"

Guster wanted to call out to her. He wanted to leap from his hiding place and tell her that he didn't care anymore, that she didn't have to do it for him.

It was too late. Mom's eyes dropped to the floor. He could tell Palatus' words had hit their mark.

Palatus clapped a metal dome triumphantly over the plate of chocolate. "Take the ingredients to the kitchen; we begin at once!" The Budless opened a heavy wooden door on iron hinges. One of them took the platter of chocolate, the other the ice chest, and like pall bearers marched them inside.

The guards shoved Felicity and Mom through the door behind them. Palatus stopped Uvula before he could enter. "Not until *after*," he said. Uvula and his men turned reluctantly away.

Mom took one glance back toward the hall where Mariah had gone. It took two Gastronimatii to shove the door shut. Then they were gone from Guster's view.

"Don't let them out until they are finished," Palatus commanded the guard who took up position in front of the door.

Guster slid to the floor. He'd never felt so weak and small — a real 'Capital P'. What good was he against hundreds of Gastronimatii? He had to follow Mom; he couldn't leave her alone.

He felt his way along the stone. The passage wasn't exactly going in the right direction — it veered off too much left, but it was his best shot.

The ceiling got lower as he went, until it dead-ended in a hole that was only as high as his waist. A faint glow low and to his right caught his attention. As near as he could tell, it was coming from the general direction they'd taken Mom. He crawled through the hole.

The tunnel was low, so he had to stay on his hands and knees to keep his back from scraping the ceiling. At the end, the glow got brighter. As Guster crawled closer, he instantly recognized the source — another tiny door covering a set of eyeholes.

When he got to the end he stood up carefully — he mustn't be heard. The tunnel dead ended in a room the size of a phone booth. On the same wooden wall as the eyeholes were three rusty hinges.

Judging by the size of the room and the way the hinges were fastened, he was standing behind a secret door that swung outward, hidden by a portrait on the other side.

He heard the muffled arguing even before he'd slid the tiny door covering the eyeholes open. Sure enough, it sounded like Mom so he pressed his eyes against the holes to get a better look.

On the other side was a spacious tiled room with gleaming countertops, brass sinks, dark wooden cutting boards, and silvery pots and pans hanging from the ceiling. A huge bronze oven stood in the center of the wall on the left. Two yellow, blue and red stained-glass windows made up the far wall that faced the courtyard. Every bit of wooden trim was ornately carved. Every tile was polished like marble.

Felicity's secret, state-of-the-art kitchen. Guster didn't care much about cookware or home decorating, but the way it gleamed and shined, it was like it had been carved from a pearl. Had circumstances been different, this would have been Mom's dream come true.

"How long have you known about this?" demanded Mom. She stared at Felicity with the hot fury he'd only seen her use on Zeke.

Felicity kept her cool. "Ever since I saw the eggbeater in Prison."

"And you didn't tell us?"

"Would it have made a difference? When you started out on this journey, who did you think would make the recipe?" asked Felicity.

"I…I don't know," said Mom. "But when we met up with you, I guess I thought that you would. You're the Celebrity Homemaker. You're the gourmet. You are FELICITY CASA! I shouldn't be the one to make this. I can't cook like you can."

"I would make it if I could," growled Felicity. She looked frustrated, like something had been taken from her.

"Then why don't you?" said Mom.

Felicity snatched the eggbeater from Mom, gripping it in her fist. "Because, roughly translated, the last few lines of the recipe say this: '*Mixed not by the hand that pleases for wealth, but by the hand that nourishes for life; Confirmed by the tongue of the Harbinger of Peace*,'" Felicity recited.

Mom looked blankly at her. "So? What does that mean?"

"I cook for money. It means I don't qualify. Neither does Palatus. In fact, there is only one person in this castle who does. 'The hand that nourishes for life.' That's what the last line of the recipe means: only a mother can make this soufflé."

Mom pressed her hand to her bun. She looked overwhelmed, like every danger they'd faced since leaving the farm had all come crashing down on her at once.

"If we don't follow Archedentus' instructions exactly, the soufflé could fall, and the ingredients would be wasted. Palatus doesn't want to risk that. And frankly, neither do I."

Mom looked incredulous. "You think this Archedentus is some kind of saint."

Felicity nodded her head. "He's as close as they come."

"But all this time you knew!" shouted Mom. "You came after Guster and I so you could get us to make this!"

Guster felt himself boil. Mom was — no, both of them were — pawns in Felicity's game. Everything she'd told the Lieutenant in the jungle now made sense.

Mom shook. It wasn't anger this time. It looked like anxiety. "By now Guster is far away," she said. She smoothed her blue apron with her hands. She stared at the oven. "And I've never actually made soufflé before," she said quietly.

"You've seen my program. You have the recipe. I'll show you how to do the rest."

After a long while, Mom nodded. She crossed the kitchen toward the Budless — she looked like an ant compared to the two giants — and took the silver platter with the chocolate on it back to the counter. They did not protest. She did the same with the ice chest.

"I'll set up for you," Felicity said, throwing open a pair of cupboard doors behind her head and retrieving a stainless steel mixing bowl. She set it on the counter in the middle of the room, then whirled to the other side, where she turned the oven on. She grabbed wire whisks, glass bowls, and little scales from every corner of the kitchen and set them on the counter as she went.

Mom put the ingredients on the counter, one by one. Felicity held the egg beater and read off the instructions, translating them into English. "'The Fruit of the Fowl, sunshine and cloud,'" she said. Mom cracked the watermelon-sized egg open with a small mallet. Guster could smell the meaty sunshine of the yolk burst into the air of the kitchen as soon as she broke the shell. It had been so long since he'd eaten that egg plucked fresh from the tree in the orchard at Machu Picchu. Too long.

"Split the egg whites from the yolks carefully. You mustn't break either one too soon."

Her hands shaking, Mom poured the contents of the egg into a gigantic bowl. She stopped to steady herself before separating the egg yolk from the egg white. He'd never seen her more nervous.

"And then 'Twenty-one shekels of the Buttersmith's Gold.'"

"What's a shekel?" asked Mom.

"Here, use this," said Felicity handing her a small balancing scale. "Scoop it out of the barrel, weigh it, then melt it on the stove," said Felicity. Mom opened the barrel of butter and carefully weighed several spoonfuls. Guster could almost smell the sweet crispness of the clover.

Felicity turned on the range next to the big bronze oven. Mom put the butter in a pan. "Stir it once, then three times the opposite direction."

Mom stirred. "The *opposite* direction," snapped Felicity. "It has to be perfect." Mom stirred the other way.

"'Fifteen and a half Shekels of The Mighty Apes' Diamonds'," said Felicity. "Crush the nuggets up into granules the size of Saharan sand." Mom unscrewed the jar, and with a bowl and a porcelain grinder, she broke up the diamonds. "Not too fine!" said Felicity. Mom stopped crushing.

"I'm not sure I can do this," she said.

Felicity gripped the countertop with both hands. "Mabel, if you do not, you may never see your children again."

"And if I do, I'm not sure I will either," she said. She closed her eyes, "Guster," she said.

She measured out fifteen and a half shekels of sugar-diamonds on the scale and set them aside.

She cut off chunks of the Dark Milk Bricks from Arrivederci's Bean. She measured those on the scale, then put them in a pot on the range to melt.

"'Beat the cloud of the fowl to soft, white peaks,'" read Felicity. She took an electric mixer from the cupboard below. "Here," she said, handing it to Mom.

Mom shoved it away. She reached over and grabbed the eggbeater from Felicity instead. “This one seems more fitting.” Felicity’s lips curved; it was almost a smile.

Mom turned the crank of the eggbeater, mixing the egg whites into a frothy foam. She added sugar bit by bit to the mixture. “Good,” said Felicity when she was done. Mom set the eggbeater down, rushed to the stove and removed the butter from the heat.

She continued to move pans here and there as she mixed this and that, then buttered the surface of seven small, white cup-like dishes. She squeezed out seven generous drops of the Sweet, Black Tears into a mixture of yolk, whites, sugar and chocolate, until finally, she had a bowl of thick, dark, foamy mixture. She poured it evenly into the seven dishes.

The smell soaked through the eyeholes of the portrait into Guster’s nostrils. He had never imagined the combined ingredients could be so perfect. He had never imagined he would want something so badly. He wanted to jump from his hiding place and drink it up, but he couldn’t; he knew he mustn’t — not with the Budless standing guard. Not with the Gastronimatii swarming the castle, waiting to pounce. *Control*, thought Guster. He bit his lip.

Mom, moving a bit more slowly now, donned a pair of oven mitts, opened the oven, and pushed the dishes inside, one by one. She closed the oven door. Mom had come this far — he hoped she’d done it right.

“There,” she said in a honey-covered voice, dusting off her butter-covered apron. “Oh, I do feel quite relaxed now.”

“A job well done will do that,” chimed Felicity. It wasn’t something Guster expected her to say. Perhaps, since her soufflé was finally in the oven and the One Recipe was at her fingertips she was lightening up. Either way, it was about time.

But then again, maybe Guster had been too hard on her. Maybe she wasn't so bad after all. There was no time for grudges with such a wonderful smell in the room.

"In so many ways, I envy you," said Felicity. She looked different, like someone who'd just woken up, or was home from a long vacation; her shoulders slumped and there was a grin smeared across her perfect face.

"Oh?" said Mom, leaning on the counter and resting her chin on her hand nonchalantly. They were all acting so… so comfortable.

"You've got a great job. As a housewife I mean." Mom looked puzzled, but happy. "You know, with Mariah, Zeke, Henry Junior." It was the first time Guster had heard Felicity use their names.

"But I've never been on TV," Mom said cooing, like she did with Henry Junior. "You have one of the highest-rated shows in television history. You've served dinners at the Whitehouse! You have millions of fans and an empire that spans the globe!" It was like she was talking to her old hero again.

Guster wished Mariah was there to interpret — was this something women always did when they cooked?

"None of that matters! Haven't you noticed?" said Felicity, smiling intently, the first hint of warm soufflé rising out of the oven. Oh it was glorious.

She grasped Mom by the arms and looked her in the eyes. "I don't have children like you do. I may have millions of fans, but it was the best I could do. To them, I'm a mere hobby — a passing thought. For all the success I've attained, I have never shaped four lives as deeply nor as permanently as you have the lives of your children.

"It's the power of food — the power of the things that you feed them, day in and day out! I'm not talking about gourmet dishes. I'm not talking about exotic flavors, custards, tarts, or frilly sauces. I'm talking about life! Think about the rolls you've kneaded with your palms, the nuts you've sprinkled with your fingers, the cuts you've grated into your own skin without so much as crying out! You've made these children. They are you."

Mom looked startled at Felicity's words.

"Everyone running the world was once a child, Mabel, and you are shaping yours. 'Mixed not by the hand that pleases for wealth, but by the hand that nourishes for life' Like it says! Only a mother could make this soufflé," said Felicity.

Mom leaned back on the countertop. She looked like she'd only thought about that just now, for the first time. "That's kind of you," she said. "And perhaps, well, maybe you are quite right."

The smell grew stronger — not like before. Not like anything Guster ever knew.

"I do wonder if everything in the end will turn out alright here," said Mom.

"Perhaps. Perhaps not," said Felicity nonchalantly. She looked straight up at Guster. "Archedentus, you ol' trickster. This was all very clever of you. Very clever."

Guster held his breath. She'd looked him right in the eyes; did she know he was there?

He nearly choked when he breathed again. It was like the Patisserie back in New Orleans had baked all its treats at once — no, that did not do it justice. It was like the baked goods of the ages from the creation of the earth to the very end had all combined in one buttery sweetness.

Then there was a scuffling noise. The faint sound of scraping on stone somewhere way back in the tunnels behind him. Had the

Gastronimatii found their way into the tunnels? Were they searching for him? Somehow, it didn't matter.

Felicity dusted off her hands. "Well, we have a few minutes before our doom," she said, taking a seat next to Mom. Mom swung her head back and forth, like she was listening to a melody only she could hear; it was like she was in a dream just like Guster had been at the pillar of sugar-diamonds. He didn't realize until now how silly he must have looked. *It's controlling her*, he thought.

Did it matter though? Maybe Mom was right. Maybe everything would turn out alright. Certainly with such a delectable smell like that, there would be no harm in running out there right now and having a lick of the batter. He could use the secret door. *To test it before it's finished*, thought Guster.

Guster stomped on his own foot. *No*. He couldn't. He mustn't. Not with the Budless standing there. They would capture him in a heartbeat, and all would be lost. He had to wait for the right opportunity. He pulled his shirt up over his mouth and nose again.

"My dear Felicity, when should we take the soufflé from the oven?" said Mom.

"Oh, I don't know. A moment too soon, and the air bubbles inside the soufflé will burst, causing it to fall. A moment too late, and it will suffer the same fate. Either way, it will be a failure." Felicity looked like she was on the verge of giggling now too.

How could they say that? It couldn't fall. Right now it was the only thing in the world that mattered. *I have to snap out of it*, thought Guster. He couldn't let it get to him.

"Well, what do the instructions say?" asked Mom.

"'Be vigilant! Bake until it is time,'" read Felicity.

Mom rolled her eyes. "Until it is time? He tells us which direction to stir the melting butter, but won't tell us when to take it out of the oven? Silly ol' Archedentus couldn't get more specific than that?"

"Probably not. Soufflés are subtle. They are influenced by the whims of the oven! You will have to decide when the time is right."

Don't mess this up now! thought Guster. *Please Mom, just this once*! His hands were locked on the stone walls. A thin strand of drool fell from his lips.

"Should be any minute now," said Felicity.

Mom knelt next to the oven door and peered through it. Guster wished that he could see into the oven, but he couldn't from his vantage point behind the portrait. Mom flexed her hands, like a batter waiting for a pitch. "It's risen so nicely!" she said. "A few more seconds…"

Palatus burst into the room. The gray bandana was tied tightly around his face again. "Is it time?" he cried.

Mom held up her hand. She counted to herself silently, then said, "It's time."

Palatus gripped the countertop tightly, his knuckles white. "Bar the door," he said to the Budless. "No one gets through." The Budless closest to the door moved toward it and dropped a heavy wooden beam down, locking it off.

Mom opened the oven door. She reached inside, and swiftly, like she was setting the table back at the farm, pulled the seven dishes from the oven and set them on the countertop.

As soon as Mom opened the oven, the sweet aroma slammed into Guster like a wall of water. He fell to the ground, consumed by the smell. He bit his arm through his shirt, writhing, trying to gain control. He could not let Palatus discover him now. He was the only one left.

Concentrate. He put his face up to the eyeholes again. A firm, nearly cake-like substance, dark, rich and brown blossomed out of each of the seven dishes like bubbles of ambrosia.

He had never seen anything he wanted so badly in his whole life. It took all his energy to keep himself from bursting out of the hole and consuming all seven soufflés.

Felicity sat on the floor and held her knees, her face serene, a far off look in her eyes. Mom sat back on a stool, still facing the countertop, her hands quietly folded.

Palatus gripped the countertop ever harder, battling within himself, his eyes watering as he stared at the dish. His knuckles looked like they were about to snap. His ribs swelled in and out, like he was trying very hard to resist the soufflé even though the bandana masked the smell. "O, Delicious One," he whispered quietly, on the verge of tears.

Guster wedged himself between the stone walls. Whatever desire he had to taste it, Palatus' was worse. The soufflé was the master, the Arch-Gourmand its slave, willing to do its bidding, whatever it bade.

"I see that your Harbinger of Peace has not yet come to save you," Palatus said, mustering every bit of self-control he had. "No matter. In three minutes, the soufflé will fall. If he does not come, so be it. I will taste it before then, and you will all suffer the consequences. Even the smell that seeps through my mask cannot lie."

Was this what it meant to be an Evertaster? To be so obsessed with perfection you were enslaved by it? To be consumed by the Gastronomy of Peace —

That's when the noises in the tunnels behind him did not matter anymore. Neither the Budless, Palatus, nor the hordes of Gastronimatii. Guster knew what he had to do.

He shoved his shoulder against the stone wall, swinging the secret door slowly open. He stepped into the kitchen.

Chapter 23 — The Gastronomy of Peace

Guster's knees nearly buckled when his feet hit the kitchen floor. Despite the shirt pulled up over his nose, the smell of the One Recipe was so strong, it was like he was already tasting it.

Surprise washed across Palatus' face. "Aha!" he cried, "So zee boy 'as returned to face his ruin!" Palatus motioned to the large gray guards, "Seize him!"

The Budless charged; it was remarkable how immune to the smell they were. In that split second, Mom looked at Guster vacantly, like she had just finished a hot bath and was only mildly surprised to see him. She did not rush to help him; he'd almost expected that.

Guster held up his hands. "Stop!" he said.

For a moment the Budless faltered. "I said seize him!" cried Palatus. Only the counter in the middle of the kitchen and the seven dishes of soufflé stood between the two of them.

"You will not!" boomed Guster, trying his best to sound important. "I am the Harbinger of Peace. As decreed by the great chef Archedentus, I come to claim that first taste of the One Recipe which is rightfully mine!"

Palatus drew his knife and stabbed it into the wooden counter top. “Mmm!” he grunted. Everything was riding on Palatus’ loyalty to the recipe; for the moment, it seemed to be paying off.

The chef motioned to the Budless and they stood down. “Very well boy, go ahead, taste the One Recipe. Be the guinea pig in the experiment. Then, as soon as I see the effects, I will know that your simple mother has completed her task.”

There was movement — bodies on the other side of the kitchen window pressing up against it.

“That would be a delight, my dear son. You have a taste, and then we can all have some,” said Mom lazily.

“The rules say you have to go first,” Felicity said.

Guster was fighting to remain in control, to appear like he knew what he was doing. He had to keep his hands from reaching out, from grabbing the seven dishes.

“Casa, give the boy a spoon,” said Palatus.

“A spoon? Oh of course,” said Felicity. “I have just the one.” She reached into a drawer and pulled out a shiny, silver spoon with a handle twice as long as any normal spoon. She held it up to Guster between her thumb and forefinger.

Didn't she see the danger of the situation? The aroma of the kitchen was so pleasant he was rather glad he'd come, even with Palatus there, the threat of impending doom, and the Gastronimatii on the brink of triumph. Oh, it was such a happy kitchen to be in.

He pulled the shirt down from his nose. It was like dipping his face in water — only this water was the sweet smell of baked goodness. Was that Dark Milk Bricks he smelled, seeping into every crack in the walls, into every pore of his nostrils? He wanted to fall upon the source of that smell, get as close as possible to it, become one with it — to have it soak into his soft insides like cocoa washing over a cookie, filling all emptiness. It took him a moment before he realized that he'd stopped breathing.

Must control myself, he thought. He took the spoon from Felicity.

Palatus stared at him from across the counter, like he was about to leap, grinding his teeth together beneath the mask. "Well?" he said.

Guster held the spoon gently, resting it on his index finger like he was about to taste soup. He dipped it down into the dark soufflé. The silver tip pierced — no, slid gently through the mixture like it were freshly fallen snow. He turned the handle and brought a spoonful to his slightly open mouth.

Concentrate, he thought. *Cannot let it overwhelm me —*

He could taste it before it even touched his lips. A rolling chocolate cloud captured in a single moment in space. In an instant, the room vanished. He could not feel the floor beneath him, nor his fingertips, nor his legs. All things were as if they were nothing, except for the one thing — his mouth — the only remaining reality in the great void of the Universe; the only three inches that mattered. 28 teeth, a palette, the impressionable insides of his cheeks, and his tongue — his oh so vulnerable tongue.

And then it touched the first of his taste buds — they reached up to the coming tide of change — a porous mixture that was light, but real. A lingering touch that gripped them, embraced them in a warm, buttery sweetness that was so firm and layered, the bumps of his tongue welcomed it like delicious lava flowing across their backs.

And then there was nothing. No family in danger. No threat of Palatus. No kitchen. No castle. There was only the chocolate soufflé, and Guster's mouth, which had the sole purpose of tasting it.

Then the first wave of flavor, as remarkable as it was, transformed. It was a sunshine-lit peak overlooking a far-off jungle-scape. There were armies approaching, their spears aimed skyward, their drums beating, and the crisp smell of a new continent and the fresh fruits that it bore. High above the coming war, on the edge of a cliff, bloomed a golden blossom of new life, ambivalent to the turmoil below. It was delicate, wrapped in a clear elixir of life, protected in a shell where it ripened until it burst into the mixture in Guster's mouth.

And then there were gleaming clear bursts of light, popping through perfect harmony with the golden blossom, as sweet as can be, born in the depths of earth and ripened before the crust was ever torn by machines. Raised below human feet, forgotten for centuries, discovered again and crushed into powder, dissolved into a succulent mortar.

A hint, ever so slight, of a touch of something new — it wasn't the chocolate, it wasn't the sugar — it was sweet — and then it was gone.

Then there was a landscape where no pollutant could fester, purified by ice. A sudden soft warmth — slightly salty — all massaged and tender, a gift from a beast fed on pure greens watered straight from heaven. The soft warmth melted the others together, so that no one sensation sang alone, but all found their voices together.

Then there was the chocolate, made by the hand of a master. Just bitter enough to tell the truth of itself; but smooth as it did so, a soothing friend bearing up his soul.

And then all the tastes were one, something entirely new, no longer individual trees, but a forest. No longer single voices, but a chorus. No longer words, but a poem. And Guster forgot them all because something entirely new and as pure and complete as any element had come into his mind and taken hold of his heart: soufflé.

Rich. Dark. Soft as a summer's morning.

How could he have lived without tasting this before?

He was flying — floating — looking down on the earth, a blue speck growing smaller in the distance. There he was, drifting in an empty universe with the taste of that soufflé being the only tangible thing that existed or ever needed to exist. Everything else grew meaningless. Nothing else mattered. Not the rest of the world. Not himself. Not danger. Not his family. He did not care if he lived or died. The world could destroy itself if it wanted. He only wanted to stay in this moment forever — when suddenly the scene changed.

He was standing at the back of a chateau, much like the Chateau de Dîner, but the trees and grounds and colors were different. There were wisps of dandelion floating on the summer air. The light shone thickly, coating the manicured trees and carved stonework and glinting off the lake at the back of the porch. He could not tell what century it was, nor could he tell if it was late in the afternoon or late in the morning; the air and sun both felt like they were moving on to somewhere new and leaving the old behind. The day was perfect.

He leaned himself up against the stone banister at the back of the porch. The soufflé rested atop it at chest level, the silver spoon protruding from it like a sword in stone.

"Why don't you take another bite?" said a voice.

Guster turned his head. Standing there, like he'd been there from the beginning, was a chef clothed in white chef's jacket, hat, and apron. His hair was black, and his skin olive. His face was smooth, as if a hair had never grown upon it. He had a pleasant quality about him, like a man who'd lived as he knew he should, and wanted to allow others the same privilege. In an instant, Guster knew who he was.

"I want to very badly," Guster said.

"How badly?" asked the chef expectantly. Somehow, even his presence soothed Guster.

"More than I think I've ever wanted anything."

The old Chef smiled. "I suppose I did alright then," he said, chuckling to himself. "I'd always wondered how it would turn out."

Alright? That was a funny word to use, considering that Guster's body cried out to him, each particle of his being calling out like a massive crowd begging for one thing and one thing only, promising to crown him king and pledge their devotion if he would give them but one more taste.

Guster clenched his hands behind his back. It took all the willpower he had not to take hold of the spoon again. He must not — not yet. He needed to know something first. He struggled to concentrate on forming the words. Before he could, the chef spoke again.

"Are you at peace?"

Guster smiled. Yes, he was. Very much so. He couldn't remember what he'd been so worried about before he'd taken that bite, before his world became perfect. He nodded. He could hear the beat of the hummingbirds' wings.

"Then?" said the chef, lifting one eyebrow.

Then Guster knew what he wanted to ask. "It won't kill me?"

Archedentus laughed. "Kill you? My friend, you can't be serious! It is a dessert! It would give you things you cannot imagine."

Guster's last worry slid away. It was as he dreamed. He melted into the beautiful day.

"You feel a little like them, don't you?" asked Archedentus. He pointed to the lawns below the porch. Dozens of men and women milled about dressed in fine suits and gowns, hair piled high in ringlets, layers of collars blossoming from their jackets. They lounged on benches or stood by the lake shores. Some were laughing, others strumming tiny guitars. One of the men wore a well-tailored pale yellow coat. He flicked droplets of lake water at one of the pretty ladies standing nearby. She giggled and turned away. They looked like they had been picnicking for quite a long time.

They all had one thing in common: beside each of them was a small white ramekin filled with a rich, dark soufflé and a silver spoon protruding from it.

It seemed to Guster like they'd always been there, though he was certain that he hadn't seen them before.

Two boys about Guster's age ran from the woods and jumped onto a swing that swung them out high over the lake and back.

"They love it here. You could stay with them," said Archedentus.

It was inviting. A place free of danger. A place where he could pass the hours skipping rocks on the lake, or lie on his back staring at the shapes in the clouds. A place where he was finally free to taste without pain. To feel the soothing sensations slide across his tongue. Was this what it was like for everyone else all the time? To eat without agony? It was how he'd always wished it could be.

A memory struggled to the surface. A far off place. The Farmhouse — that's what they'd called it — a place where he had wished for such a taste. Where he had struggled to find it. There had been people there. Someone named Zeke. And Mom. Now it all seemed so far away.

"What about my family?" Guster asked.

Archedentus shrugged. "Guster, you've done that thing which I dared not do. You could go back, but is this not the soufflé for which you have searched across the world?"

Guster thought for a moment. He wasn't sure how to answer. "It is," he said, "and it is as wonderful as I hoped."

"Yet I see that you have not yet finished it."

"If only I could have both," said Guster.

"And if you can't?"

Guster was quiet. "I don't know." He touched the silver spoon lightly, holding his fingertips on the edge of its handle for a long time. He remembered the pain. "Does this mean that, if I go back, that… that I won't be cured?"

Archedentus' face lost all expression.

It was frustrating: the soufflé on one hand, Guster's family and the world he knew on the other. Why should it be a choice? If only they could taste it. First Mom, then Zeke, Mariah, Henry Junior, the Lieutenant, and Felicity. And then his own town, his country — everyone. If only everyone could feel the joy he did. He could give it to Palatus and the Gastronimatii. Just like that, their war would be over. Guster spoke, "You never made it."

The chef looked far away, as if he were staring at something beyond the horizon. "I would have, if only they had been ready for it."

The lake, the grounds, the people and the chateau disappeared as the scene changed before Guster's eyes once again.

There was an orchard far larger than the one on Machu Picchu, or any Guster had ever seen, white eggs gleaming like pearls as far as the eye could see. There was an army of men dressed in red aprons, tending to the trees like masters over slaves, harvesting the fruit, sending it away by the bushelful.

Then in a blink, Guster was underground, surrounded by glistening pillars of diamond sugar. The Budless were there, huge and draped in gray rags, driving their pick axes into the rock, mining nuggets of precious sugar-ore and piling them into mine carts, then pushing them away on tracks that crisscrossed the caverns.

Another blink, and Guster was on a familiar island, hundreds of the Budless arriving on its shores. They surrounded the herds of cows that grazed there, and drove them with whips toward the sea where they beat them until they gave up their butter. Two giant men with beards and horned helmets struggled against the chains that bound them while Palatus looked on.

Again the scene changed, this time Palatus was bowing before a king, presenting him with a gift. It was like a dream. Guster could not hear what was said, but he did not need to; he could feel their intentions. They ate. They were pleased, and they granted Palatus his wish.

Then there was a parliament chamber filled with statesmen contending against each other, malice in their words as they debated the fate of the nations. Palatus entered, his face masked, an army of red chefs spilling through the doors, serving gifts of chocolate soufflé to the legislators. One by one they ate, and one by one their anger toward each other melted away; they shook hands in reconciliation.

Then there were people filling the streets of the great metropolises, waiting for just one sniff, if not a taste of the soufflé. Palatus gave it to them. The horns stopped honking. Angry voices turned to whispers. Children ceased to bully. Fathers praised their neglected sons. Corporate men embraced the humble homeless, and the homeless cleaned the streets on which they'd slept.

There was happiness, there was laughter, there was serenity. There were soldiers discarding their weapons, engineers dismantling the tanks and the bombers, admirals turning their battleships for home, and generals signing treaties with one another.

The world unfolded below him, people everywhere eating the soufflé, enraptured in the same joy and ecstasy he felt. There were billions embracing each other, filled with love, bowing down to the dessert that had changed their lives. They wanted nothing more. They would live only for that. They were at peace.

The battle was finally over. He would never fight again! He could taste!

And then there was Palatus giving a mighty minister of a nation a buttery Hollandaise sauce that plugged his arteries in one night, and he was dead.

Then Palatus seized the food of the nations by force, grocer by grocer, farm by farm, factory by factory.

There was no one to oppose him — the people were so busy with their soufflés. They would not — they could not — stop tasting their peace. Like a black plague, starvation spread.

The bombs fell from the sky again, seasoning the land with destruction. Palatus stood on the head of a gray mountain, a pile of discarded ramekins at his feet, bleached white like skulls, as he overlooked the plains and his armies advanced and the fields burned and the people starved to death. But none would oppose him, for they had their peace.

"No!" shouted Guster. He was back at the porch of the chateau again. He was exhausted — he'd somehow managed to realize his nightmare wasn't real while he was having it — but he was still in a dream.

"That isn't the way it has to be!" Guster shouted. "I could do this! It could be different. I am the Harbinger of Peace."

"And even if you did, even if you somehow were different, would everyone respect the peace you had made? Would everyone allow it?" asked Archedentus. "Whose version of peace will it be Guster? Palatus'? Mine? Guster Johnsonville's?"

Archedentus' face fell. "I too, had the hopes you did."

For a moment, the gray head of the mountain overlooking the plains flashed into Guster's view again. He watched in horror. This time, instead of Palatus, Archedentus stood triumphant, a pile of ramekins at *his* feet, as he overlooked the plains and the fields burned.

Then it flashed again, this time Mom stood on the gray mountain, rolling pin in hand, the world below her neat and tidy, every last human starting his chores and minding his manners.

Then another flash, and Zeke stood on top, the plains below covered in hot rod cars and rock and roll.

Then there was another, and Felicity stood there, a perfectly manicured, embroidered landscape of art and craft spread below her.

The visions melted away. Guster was trembling.

Finally, he understood. It all made sense now, though he did not want it to. "So that's why you walked away," he said.

Archedentus shrugged his shoulders. "It's just a soufflé, not a casserole!" he said, forcing a chuckle.

Casserole, thought Guster. Like Mom used to make. The Farmhouse.

For the first time since tasting the soufflé, Guster's thoughts turned back to the kitchen where Mom stood waiting, and the threat of Palatus lurked nearby. A new flavor unfolded at the back of his throat. It was more salty than sweet, but it was familiar. It tasted like home. It was something he had not yet perceived in the soufflé that day — ingredients touched by his mother's hands. He wanted more of it.

"What should I do?" asked Guster. He felt hot tears pressing up against his eyes. If he *did* finish the soufflé, he knew what the outcome would be. Seeing Palatus on the mountaintop made that clear enough.

"My time has passed. That is for you to decide," said Archedentus.

Guster's throat suddenly felt heavy. He coughed back the tears, but they came anyway. There he was, with the wisest chef of all time, and now Archedentus was leaving the decision up to him? He searched for the slightest hint of what to do in Archedentus' face. There was none.

Besides, Guster knew as soon as he'd stepped out of the safety of that secret passageway into the kitchen, this was a choice he was going to have to make alone, and no matter what that meant, he would do the right thing.

An insect buzzed from somewhere in the bushes. "Well?" said Archedentus, holding both hands, palms up, toward the soufflé.

Guster closed his eyes tight and shook his head. "Thank you, but no," he said, and pushed the soufflé away from him. The ramekin ground across the stone, the spoon still sticking straight out of the dish, only one of so many succulent bites eaten. Guster turned his back to the remaining dessert.

Archedentus nodded, "You've made your choice then?" he said.

"Yes," Guster forced the word from his lungs.

Though Archedentus frowned, Guster thought he saw the faintest trace of a smile in the old chef's eyes. "Then my work here is done," he said.

"Will I ever see you again?" asked Guster.

"I suppose that depends on what other choices you make."

It was a strange statement, but so was most of the encounter.

"Look!" Archedentus pointed to the far side of the lake where the sun had dipped below the horizon and the first shades of evening approached.

"I don't see anything," said Guster, looking out over the horizon. When he turned back, the chef was gone.

Then there was a flash of light as something exploded where Archedentus had pointed. Guster whirled around. In the distance, cannons boomed and muskets fired. An army approached, marching around either side of the lake toward the lawn where the people sat.

"What's that?" said the man in the pale yellow coat.

"Some fellows come to see things over here," said a man lying on a stone bench. He barely raised his head.

"What do you suppose they want?" asked the first, as he shoved another spoonful of soufflé in his mouth.

"Oh, surely just to have a look," said the man on the bench. *Why don't they run*? thought Guster.

"Ah. Well that's nice. That's just nice," said the first, licking his spoon.

The scene erupted in a violent volley of musket fire, then faded from Guster's view.

Gradually, he felt his hands gripping the countertop in the castle kitchen once more. Guster opened his eyes. The first thing he saw was his mother standing next to the wall, looking content.

Palatus stared across the counter at Guster, ready to pounce, his teeth bared like a tiger, his hands clawing the countertop. "Well?" he said.

Guster casually tossed the silver spoon onto the countertop, the remainder of his soufflé untouched. "Needs salt," he said, shrugging his shoulders.

Palatus drew himself up to his full height. "Impossible! I do not believe you! I can smell it myself!" he screamed.

Guster grimaced. "You can have it. I don't want the rest," he said, pushing the soufflé away from him.

Palatus roared. "You lie!" he said, tearing the mask from his mouth and nose. As soon as he did so, his eyes flashed red. He bore his teeth and drool foamed down his chin. Like a wolf, mad with the smell of blood, he dove onto the countertop, his arms outstretched, reaching for Guster's unfinished soufflé.

Guster was quicker. He snatched the ramekin out from under Palatus' fingers, and hurled it over the Chef-in-Red to the closed kitchen window, where it smashed through the glass.

Palatus watched it sail over his head. "You 'ave disgraced zee Gastronomy of Peace!" he hissed.

Moans of delight came from outside the shattered window as the potent smell of the kitchen rolled into the courtyard. "It's here!" cried one voice.

"I want it!" said another.

"The rapture!"

"Parfait!"

"The ecstasy!"

Guster heard a striking sound, then a shriek of pain, followed by violent blows. "More!" shouted a chef. Suddenly what was left of the window shattered into tiny shards as dozens of bodies cloaked in red, their mouths open wide, burst into the kitchen, knocking over the Budless as they came.

For the first time, Guster saw fear on the wicked chef's face. "What 'ave you done, boy?!" Palatus cried, and turned to look behind him.

In that instant, as the Gastronimatii streamed down upon him, Guster kicked down with the back of his heel, opening the oven door, and swept all six of the remaining soufflé dishes into the still-burning oven. The dishes spilled over, the six remaining soufflés dumping all over the molten metal rack and walls of the oven.

The Gastronimatii shoved and scrambled over each other, their faces bleeding from the broken glass, gouging each other's eyes, elbowing each other in the face, fighting to be the first to reach the oven. Some stopped as they crossed the windowsill, hit by an invisible force, zombies transfixed by a tangible aroma.

A pair of them leapt onto the counter, treading across Palatus' back with their feet.

"Scavenger!" Palatus screamed at Guster. He winced in pain as more Gastronimatii trampled across him on their way to the oven.

To Guster's horror, the first of the Gastronimatii did not stop when he reached the open oven, but shoved his head inside, licking what was left of the soufflé as it clung to the burning walls. He cried out in pain, recoiling, then tried to taste it again as another chef leapt over him and shoved his head inside as well.

Guster grabbed Mom's and Felicity's hands and pulled them toward the kitchen door. He side-stepped the Budless who were crawling on the floor, and led his Mother and Felicity upstream, doing his best to dodge the swarm.

As they reached the kitchen door, more Gastronimatii streamed past them from the window to the oven. Guster heaved up against the heavy wooden beam that barred the door, trying to wrench it free. It stuck fast.

"Help me!" he cried to Mom. She looked like she was daydreaming. "Mom!" cried Guster.

"Oh! My!" she said, snapping from her hypnotic state. She set her shoulder below the wooden beam, and together with Guster, the two of them heaved it free. They pushed open the door and ran from the kitchen, leaving the brawl behind them.

They ran down the castle corridor, Felicity becoming more alert with every step, like she was waking up from a nap. "This way, to the dungeons," she said. They turned right down a corridor and descended a steep, winding stairway. At the bottom, Felicity kicked open the door.

The dungeon was dark and damp, a row of barred cells lining either side of a long room. A single Gastronimatii stood guard near the open door. Felicity punched him hard in the face and he dropped to the ground.

"I think I'm in love," said Zeke from behind the bars. Mariah was there too, with Henry Junior in her arms.

Mom grabbed a ring of rusty iron keys that hung on the wall and opened the cell, freeing her children. They rushed to her and hugged her.

Felicity took the keys and opened the other cells one by one, until there were more than twenty of her mercenaries free and standing at attention.

"Lieutenant, there's a stash of weapons hidden on the second floor. Let's re-secure the estate," she said. The Lieutenant saluted her. He charged up the steps and out of the dungeon, the entire force marching behind him. Shouts and crashing followed.

Guster felt himself collapse on a bench next to one of the cells. He shook his head, trying to clear it. Suddenly, he realized just how very, very tired he was.

Chapter 24 — The Farmhouse

One half hour later, Guster woke as Mom gently shook him. He had fallen asleep on a soft couch next to a suit of armor in one of the sitting rooms in the castle. Zeke snored on the couch next to Guster, while Mariah sat dozing in a chair. Felicity had told them to wait there. Not long after, the Lieutenant returned.

He saluted Felicity. “The Gastronimatii are all in custody!” he reported. There was a rifle strapped to his back.

Guster opened his eyes. He was too tired to move, but wanted to hear what had happened.

“It was easy enough to overwhelm them in their frenzied state,” said the Lieutenant. “It wasn’t much of a scuffle at all. They had nearly destroyed themselves fighting over a chance to lick that oven.” Guster felt nauseous at the memory.

“We have them all locked away in the dungeon, and Interpol is on their way. Apparently they‘ve been tracking the Cult of Gastronimatii for some time now.”

“And Palatus?” asked Felicity.

“Gone. If we’re lucky, he didn’t survive the trampling. There was nothing left but the shredded remains of his apron.”

Guster winced. He was glad he hadn’t been there to see it.

"By his own Cult —" said Felicity to herself. She shook her head. "Lieutenant, prepare the vehicles and have my jet waiting at the airport. Have the same done for the Johnsonvilles." She sighed. "It's time we headed home."

The Lieutenant saluted, turned on his heel, and left the room.

Guster pushed himself slowly up from the couch and stretched his tired bones. Zeke had woken up and was hovering nearby like he'd been watching over Guster. Zeke bit his lip like he wanted to say something, but didn't.

"Hey Zeke," said Guster.

"Hey." said Zeke. He hesitated. "So… are you cured?" he asked, scratching the back of his head.

Guster shook his head. He tried to fight back the tears. "I didn't finish it," he said, looking at his cowboy boots. He'd missed his chance.

"You're awake," said Felicity, turning to Guster.

Her stern tone had returned. The light-hearted Felicity from the kitchen was gone. "You threw it away," she said. She did not seem pleased. Nor was she entirely angry. He couldn't tell what she meant by that.

He *knew* that he'd made the right choice, but how was he going to explain that to the rest of humanity? A weight pressed down on his heart. He felt his face get hot.

"The soufflé to end all war," she said. Her eyes were full of fire — and to a certain extent — understanding. "You saw the danger in that when no one else could."

Guster remembered the look of sadness on Archedentus' face. He knew they had both done the best they could.

"What did it taste like?" she asked. She looked pained, like a prisoner asking how freedom felt.

Guster thought for a moment. There was only one way to describe it in words. “Like a story,” he said. “A true one.”

Felicity smiled, longing behind her eyes. It lingered for a moment, then fled from her face. “We found your Aunt. She called a cab as soon as we set her free. She’s probably at the airport by now,” she said. “Better wake your siblings. It will be time to go soon.”

“Wait,” said Guster. “There’s one more thing I need to do.”

“You want to see the kitchen before you go, don’t you?” she said. He nodded. “I’ll take you there.”

Guster forced himself to stand. Felicity led him through the long castle hallway, past several suits of armor, and back to the heavy wooden door. It was still open, the beam that barred it tossed aside where Guster and Mom had heaved it.

Felicity stood back and let Guster enter alone. The kitchen was in ruins, like it had been torn apart by a tornado, then smashed to bits by a raging bull. The counter in the middle had been dented and smashed until the legs underneath it collapsed. The drawers and cupboard doors were ripped from the cabinets, and the floor was strewn with red shredded apron. Pots, pans, and utensils were thrown everywhere. The oven itself was dismantled, every last strip of metal and bolt torn apart and licked clean. Only a gaping hole and the bolts that had held it to the floor were left where it once stood.

Guster picked his way carefully through the wreckage. There, under a fallen cabinet door, he spotted the carved wooden handle of the eggbeater, right where Mom and Felicity had left it. Guster kicked aside the cabinet door and lifted it from the wreckage.

As he did, he looked up at the wall where the secret passage opened into the kitchen. Someone had closed the painting over the hole again, so that the passage was covered. Guster had not been able to see the face painted on the portrait before since his back had been turned to it. His heart flipped inside him.

On the canvas, framed in gold, was a tall, olive-skinned man with a sharp nose and a smooth face. He wore a white cap and a white jacket. A nearly imperceptible smile graced his lips. In the crook of one elbow he held a bundle of brown wheat. In the other, an olive branch.

No wonder Felicity had been addressing Archedentus while Guster was hiding in the passage. The man in the portrait was him — the very same chef Guster had seen and spoken with on the back porch of that old chateau. Just like the one he'd imagined while under the influence of the Gastronomy of Peace.

"Do you realize you've dismantled a centuries-old secret society?" said Felicity.

Guster shrugged his shoulders. He didn't think he could take credit for that.

"They won't be searching for the One Recipe again. They'll be in jail soon, and if they ever did achieve their freedom, they would never be able to taste again anyway, not after what they've done to their tongues. They'd be lucky if they could tell the difference between a rotting pickle and cube of sugar."

Guster tucked the eggbeater under his arm. Felicity looked at it longingly. Instinctively, Guster backed away.

She reached out for a split second, then dropped her hand. "You should probably keep it," she said.

Guster relaxed. He did want to know where it was at all times; it may not matter so much anymore, but still, it was his duty to protect it.

"Come, your mother and brothers and sister will be waiting outside. It will be a long journey back to Louisiana."

Guster turned away from the kitchen and headed down the hall and out of the castle to where the limousine was waiting.

***

Dinner at the farmhouse was never the same for Guster Johnsonville after he'd decided the fate of humanity with the end of his spoon.

Henry Johnsonville Senior returned home from selling insurance the day after Guster and the family got back to the farmhouse. "Did I miss anything?" Henry Senior asked.

"Dessert," said Mariah with a wry smile.

Guster laughed. It was good to have him back.

"Oh," said Henry Senior. He looked confused. "You know, I was thinking, why don't we plan a vacation to someplace far away and exotic next year, like California?"

Mom kissed Henry Senior on the cheek. "I love you, my dear," she said. "We need to have a very long talk as soon as you unpack your things."

After dinner Guster overheard him speaking excitedly to Mom in their bedroom. "And then he did what?" he said, followed by a "They were how big?" or "A jungle where?" He finished it all by saying, "All that for one little taste?" He was quiet for a long time after that.

When Henry Senior came out of the bedroom, he seemed astounded at the very sight of Guster. "Well, I'll be —" he said, his hand on the back of his neck and his face full of admiration.

Guster didn't know why anyone would make such a big deal about him, nor did he know what to say, so he just looked at the floor and tried to keep to himself for the rest of the evening.

The next afternoon, the phone rang. It was Aunt Priscilla. Guster picked up the receiver in the kitchen so he could eavesdrop on the other line.

Mom jabbered with her for a full minute, asking if she got home safely, if she was well after all that excitement, and on and on. Aunt Priscilla explained in turn how she was negotiating for a seat on the board of Casa Brand Industries because she felt that company needed a financial genius of her caliber to help turn it around and so forth. She told Mom how glad she was that Mom could get out, see the world, and finally get a little life experience. Mom listened politely, until Aunt Priscilla finally got around to asking her question. "Whatever happened to my plane?" she said.

"Oh, it blew up," said Mom in the most genial voice.

There was silence on the other end for a very long time. Then the receiver exploded with all the fury Aunt Priscilla's angry words could muster.

Guster didn't feel like hearing it, so he hung up the phone as quickly as he could. A minute later, Mom did too. She was grinning from cheek to cheek when she came into the kitchen.

Mention of the plane made Guster wonder — what *had* happened to Braxton and the Buttersmiths? It pained him that his friends had been lost at sea.

As the summer wore on, Guster could not help but feel changes at the farmhouse, all happening right under his feet. Henry Junior started saying real words like "No" and "Yucky." Zeke decided to visit the dairy to see where milk really came from. Mariah was determined to get her pilot's license one day.

Mom seemed the most different of all. She moved about the kitchen more easily now. As a gesture of goodwill, Felicity had sent Mom home from France with all of her published works, as well as a few of her secret recipe books. They took a special spot on a shelf above the stove, covered in blue and red canvas with golden letters. Sometimes, when Mom approached a new recipe that she did not understand, Guster could overhear her muttering to herself in the kitchen, "Mixed not by the hand that pleases for wealth, but by the hand that nourishes for life —"

Mom seemed to have more of a knack for cooking now; maybe it was because she had cooked with her hero and seen a real pro at work. Or maybe it was because she had been the one to make the greatest recipe of all time. Guster could still taste the dirty corn fed to the chickens Mom used in her casseroles, or the foul rain that fell on the almond trees, but there was something different about her meals now. A new confidence and conviction that Guster could taste.

On certain nights that summer, when it was late, Guster would tiptoe down to the kitchen and sit under the window where he could stare at the moon. He would take the eggbeater with him and wind its crank back and forth, the silvery glow of moonbeams shining over its metal gears. It was at those times that an incredible amount of stillness filled his heart as he remembered the most delicious spoonful he had ever tasted. Sometimes, it was with sadness. Always, it was with fondness.

He knew, ever since he'd found the eggbeater in the wreckage of the kitchen, that such nights could not last: the time would come to bury the eggbeater. In the middle of July, he wrapped it in an old tablecloth and locked it in a metal box. He scratched the words "When all men make peace, this shall be their dessert" into the side of the metal, because it was something Archedentus would say. Then he lowered the box down the abandoned well in the backyard.

On his way back to the house, a switch flipped inside his mind, soft as a whisper, as the memory of a single, subtle taste from the

Gastronomy of Peace returned to him. It was a tiny taste — a taste he'd almost overlooked in the soufflé's myriad of flavors. It had been faint among so many rich ingredients, like a single voice in a crowd, or an ant calling from a leaf on a tree across the canyon — faint, but true. It was a taste as real as the Johnsonvilles; it was the taste of the farmhouse; it was the taste of Mom's fingertips as she cracked eggs or sprinkled sugar. It was the taste of her sweat, as she labored to give them their daily bread. It was the taste of one who had created his life. A taste he would have taken for granted, had it not been mixed with the soufflé.

The memory of the tiny taste grew, day by day, as did Guster's craving for it. He wanted it; he needed to taste again from the hand that had made it.

Finally, at the end of that summer, Mom pulled a loaf of home-baked bread from the oven. It looked too dry and heavy, but Guster thought he could smell a hint of something in it — the touch of his mother's hand. "Can I have a slice?" he whispered to her.

She gave it gladly. It was delicious; it sustained him; he had another, and then another. For the first time he could remember, his tiny belly was full. And he never felt more at peace. From then on, he wanted more.

A week before school started, Guster lounged on the porch after one of Mom's hearty lunches when a plane buzzed overhead. Minutes later a sleek black car pulled up in front of the farmhouse. Guster looked up from the checkers game he and Zeke were playing to see who was driving it.

An old man dressed in a dark suit with a twinkle in his eye stepped out. "Is your mother home?" he asked.

"Braxton!" cried Guster. He and Zeke rushed to hug him.

The old pilot patted the boys on the back as he followed them into the house, a picnic basket slung over one shoulder.

"I came as soon as I could," he said. "The Buttersmiths took me to the mainland after they woke up from their naps. They send their greetings."

A little piece of Guster mended itself back together. He never thought he'd see Braxton again. And from the sound of it, Torbjorn and Storfjell had gotten home safely too.

"After Ms. Casa took control of Casa Brand Industries again, she hired me to be her personal pilot. We let bygones be bygones and all," he told them as soon as they were seated at the kitchen table. He laughed. "She sure made a killing on the documentary about the Cult of Gastronimatii and the story of the great Archedentus that aired on her show. That alone rocketed her back into the limelight and won over her fans. I don't know if anybody believes it, but they eat it up anyway. She never mentioned the Gastronomy of Peace. So no one knows the full story," he said, winking at Guster.

"Nor does she know, that I've been saving this for you," He set the picnic basket on the table. "A gift," he told Mom, sliding it toward her.

Mom opened it. Astonishment crossed her face. Inside were a few shavings of rich, dark chocolate. Guster recognized the smell immediately.

"Mr. Arrivederci is none the worse for wear about him and Ms. Casa's arrangement, especially after he found out she wasn't the thief. She supplies him with a small amount of sugar every year, since she knows where to get it. In return, he supplies her with some of his special chocolate from the vault. For the life of him, he can't figure out what makes Felicity's sugar so much better than anything he's ever tasted," Braxton said, grinning. He chuckled. "I think you and I both know the answer to that."

"Which brings us to this here," he said, motioning to the chocolate. "Not exactly the One Recipe, but if you add a few ingredients to these ol' Dark Milk Bricks, Mabel, I'm sure you can whip something delightful up."

"This stuff's worth a million dollars a pound," said Mom. Her eyes lit up. "You mean it Braxton?"

"I do," he said, nodding. "There are always a few extra shavings left over here and there from Felicity's work."

Mom took the basket, chopped the chocolate into bits, and emptied them into a metal bowl where she mixed it with cookie dough. She took a small vial of vanilla extract from a necklace around her neck, unscrewed it, and added a few drops. Then she dropped a dozen spoonfuls of dough onto a metal sheet and baked them until a warm, near-perfect aroma held the kitchen in its arms. Mom opened the oven and removed the fresh chocolate chip cookies a few minutes later.

The family ate their cookies on the porch in silence, engulfed by the magnificent flavor of the chocolate that so few had known.

Braxton promised that, from then on, he would come once a year, at the end of every summer, to bring fresh ingredients and news from Torbjorn and Storfjell.

Zeke said with mouth full of awe that he would never tease his sister again. Mariah hummed to herself, and Henry Junior cooed softly. Henry Senior was flabbergasted. They savored each bite carefully, until all the cookies were gone, and one by one, they went inside to ponder the things they had tasted. It was a glorious night on the farm.

Guster and Mom did not leave the porch for hours. They sat, licking the last bits of chocolate from their fingertips. The night crept up, and the fireflies began to glow. It got quiet, and Mom asked Guster a question, "Do you think the world will ever be ready to taste the Gastronomy of Peace?"

Guster did not know what to say. He was a little surprised that his mother would ask *him* such a question. Archedentus had probably wondered the same thing before he disappeared, centuries ago. "I certainly hope so, Mom," said Guster. Whatever happened to the world, whatever came of it, for that moment, it didn't matter. Then and there — with Mom, with the Johnsonvilles, on the farm — he had never felt such a full measure of peace.

Further perilously delicious adventures for Guster and the Johnsonvilles coming soon in:

The Delicious City

&

The Final Season

Come LIKE Adam on Facebook or follow him on Instagram to find out more about his books!
www.facebook.com/AdamGlendonSidwell
Instagram: @AdamGlendonSidwell

An Evertaster companion novel:

The Buttersmiths' Gold

Chapter 1 — Torbjorn and Storfjell

Almost every historian you ever meet will tell you that there is nothing Vikings love more than blueberry muffins. Blueberry muffins with blueberries shining like gems atop the muffin's golden crown. Blueberry muffins with little bubbles of succulent blue juice that burst in your mouth when you sever their skin with your teeth. Blueberry muffins for breakfast, blueberry muffins for lunch, blueberry muffins for supper next to your clan's roaring fire in the longhouse.

Most historians would tell you that's what Vikings love most. Most historians would be wrong.

"You boys sure seem to love muffins more than anything!" said Braxton. The old pilot had seen it all in his day – kangaroo rodeos, bees on bicycles, and even a fish who could shoot – but never ever in his whole life did he expect to be stranded on board a wooden ship in the middle of the sea with a pair of humongous Vikings.

And now that pair had laid aside their horned helmets and were shoveling blueberry muffins into their mouths by the fistful.

"Oh yah! ha ha!" laughed the larger of the two Vikings – his name was Storfjell – with a deep, rumbly laugh that shook his mountainous belly. Golden-brown muffin crumbs fell from Storfjell's mouth into his silvery beard. He was at least eleven feet tall, with a pair of silver braids that must have been woven from moonbeams. "What you are saying is a common mistake! We are loving blueberry muffins very much! But you know what we are loving even more?" Storfjell said between mouthfuls.

Braxton's watery eyes twinkled. The cows mooed. "I could venture a guess," he said. If it weren't for these two Vikings, alive and thriving in the modern era, unknown to the rest of the world, Braxton might still be stuck on a remote island in the Norwegian Sea. Still, as strange as it all was, he had a feeling he knew what they were going to say.

"Blueberry muffins are delicious to eat of course, but it is this, the Golden Fortune of our Herds – that is the best thing to taste in all of Midgard!" said the Viking named Torbjorn. Torbjorn was the smaller of the two – he was still ten feet tall and broad as an ox. He heaved a heavy wooden barrel upright and slid it across the deck of the ship to the mast where they sat. He pried off the lid with his battle axe and dipped the edge of the blade into the soft, golden butter inside. "It is butter that we Vikings love all the best!"

Butter – creamy, rich and smooth. *I wonder what the encyclopedias would say about that,* thought Braxton. The way these boys drank down their butter, you'd think their butter was the treasure that launched the Viking Age itself. He watched their herd of cows pushing at the oars. A question began to form in Braxton's mind. There was something he had to know. "I know you love your cows and treat them right. I know you feed them on fresh clover," said Braxton. "But what is it that makes your butter so special?"

Storfjell smiled, his long silver mustache turning upward with the corners of his mouth. He looked quite pleased that Braxton would ask. "This is a good thing you have wondered, but it is not my story to tell." He pointed to his brother Torbjorn. "You must ask him, and he will tell you that and many things."

Torbjorn scooped out another mound of butter and smeared it all over the heap of muffins still left on the table, then pounded the lid back onto the barrel with the butt of his axe. He was usually the jollier of the two Buttersmiths, but now, all of a sudden, he grew quiet. “It is an ancient tale,” he said. “One that begins with our fathers and their fathers’ fathers, so many times ago, before the ships could cross the great sea, when there were fewer people on the land, and when kings were rare indeed.”

Braxton took another bite of his muffin. The butter washed down his throat. He settled back against a barrel. It was a long way to land, and this was the tale he’d hoped would get told.

“In those days, our clan churned the butter in wooden churns by hand. It was a very tiring work.

“In those days, our clansmen did not live past 40 winters old. If he did not get a knife in his back, or a battle axe to his teeth, old age would surely find him.

“My father’s father’s father, very many fathers ago, was also like me named Torbjorn. Also his brother, like mine, was called Storfjell,” said Torbjorn. His words went up and down in his sing-songy voice as he spoke. With the fresh muffin warming Braxton’s belly from the inside, and the creamy butter melting through him and coating all his nooks and crannies, Braxton began to hear Torbjorn’s words as if they were a dream. This is the story that Torbjorn told.

Chapter 2 — Smordal

Many centuries ago, young Torbjorn Trofastsonn of Smordal knew quite well that the tastiest thing in the whole world was butter. Creamy, rich and smooth. Butter was the reason his clan invented blueberry muffins in the first place – they'd needed something to smear it on. Butter was their lifeblood. Butter was the warmth in their hearts, the horns on their helmets, the tips of their mustaches.

Butter was also their greatest secret.

Torbjorn hoisted an oversized basket full of steaming hot muffins into his arms and tottered down the gangplank onto the sandy shore of Viksfjord, the merchants' village. He and his clan had sailed from the open sea into the fjord this morning, where he and his brother Storfjell had helped Father and the bovines row the final twenty miles to the sand.

He did not mind the work. He was large for only 13 winters old. Smaller than the biggest boulders, but larger than most respectable rocks, Torbjorn was already 8 feet tall. If five sheep stacked themselves on top of each other, he could stare the fourth one straight in the eye. He was from Smordal, and Smordaler were known for their tremendous size – not to mention their good humor.

"The streets of Viksfjord are filled with much peril," said Father. He stopped Torbjorn at the bottom of the gangplank and grasped him by both shoulders. "Go to find the money-clutching merchants in the village center. They will trade with you behind closed doors. Make your trade, then leave. Do not be seen. It's the Buttersmith's way."

It was the first time Torbjorn would bargain for himself, but Father didn't need to tell Torbjorn what to do. He'd seen the men come and go on trading trips dozens of times. And Torbjorn was a Smordaler through and through – it was in his blood.

"We don't want to attract attention," said Father, his yellow beard covering his belly like a thick blanket of hay. His mustache turned down at the corners – it meant that Father was frowning.

"I won't," said Torbjorn.

Torbjorn's 9-foot-tall brother Storfjell shoved past him. "Good luck, my brother," Storfjell said, punching Torbjorn in the arm. It nearly knocked Torbjorn off balance. "Do not settle for fish feet!"

I laugh my belly off, thought Torbjorn, frowning to himself. Fish feet were what you got when you'd been bamboozled. Torbjorn was not about to get bamboozled.

Torbjorn watched Storfjell chuckle as he ran up the beach into town. Storfjell was the only man 17 winters old who already had wrinkles growing out the corners of his eyes. His beard and mustache had turned silver early-on too. Father said it was because Storfjell had wisdom beyond his years. Sometimes Torbjorn wondered if that were really true. *More like stuffy beyond his years,* he thought.

Father also said Storfjell was his most responsible son. He counted on Storfjell to make reliable trades. Nothing extravagant or extraordinary, but Storfjell always brought back something useful for the clan. He was consistent, and that made Father happy.

When it came to Torbjorn, though, Father wasn't so go lucky. He was always telling Torbjorn to be a man, but Torbjorn already felt like one. He was 13 winters old! He already had a full red beard. He could do at least as well as Storfjell. Today, he was determined to do better.

Torbjorn threw his wool cloak over the basket of muffins. He paused as he passed a reddish bovine that had rowed alongside them. He patted her on the head – he so loved their bovines – then set out on the sand.

He passed a few small fishing boats, rounded an outcropping of rock, and found the wooden walkway that led into the village.

Viksfjord was big. Just from the shore, Torbjorn could see four separate, fortified enclosures, at least a few dozen lean-tos, a handful of ramshackle huts, and eleven wooden longhouses. There must have been a few hundred people living there, and even more stopping to trade. It was the biggest village Torbjorn had ever seen. Maybe the biggest village in all of the North. There was even a longhouse with carved dragon heads pointing out either end of its roof.

And then there were the streets: they were bustling with shoppers and merchants. There were people shouting from their doorways, people pushing carts. Torbjorn made his way carefully up into the swarm. This was the first time he'd gone into Viksfjord alone…

ABOUT THE AUTHOR

In between books, Adam Glendon Sidwell uses the power of computers to make monsters, robots and zombies come to life for blockbuster movies such as *Pirates of the Caribbean*, *King Kong*, *Transformers* and *Tron*. After spending countless hours in front of a keyboard meticulously adjusting tentacles, calibrating hydraulics, and brushing monkey fur, he is delighted at the prospect of modifying his creations with the flick of a few deftly placed adjectives. He's been eating food since age 7, so feels very qualified to write this book. He once showed a famous movie star where the bathroom was. Adam currently lives in Los Angeles with his wife and daughter where he can't wait to fall into the sea.

Say hello to Adam here: www.evertaster.com

Want Adam to come to your school? Contact:
publicity@evertaster.com

Bring Adam to your school!
Email publicity@evertaster.com

To find out more about his books,
come LIKE Adam on Facebook:
www.facebook.com/AdamGlendonSidwell

or follow him on Instagram:
@AdamGlendonSidwell

Watch the Evertaster Book Trailer on YouTube:
www.youtube.com/Evertaster

Other books by Adam:
CHUM
FETCH